CANDLELIGHT Ecstasy Supreme

"WHAT WE HAVE HERE IS A COMBUSTIBLE COMBINATION!" JONATHAN SLOWLY EASED AWAY FROM HER.

"It seems so." Holly lowered her voice to a seductive murmur. "But I'm sure we can come to a mutual solution on how to effectively quench the fire."

"No," he said gruffly. "That's how we made our first mistake."

"Is that how you see it, a mistake?" she asked softly.

Jonathan shook his head, cursing his unfortunate choice of words. "No, but two people should try to get to know each other better before embarking on an affair."

Holly closed her eyes. That was the last word she would ever have used to describe their relationship. To her, an affair was between two people who *didn't* want to get to know each other.

CANDLELIGHT ECSTASY SUPREMES

21 BREAKING THE RULES, *Donna Kimel Vitek*
22 ALL IN GOOD TIME, *Samantha Scott*
23 SHADY BUSINESS, *Barbara Andrews*
24 SOMEWHERE IN THE STARS, *Jo Calloway*
25 AGAINST ALL ODDS, *Eileen Bryan*
26 SUSPICION AND SEDUCTION, *Shirley Hart*
27 PRIVATE SCREENINGS, *Lori Herter*
28 FASCINATION, *Jackie Black*
29 DIAMONDS IN THE SKY, *Samantha Hughes*
30 EVENTIDE, *Margaret Dobson*
31 CAUTION: MAN AT WORK, *Linda Randall Wisdom*
32 WHILE THE FIRE RAGES, *Amii Lorin*
33 FATEFUL EMBRACE, *Nell Kincaid*
34 A DANGEROUS ATTRACTION, *Emily Elliott*
35 MAN IN CONTROL, *Alice Morgan*
36 PLAYING IT SAFE, *Alison Tyler*
37 ARABIAN NIGHTS, *Heather Graham*
38 ANOTHER DAY OF LOVING, *Rebecca Nunn*
39 TWO OF A KIND, *Lori Copeland*
40 STEAL AWAY, *Candice Adams*
41 TOUCHED BY FIRE, *Jo Calloway*
42 ASKING FOR TROUBLE, *Donna Kimel Vitek*
43 HARBOR OF DREAMS, *Ginger Chambers*
44 SECRETS AND DESIRE, *Sandi Gelles*
45 SILENT PARTNER, *Nell Kincaid*
46 BEHIND EVERY GOOD WOMAN, *Betty Henrichs*
47 PILGRIM SOUL, *Hayton Monteith*
48 RUN FOR THE ROSES, *Eileen Bryan*
49 COLOR LOVE BLUE, *Diana Blayne*
50 ON ANY TERMS, *Shirley Hart*
51 HORIZON'S GIFT, *Betty Jackson*
52 ONLY THE BEST, *Lori Copeland*
53 AUTUMN RAPTURE, *Emily Elliott*
54 TAMED SPIRIT, *Alison Tyler*
55 MOONSTRUCK, *Prudence Martin*
56 FOR ALL TIME, *Jackie Black*

LOVE HAS MANY VOICES

Linda Randall Wisdom

A CANDLELIGHT ECSTASY SUPREME

Published by
Dell Publishing Co., Inc.
1 Dag Hammarskjold Plaza
New York, New York 10017

Copyright © 1985 by Linda Randall Wisdom

All rights reserved. No part of this book may be reproduced or
transmitted in any form or by any means, electronic or
mechanical, including photocopying, recording or by any
information storage and retrieval system, without the written
permission of the Publisher, except where permitted by law.

Dell ® TM 681510, Dell Publishing Co., Inc.
Candlelight Ecstasy Supreme is a trademark
of Dell Publishing Co., Inc.

Candlelight Ecstasy Romance®, 1,203,540, is a registered
trademark of Dell Publishing Co., Inc.

ISBN: 0-440-15008-6

Printed in the United States of America
First printing—January 1985

To Our Readers:

Candlelight Ecstasy is delighted to announce the start of a brand-new series—Ecstasy Supremes! Now you can enjoy a romance series unlike all the others—longer and more exciting, filled with more passion, adventure, and intrigue—the stories you've been waiting for.

In months to come we look forward to presenting books by many of your favorite authors and the very finest work from new authors of romantic fiction as well. As always, we are striving to present the unique, absorbing love stories that you enjoy most—the very best love has to offer.

Breathtaking and unforgettable, Ecstasy Supremes will follow in the great romantic tradition you've come to expect *only* from Candlelight Ecstasy.

Your suggestions and comments are always welcome. Please let us hear from you.

                Sincerely,

                The Editors
                Candlelight Romances
                1 Dag Hammarskjold Plaza
                New York, New York 10017

CHAPTER ONE

Jonathan rubbed his fingertips over a forehead creased with tension as he leaned back in his easy chair. The raucous voices of children playing filtered in from the outside and disturbed his concentration. He swore under his breath as he reached for the phone and punched out a number.

"Bayline Property Management." The chipper voice that answered the phone didn't improve his dark mood.

"All right, Ruth, where is she?" Jonathan demanded imperiously, his very proper British accent making him sound even more intimidating than he was.

An audible sigh sounded on the other end. "Jonathan, I told you an hour ago that Liza is out with a client. I'll have her call you as soon as she walks in the door," the receptionist promised in a long-suffering voice. It was the eighth time he had called in the past two hours and her patience was wearing thin.

"Tell her to call me *today* or so help me God, I'll find a way to have her house mortgage foreclosed," he threatened with grim determination.

After knowing Jonathan for close to six years, Ruth had no doubts that he would carry out his threats. She again promised to have her boss call him and hung up, fervently praying he'd finally leave her alone.

Jonathan hung up and rose from his chair. He stood by the window that looked out over the large backyard of the duplex he lived in. There had to be at least ten children running around out there. And all of them were under the age of ten. Except for one.

Jonathan's long fingers combed through his neatly clipped umber hair. Gold highlights shot through it and faint hints of gray were sprinkled along the temples. His hazel eyes watched the children who were engrossed in their attempt to fly a kite.

It isn't that I don't like children, he thought to himself, trying to justify his irritation. It's just that I don't like them around me!

But despite his mood, he couldn't help but smile at the antics of the young woman in charge of the playful group.

He doubted that she could be taller than five feet, and she sported short, velvet-black curls that bounced along her neck. Her hair conveyed the image of a woman who found more important things to do than spend hours in front of the mirror fixing it. Jonathan thought that she looked about sixteen years old as she assisted the children with the unwieldy kite.

The ringing of the telephone roused Jonathan from his surveillance. He turned back to answer it. "Lockwood here." He spoke abruptly into the receiver.

"You're snapping again, love." A deliciously feminine voice floated in his ear.

"Do you realize what is going on out in the backyard?" he demanded.

"No, dear, you tell me," she soothed.

"She's having a damned birthday party for her damned dog!" he all but shouted.

"Now how do you know that?" Liza asked him, amusement laced through her voice.

"Because they were singing 'Happy Birthday' to him!" Jonathan clenched his teeth. "When I moved in here, did you omit one important fact?" he accused. "I was positive that you had told me children didn't live here."

"That's correct," Liza replied readily. "Holly's a single woman, therefore, no children."

"Lack of a husband doesn't mean lack of offspring," Jonathan returned sarcastically. "Even basic biology can tell you that."

"Umm, I'm glad to see that you remember your biology, Jon." Her laugh was more a throaty purr. "Although I doubt that you had ever forgotten it. You were always very good in that area."

"Damn it, Liza!" he exploded. After all these years, why did she still insist on calling him that godawful nickname? The answer was easy: Because she knew he hated it! "It's bad enough that I was hoping to get some work done, but all that yelling going on outside has shot my concentration to hell! You don't know how noisy children can be," he finished on a grumpy note.

"Honestly, Jon, if you don't calm down you'll end up with an ulcer," she pointed out on a practical note. "Besides, a temper and your stuffy attitude don't mix."

"I am not stuffy." He bit out each word.

"Darling, you were proper and correct the day I met you, the first time we made love, the day we married, and the day our divorce became final. Why ruin a perfect record now?" she declared airily. "After all, who else but a stuffy workaholic such as yourself thinks of working on a beautiful Saturday?"

"What about you?" he countered. "It's apparent that you're not home lying by the swimming pool."

"Property management doesn't necessarily end at five o'clock on Fridays. You should remember that," Liza reminded him of the long hours she had put in when she'd first started her company, although he had never complained since he had been putting in long hours of his own at the bank where he was the head of the auditing department.

Jonathan squeezed his eyes shut, picturing the tall, well-formed blond woman on the other end of the telephone line. "If I don't have some peace and quiet around here very soon, your precious Miss Sutton will find herself hanging from that damn kite she's now trying to fly! I don't care to move again."

"You'll never find a better place until your house is finished. After all, you were the one who wanted to move out of the city before it was completed. You're certainly away from most of the smog and city noise. So what is there for you to complain about?" Liza was undaunted by his threats. "Look, darling, I have to run. Harold is having several business associates over for dinner and I promised to be home early."

"That will be a switch," Jonathan commented sardonically. He could easily visualize Harold, Liza's third husband. A quiet man, because his wife didn't let him get a word in edgewise, and with a slight paunch, he looked far from the image of a mate for the vivacious Liza. Yet there was no doubt that he adored his vibrant spouse. Jonathan had been Liza's first husband, but by no means her last.

Muttering darkly, he slammed the receiver down. The sound of the doorbell pealing didn't improve his mood any. Nor did the sight of a small boy standing on the doorstep holding a bunch of brightly colored balloons brighten his day.

"These are for Sylvie," he announced cheerfully, holding the balloons out.

Jonathan's scowl wasn't the least bit welcoming. "There is no Sylvie here," he coolly informed the boy.

"Sure, she is," the small boy insisted. "I can't stay cause Mom's takin' me to the dentist. Just give these to her please. Thanks."

Without thinking, Jonathan accepted the balloons and watched the boy scamper off. He had a month's worth of paperwork waiting for him, kids outside were yelling and playing havoc with his concentration, and now this!

"Sylvie must be one of those little monsters in the back," he muttered, shutting the front door.

Jonathan felt foolish carrying the bunch of balloons toward the back of the house. He felt even more ridiculous when he pushed the back door open and walked outside. The children were so involved in their play that they didn't even see their visitor at first.

"Excuse me." Jonathan raised his voice in order to be heard over the noise. "These are for someone named Sylvie." He held up the balloons.

The children turned around and, at hearing the name, began to laugh as if they all shared a joke.

"They must be from Bobby, Holly," one little girl informed the young woman.

Holly walked over to Jonathan. "I'm sorry if Bobby bothered you, Mr. Lockwood," she apologized in a deep smoky voice that shouldn't belong to a woman so young and petite. Her voice made a man think of champagne, silk negligees, and dimly lit bedrooms.

"It has been difficult to get my work done around here

this afternoon. If anything it's tantamount to insanity," he grumbled, frowning at the incongruity of the feminine creature standing before him. Her face resembled drawings of woodland elves found in picture books. Her evident good humor was more than obvious when she smiled, although the flash of silver when her lips parted had been a surprise. None of the women he had known would have worn braces past the age of twelve! "Aren't you a little old to wear braces?" Jonathan remarked abruptly.

Holly laughed, a sound resembling a rich, full-bodied liquor that slid down a man's throat with deceptive ease and delivered the kick of a mule when least expected. "No one is ever too old for anything, Mr. Lockwood," she told him, her voice filled with mirth.

"Obviously," he muttered darkly.

Holly held up the multicolor kite with its elaborate tail. "We've been trying to get this kite up all morning, but there just isn't enough wind to keep it aloft. I'm sorry if we happened to disturb you. I guess I didn't think that anyone would work on the weekend. Especially when it's such a beautiful day."

Jonathan's lips thinned. Anyone who knew him well enough was aware that this was a sign that he wasn't pleased at all. "I am a very busy man, Miss Sutton. I have a great deal of work to do on an important project. I may not be living here for long, but I was still given to understand that children did not live in this duplex. I didn't know that it would resemble the local schoolyard a majority of the time!"

Holly's eyes, a deep shade of blue green, sparkled with her own show of temper. "Children may not *live* in my side of the house," she spoke softly, but a thread of steel could be discerned in her tones. "But they're certainly free to come here. I don't believe that there's an age limit for visitors." Her regal manner clashed with her faded jeans and T-shirt.

"The children will be returning to their homes within the next hour," she continued. A trace of amusement now danced in her eyes while his still reflected anger. "Don't worry, Mr. Lockwood. You'll have all the peace and quiet you'll want this evening. It isn't my turn to hostess the weekly orgy."

Jonathan muttered an angry, unintelligible reply, spun on his heel, and stalked back into the house.

"Gee, Holly, he sure isn't like Mrs. Donaldson," one of the girls said, referring to Holly's former neighbor.

"Probably because Mrs. Donaldson was almost deaf," Holly said wryly, wrapping the twine attached to the kite around her closed fist. "We couldn't have disturbed her if we had tried."

"He's not very nice," someone else announced with the open candor only a child could display. "Make him go away, Holly."

Holly smiled and dropped a light kiss on the top of the mussed carrot-red hair of a small boy. "I can't do that, but I can weave a magic net over him and turn him into one of us," she told him in a voice that was higher pitched than her own and sounded as if it was coated with fairy dust.

"Sylvie!" Several children yelled with glee at recognizing the famous voice of a wood nymph in a cartoon program.

"Right!" she squealed back, throwing her arms out.

Twenty minutes later, Holly watched the children leave by the side gate before heading for her back door. Her eyes glanced toward the window on the opposite side of the house.

"I bet Scrooge took lessons from you, Mr. Jonathan C.

Lockwood," she muttered, opening the back door and entering the small laundry room adjoining the kitchen. "Hmm, I wonder what the *C* stands for. Liza never did tell me. Probably cranky!" She giggled.

There was no warning when Holly stepped into the living room. Only a soft *whoof* alerted her seconds before what felt like a ten-ton weight settled against her chest and knocked her to the soft cream-color carpet.

"Ralph!" Holly yelled, pushing vainly at the large, immovable, furry object. "Get off me."

A large, smooth tongue seemed to cover her face. Soft barks sent out chocolate-scented breath.

"You fiend!" Holly scolded the ungainly St. Bernard as she finally managed to push him off her stomach and legs. "You found my M&M's!" she cried as she scrambled to her feet none too gracefully.

When Holly had gotten the three-month-old puppy she had dubbed Ralph, she hadn't realized that he had an insatiable craving for sweets, especially peanut M&M's, which were, ironically, her favorite candy. No matter where Holly hid her booty, the dog found the brightly colored candies and gobbled them up in record time. It had become a game between the two as to how long Holly could keep the candy hidden from the chocolate-sniffing hound. Especially because she allowed him very few candies since sugar wasn't good for dogs.

Holly looked down at the properly repentant dog. He whimpered mournfully, hanging his head in shame more at being caught than in sorrow for his crime. Holly propped her fists on her slim hips as if she were angry, although she could see only humor in the situation.

"Don't try that sad-sack routine with me, you old

faker," she scolded. "You're not really sorry and we both know it."

Ralph immediately whined and lifted an apologetic paw. From past experience, he knew that if he looked properly contrite, his mistress would forgive him . . . until the next time.

"Why can't you be like other dogs and eat dog biscuits?" Holly demanded, walking into her bedroom. The blinking light on her telephone answering machine was a silent beacon informing her that a message awaited. She twisted the knob to rewind the tape then switched it to playback.

Beep! "Hi, Holly, it's Steve. I just got word for us to be at the studio at nine on Monday." He chuckled. "Work on your witch's cackle, babe. See ya then."

Holly sighed as she flipped the button to erase the tape. She disliked the thought that again she had been chosen to play a witch when she really preferred playing more lovable characters. She pulled off her running shoes and walked barefoot into the kitchen. In a short time, she set a bowl filled with dog food on the floor for Ralph and prepared a large salad for herself. That, along with a slice of toasted garlic bread and a glass of wine, was her dinner.

Holly's low-calorie meal didn't mean that she had to watch her weight. Her active lifestyle took care of any excess calories she might consume. The reason for her choice of meals was that Holly and stoves didn't get along. It had taken her a long time to learn how to warm garlic bread under the broiler without burning it to a cinder. As for a microwave oven, well, she could certainly prove that food could easily be cooked to a lump of charcoal in one! It was easier for her to toss together a salad or steam vegetables. She seemed to have no trouble with those culinary accomplishments. She was also well known at the local fast food restaurants when a hamburger or a steak sandwich was the order of the day.

"What do you think of our neighbor, Ralph?" Holly asked the St. Bernard who was busily devouring his own dinner. "He's not bad-looking, but he's a grouch!" She speared a cucumber slice with her fork and brought it to her lips. "He's Liza's ex-husband and works for a bank in charge of their auditing department. He's also the typical English gentleman. Sort of a combination James Bond and Sir John Gielgud. It all figures, along with the dark three-piece suits he wears to work and that 'narc' car he drives." The latter was a dark, nondescript sedan she had seen Jonathan drive away in the past few mornings. It was the kind of automobile undercover agents might drive in order to blend in with the scenery. Though that was something they didn't really accomplish, since they were easily spotted among all the flashy foreign sports cars and brightly painted vans popular in Southern California. "As to the rest of him, he's very nice-looking and sexy to boot, but I wonder if he's ever done anything daring in his entire life."

Holly ate her dinner slowly and looked around thoughtfully. She had been living there for a little over two years, since she and her boyfriend Rob had broken up. She had met Liza through a friend, and the older woman had directed Holly to the duplex. The two women had remained good friends over the years.

Holly had been surprised when Liza told her her ex-husband would be occupying the other half of the duplex for several months until his new house was finished.

"Jon's a little temperamental," Liza had told her. "But down deep, he's a regular softie. Just don't be surprised if you have to dig deep."

"When she told me to dig deep, she didn't explain I'd

need the kind of drilling equipment they use on oil rigs," Holly mused, while washing up her dishes before moving into the living room.

She collapsed on her Dresden blue couch, her legs sprawled out in front of her in an unladylike position. With a bright smile of pride, she stared at the pictures gracing the opposite wall.

At first glance, they looked like brightly colored sketches. On closer observation, though, the sketches were, in fact, cartoon cells, color pictures drawn on a type of cellophane. All were scenes from popular and not-so-popular Saturday morning cartoon programs and a few feature-length cartoons.

Holly wasn't the artist of those cells, but she was the person to give the various characters life. She provided them with vocal cords.

Holly had been an excellent mimic since her teen years. She only had to hear someone speak a few words and she could duplicate the voice perfectly. But she'd never thought of doing it professionally. Finding a job as a cartoon voice had been a fluke.

During her last year of college, Holly had been living with a layout artist who worked for a well-known cartoon production company. Knowing of her gift for mimicry, he had gotten her an audition where he worked. She was aware that her talent, rather than her relationship with Rob, had landed her the job of a new cartoon character. She still thought fondly of Rob. They had lived together platonically for three and a half years, then their relationship had gradually turned intimate, lasting only six months. What they had thought was love turned out only to be a strong infatuation, though. Rob had met would-be singer Melanie Richards and proposed to her on their first meeting. Now Rob and Melanie were married and expecting their first baby. And Holly was friends with both of them.

After that first job, Holly continued with that kind of work. She enjoyed letting out her inhibitions with the characters she felt she identified with and loved getting paid for having so much fun.

In the past seven years, Holly had given voice to various animals, a couple of fairies, a fantasy witch, the audio part of a computer in a popular science fiction movie, and a college-age seductress. With each character, she gave herself a new personality and enjoyed doing it. She also donated time to children's public television programs for educational voiceovers where she would count to ten, count by tens, recite the multiplication tables or say the alphabet in a slow, modulated voice. It was a mundane chore for someone as quick-thinking as Holly, but a chore executed with love.

Holly smiled as she studied one particular sketch on the wall. An artist friend of hers had drawn Sylvie, a wood nymph from a cartoon program, but had used Holly's face. There were many differences between the two women. Holly didn't have the sharp chin, the large watery blue eyes, the pale-blond hair and the willow-wisp of a figure that Sylvie had. Instead, Holly's features were soft and delicate, with slightly almond-shaped blue-green eyes and cropped black curls adorned with gold star barettes. Sylvie's gown was fashioned of cobwebs and her feet were bare as she reclined gracefully on a large mushroom that served as her throne. The picture of Holly as Sylvie didn't give her the otherworldly look the cartoon Sylvie had. Holly portrayed as Sylvie looked very real and very desirable, and now she couldn't help wonder if Jonathan would ever see her that way.

Sunday was a quiet day for Holly. She rose early, jogged three miles, and then returned home to shower and change her clothes in time for the late-morning church service. When she parked her car in the garage two hours later, she still hadn't seen a sign of her neighbor.

When Jonathan had moved into the house the week before, Holly hadn't been able to contain her curiosity about the new occupant in the other half of the duplex. She had met him the day after he had moved in, but his terse speech and aloof manner only piqued her interest more. Jonathan may not have been the type of man Holly usually went for, but for some odd reason she found herself wanting to know more about him. She knew that her best source of information was Liza, but she was also aware that she would have to be discreet with her questioning. If Liza knew that Holly was interested in her ex-husband, she would tease Holly unmercifully.

The day Jonathan had moved in, Holly had secreted herself behind the security of her living-room ruffled curtains to watch the movers carry in an assortment of dark wood furniture that to her taste was ultraconservative. She remembered how Jonathan had directed all the activities. She had studied the dark-haired man of medium height and of about thirty-five with sharply angled features and eyes that should have belonged to a hawk. His voice was crisp and authoritative—that of a man used to having his orders followed without question. Dressed in dark slacks and a navy-blue V-necked sweater, Jonathan exuded an aura of command.

Holly brought her thoughts to the day before when Jonathan had stormed outside holding that bunch of balloons. She had felt the very strong physical attraction a woman feels for a man. And they were clearly not the thoughts a woman should be having after listening to a sermon on brotherly love!

She went inside and changed into red athletic shorts trimmed in white and a white sleeveless T-shirt. As she left the bedroom, she caught sight of herself in the mirrored closet door.

"Real cute, Sutton," she admonished, placing her hands on her hips. "Not only are you a shrimp, but you have a mouth full of braces and still have another two months to go before they can come off. What man would look at a twenty-seven-year-old woman whose metal-encased mouth resembles a twelve-year-old child's? As for the body, well, if you keep up with your exercises, you just might, *might* eventually fill out a B-cup. Just don't hold your breath." She laughed softly. "Hmm, that just might be the way to fill out!" Holly stuck her little fingers in the corners of her mouth and pulled a face better suited to a five-year-old. "I guess I'll just have to live with the description of being a 'cute little thing,' which will probably be a millstone around my neck until I'm eighty!"

Holly's critical self-appraisal was interrupted by three staccato bursts from the doorbell.

"All right, all right," she informed her unseen visitor as she moved through the living room to the front door and opened it. She was taken aback to find the object of her thoughts standing on her doorstep. Her bright smile disappeared under Jonathan's scrutiny.

"Okay, what did I do wrong this time?" she asked, leaning her shoulder against the door jamb.

"If you'd like I'm sure I could think of something," he told her.

CHAPTER TWO

Holly stepped back and swept her arm inward. "Would you like to come in?"

She guided Jonathan into the living room. "Would you like some iced tea to drink? Or coffee? I'm afraid I don't have any carbonated drinks." She grinned. "Braces and bubbles don't mix and it would be too tempting to have any soda in the house."

Jonathan shook his head in an abrupt gesture. Dressed in navy slacks, a pale-gray shirt, striped tie, and a gray and navy tweed jacket, compared to Holly he looked overdressed.

Holly sat down on the couch, her clasped hands hanging loosely between her knees. She looked up toward Jonathan, tipped her head to one side, and studied her visitor. "And to what do I owe the pleasure of your visit?" she asked in her throaty voice.

"I thought it might not hurt to find out about my neighbor," he replied politely. "That is, if you have a little free time. Liza intimated that I shouldn't be my usual gruff self with someone who has the unusual background that you have."

"And she gave you no more of a hint than that?" Holly laughed. "No wonder you think that I belong in the local asylum."

Jonathan sat back in his chair and just listened to Holly's voice. This fey creature had a voice that sent shivers along a man's spine. Of course, she was far from the type of woman that attracted him. He preferred tall, shapely blondes with the sophistication to match the designer clothing they wore and their excellent skills in bed. He doubted that Holly had any of those attributes. She was diminutive, dressed in clothes that he felt belonged more to a teenager. Not to mention that she wore braces. Yet she had a voice that belonged in the bedroom and eyes that beckoned to a man. He wondered how she would sound when crying out words of passion. Disgusted with himself for his sensual musings, he brought himself sharply back to the present and to his mission of finding out more about the perky Miss Sutton.

Jonathan had been more than ready to leave the hustle and bustle of L.A. even though his new house wouldn't be ready for several more months. Finding a rental for six months was difficult to accomplish unless he was willing to settle for a studio apartment that rented by the day, week, or month, and that certainly wasn't his style! Since he and Liza still kept in touch, she was aware of his predicament and called him with the perfect solution. She managed half of a duplex and the owner wasn't adverse to letting Jonathan have it for six months or less. Jonathan was pleased to take it because it saved him the time of looking.

"Why do the children call you such strange names?" he asked curiously.

A smile tipped the corners of her lips. "Because that is how they see me." She went on to explain. "I'm a cartoon voice."

"I assume you're talking about those ridiculous programs on Saturday mornings," he replied stiffly.

"I admit the plots of some of the episodes are a bit much, but I wouldn't exactly call them ridiculous," Holly said mildly. She certainly wasn't going to tell him what she thought of bankers! "Tell me, how many cartoons have you watched lately? I didn't realize that you had so much free time since you have such a busy work schedule that you work on Saturdays."

"I wouldn't watch them if you paid me," he snapped back. "They only cater to the lowest mentality, condone violence, and show that the villain can win."

Holly knew it was useless to argue with this man. He would always have the logical comeback, and no one could win a war of words with someone that bull-headed. Her training in psychology told her that she was better off battling Jonathan in short skirmishes. A sneak attack would even be more beneficial, but she doubted that he was ever off guard.

"Perhaps there are some cartoon programs like that, but there are also shows that have their educational uses," she argued calmly. "Even *Sesame Street* uses cartoons as part of their learning aids." And well she should know! She had worked on enough educational programs to know of their workings. "Some children have trouble learning the traditional way, by reading books and having a teacher standing over them. By using television as a learning tool, children won't be watching shows about spies trying to take over the world or monsters eating the earth. Instead they're learning the alphabet or how cloth is made or even how to shoe a horse. They're able to see the world in a new and more exciting way. Isn't it better to watch something being done and learn about it that way than to read about it in a book?" she demanded.

Jonathan sat back, amazed by the sudden change in

Holly's manner. This woman definitely knew her own mind! "You're quite a fireball on the subject, aren't you?" he drawled with a trace of insolence in his tone.

"If you only knew," she retorted, now spoiling for an argument.

"Didn't you offer something cold to drink when I came in?" Jonathan asked suddenly.

Holly blinked at the sudden deflation of her argumentative balloon. "Of course," she murmured, her good manners surfacing at his request. She rose to her feet and headed for the kitchen. "Is iced tea all right?"

"That will be fine." Jonathan found himself watching the slight wiggle of Holly's slim hips as she walked away.

"Would you like lemon or sugar in it?" she asked politely.

"Just plain please." He looked across the room toward the wall decorated with the sketches. Jonathan rose to his feet and walked over to study the pictures more closely. The one that caught his attention was the colorful drawing of Holly dressed as a fairy queen.

"Those depict some of the programs I've worked on." Holly's voice came from behind.

Jonathan turned and accepted the ice-filled glass Holly held out to him. "Interesting," he commented indifferently.

"Please spare me the false praise," she said sharply, raising her own glass of iced tea to her lips. "Fine, you don't approve of what I do for a living. Not all of us can have a position of great importance such as yours. Perhaps I don't have the responsibility of taking charge of other people's money, but as far as I'm concerned, my work is just as meaningful, if not more!" Her eyes shot aquamarine sparks at him with unerring accuracy.

Jonathan's eyes widened with surprise. She had more spirit than he gave her credit for. The sweet-natured Holly he had watched yesterday playing with children was now a fireball! He respected her courage to stand up to him for her beliefs. Many women he knew tended to argue subtly with him only to give in in the end or just agree with any point he brought up. They didn't stand up to him the way Holly just had, and he discovered that he liked listening to a woman speak her mind. It was refreshing to have someone talk back to him. This woman had a sharp mind, and he knew he would enjoy trading words with her.

"Do you always argue with your neighbors?" he asked mildly.

"Only the bad-tempered ones," she shot back.

Jonathan swallowed the sharp retort that crowded his throat. He knew that his temper wasn't the mildest in the world, and he especially hated to hear that revelation from others. He leaned back in his chair and watched Holly closely. "Didn't you ever think about doing anything useful with your life?" he asked curiously.

"I'm not doing something useful now?" Holly asked with amusement.

"Working with *cartoons?*" He spat out the last word as if it were an obscenity.

"I only do the voices. I have nothing to do with the scripts," she explained.

Jonathan frowned. "It's obvious that you're an intelligent woman. Surely you could do something more worthwhile with your life," he stated pompously.

Holly choked on that bit of well-meaning advice. "Would you happen to have any suggestions as to what I could do?" she asked in an all-too-demure voice.

"I'm sure a secretarial course would provide you with some necessary skills," he told her.

Holly remembered all too well the last time she had used a typewriter. Somehow, she had managed to break a part that the typewriter service technician swore never broke! After that fiasco, she had engaged a professional typist to type her college term papers and thesis.

"Actually, I do quite well for myself." Her murmured reply was lost in a *whoof!* then an *umph!* when over one hundred pounds of dog landed in Jonathan's lap.

"Ralph!" Holly ordered in a stern voice while trying not to laugh.

"Get this horse off me!" Jonathan wheezed, pushing at the dog who had suddenly turned into dead weight.

"Ralph, come here," she instructed in a severe voice, but the St. Bernard had decided that he preferred staying with his newfound friend and refused to listen to his mistress. Holly decided that bribery was the only answer. She opened a cabinet door in her coffee table and reached inside. "Ralph," she cooed, holding out several brightly colored candies. "Wouldn't you like some M&M's?"

The large dog was off Jonathan's lap in a flash and gobbling up the sweets. Jonathan tried to brush the loose dog hair off his jacket and slacks without success.

"Did you ever think of sending your dog to obedience school?" he asked tersely.

"I did send him," she admitted readily. "He flunked."

"I should have known," Jonathan muttered, still trying to brush white and dark-brown hairs from his jacket. "Damn dog is all fur."

"He's better protection than a toy poodle," Holly retorted with a sassy grin.

Jonathan expressed his opinion of that comment as he

stood up. "A dog who eats candy and flunked obedience school," he muttered with disbelief shadowing his voice. "Are there any other surprises in store for me?"

Holly's brow furrowed in a displeased frown. "I didn't realize I had to answer to you regarding the activities in *my* house, Mr. Lockwood." Her voice frosted over.

"Only when it interferes with my peace and quiet," he threw back at her, striding toward the front door and opening it. "Good day, Miss Sutton." The door swung shut after him.

"How can a door not slam, yet sound like it?" Holly wondered out loud. "If I tried it, I would probably lose my grip and slam it so hard it would shatter the wood!"

Once back in his half of the house, Jonathan stripped off his jacket and slacks, replacing them with black slacks and a cranberry-color lightweight wool sweater. He poured himself a much-needed scotch and water and settled down in his easy chair with a recent issue of *Forbes*. But the lead article wasn't proving to be as engrossing as promised. Thoughts of gaminelike Holly Sutton kept cropping up to interfere with his reading.

She couldn't be normal! Vans painted lurid colors were parked outside her door at odd hours of the day or night, and her own car looked as if it were held together with matchsticks. Every child in the neighborhood treated the backyard as his own personal playground and the dog was as big as a horse. Yet why did visions of Holly's laughing face keep cropping up? No man in his right mind would have anything to do with a kook like her. Come to think of it, some of those long-haired types he had seen driving the vans would certainly qualify as companions for her. Then why did it bother him to think of her intimate with any of those men?

"And here I thought Liza was detrimental to a man's sanity," Jonathan muttered, taking a big swallow of his drink. "That little pixie must constantly run on all cylinders." His usually stern face unconsciously relaxed as the memory of Holly's delightful features swam before his face. Black curls that shone with a life of their own, eyes that resembled a rare blue-green gem, and a mouth that revealed a sensuous curve if a man chose to ignore the braces. With the incident behind him, he could now chuckle at the memory of Holly using candy to bribe that horse of a dog to climb off his lap.

Jonathan grimaced, forcing his thoughts away from the petite brunette and concentrating instead on the lovely redhead he was taking to dinner that evening. Patricia was just the cure to help a man forget a woman he didn't need or want in his life.

Early Monday morning, Holly coaxed her sickly VW Bug out of the garage and down the street to the freeway. Jonathan had been leaving the duplex at the same time. She would never forget the wince on his face when he looked at the scarred Beetle with its gray-primered fenders and painted lines criss-crossing the edges as if the metal had been neatly stitched together with a strong black thread. Once the car had been painted a cheerful yellow; now only one door remained that bright color while the other parts were either a sanded gray or, like the trunk, a vibrant blue. Holly could afford a new car, but her cautious self suggested that she drive her little Bug until it choked out its dying gasp.

Holly drove into the parking lot of Carousel Productions. The ornate two-story stucco building's distinction was that it had held offices for a well-known movie studio in the thirties and forties. It even carried a plaque with its history next to the large double doors. On the outside, the building was a part of the past, but on the inside, magic and the future were the order of the day.

After she parked, Holly walked inside the building and waved a cheery hello to Sherry, the receptionist, and passed down the hallway to the offices and conference rooms on the first floor. The technical offices and recording studio were upstairs. The room she entered was filled with six people all talking at once.

"Here she is!" One man looked up and greeted Holly with a broad smile. "Hey, babe, how ya doin'?"

"Not too bad for a Monday." She stopped at a small tray to pour herself a cup of coffee, then flopped down into an old easy chair. She picked up the man's hand that had settled on her leg just above her knee and put it back on his own knee. "Really, Steve, you need to take hold of yourself," she crooned.

Steve grinned unabashed. He looked like the typical surfer with his Hawaiian floral shirt, ragged cut-offs, thongs, dark tanned skin, and shaggy blond hair down to his shoulders. He had known Holly for almost a year and had tried to get her into his bed for the same amount of time.

An average of once a week, Steve propositioned Holly. Though each time she rejected him, he never gave up.

"I'm planning to have another barbecue down at my place soon," he told her. "Naturally, I wanted to invite you first."

"Just another one of your beachfront orgies and drunken brawls." Chris spoke up with an exaggerated yawn behind her words. She and Holly shared the female voices in the cartoon programs. A tall woman in her mid-twenties, her one vanity was her waist-length sandy-brown hair, which was usually styled in a single braid down her back. Her faded jeans and equally faded plaid cotton shirt were also a part of her laid-back personality. She and Holly had been close friends for the past five years. Chris tossed a stapled sheaf of papers into Holly's lap. "Ferdie wants you for the witch, the squirrel, and the rabbit. I got the little girl, the owl, and a deer. He'd like us to read it through before he gives it to Hal for consideration."

"Don't tell me we're stuck with another one of his so-called masterpieces!" Holly groaned.

The "then we won't tell you!" shouted in unison crashed down upon her ears.

Holly hastily scanned the script and groaned again. "Ferdie can't write a letter, much less a cartoon script. When is he going to learn that?"

"Never," Warren, a tall, lanky man in his early thirties, drawled. He had preferred faded jeans, chambray shirts, boots, and a Stetson before the urban cowboy look had become popular. It was a source of wonderment to the others since they all knew that he hailed from Maryland and was allergic to horses.

The Ferdie they were discussing was one of the layout artists for the company, but he fancied himself a writer. Every few months he would come up with a story idea and call in the group for the voices of the characters to read his new script. His ideas were always bad; the stories even worse. The trouble was that no one had the heart to tell the gentle giant of a man that his writing was atrocious. Instead the group would come into the building, read the script, then quietly recommend that the script needed some work before the executive producer read it. After that, the script was never heard of again. But Ferdie never gave up his dream of writing the ultimate cartoon script.

Carousel Productions had been in existence for only three years and produced a few Saturday morning cartoon programs and a series of weekday specials for children. Hal White, the head of the company, had always dreamed of producing his own cartoons. After working for other, much larger and better-known companies, he finally struck out on his own and began Carousel. He spent a great many long hours of talking to the local networks and luring new talent to work for low pay with promises of bonuses in the more lucrative future. He also displayed a willingness to listen to even the most offbeat ideas from his writers. It wasn't long before Hal had seen three of his programs shown on network television and two feature-length cartoons released for the viewing public. Carousel Productions was finally making a profit and paying its employees excellent wages.

An hour later, another one of Ferdie's scripts had died and would receive a quiet funeral. Holly bade her coworkers farewell and headed outside to her car. Since she wouldn't be needed until the next day, she decided to stop by the library for some new books before heading home.

The balance of the day wasn't one of Holly's best. Her car had trouble starting when she left the library and was even more cantankerous when she started it again after stopping at the grocery store.

Then when she arrived home she found that Ralph had decided to run through the garden, something he normally didn't do, and had left trampled flowers in his wake.

Her mood didn't improve when she put on water to boil

for tea and later discovered that there wasn't any water in the kettle. The teapot was burned beyond repair and she had to throw it out.

That night as she got ready for bed, Holly vowed that nothing else could go wrong. She couldn't have been more wrong.

Ralph was outside howling, and she ran to him in a flash. She found him sitting in the middle of the lawn, his head thrown back as he serenaded the neighborhood.

"Ralph!" Holly pleaded with her dog. "Be quiet!"

"Damn it all to hell!" An angry male voice was heard from the other half of the house.

Holly spun around. "Oh, no," she moaned, pressing her fingertips to her lips. "Now you've done it, Ralph."

Oblivious to his surroundings, the large dog continued his canine concert.

"Oh, Ralph, please, not tonight," Holly begged. She flinched when a door slammed.

"What is going on here?" Jonathan demanded, reaching Holly in a few strides. "Or are you going to tell me that your dog is actually part wolf and he enjoys baying at the moon? There's only one problem: *there is no moon!*"

"It's not that," she protested, even as she walked over to the St. Bernard and tugged on his collar. He refused to budge. "Actually, uh, it's just that Ralph is in love." Involuntarily, her eyes roamed over Jonathan's figure, compelling even in a dark-burgundy velour thigh-length robe.

Jonathan's jaw worked convulsively. "Your dog howls when he's in love?" He wasn't prepared to believe that story. Especially when a slip of a woman dressed in a skimpy nightshirt with a picture of Garfield on the front was telling the tale.

35

Holly took a deep breath. "Ralph is in love with the poodle two doors down and when she's—ah"—she wondered if her face was as red as it felt—"she's in heat, Ralph turns all mopey. He's a very despondent lover, if there is such a thing. He can't seem to understand that dogs are usually very aggressive during this time. The one time he approached her, she nearly bit his nose off so now he tells her, in his own way, how much he loves her."

"Your dog is in love with a poodle?" Jonathan asked flatly.

"A toy poodle," Holly mumbled, still vainly pulling on Ralph's collar. "Come on, Ralph. I'm sure Missy is sleeping soundly although the rest of us aren't, thanks to you. I'm sure Mr. Lockwood wishes he was back in his bed as much as I want to be in mine." She turned to Jonathan. "Once I get him into the house, he'll be quiet."

"Ralph, into the house!" Jonathan commanded.

Even a lovesick dog couldn't miss the voice of ultimate authority. Ralph lumbered toward the house.

Jonathan turned to Holly. His eyes skimmed over her curves under the soft cotton nightshirt and on down to her bare legs and feet.

She flushed, feeling that he could probably see the bikini panties with part of the lace missing around the waistband. She had been meaning to throw them away for some time now, but her mother's rules that nothing was discarded until it was absolutely beyond repair had stuck too firmly in her mind.

"I—ah—I'm sorry Ralph woke you up," Holly apologized, moving backward a step at a time. The signals she was receiving from Jonathan were decidedly not those of an angry neighbor! "I'll keep him inside for the next few nights," she promised, finally escaping to her door and pushing the large dog the rest of the way into the house. "Good night."

Jonathan remained outside for a few moments, shaking his head in disbelief. He could hear Holly scolding her errant dog, then watched the living room light go out.

"Amazing," he murmured, turning toward his own back door.

It wasn't just the lack of sleep that brought about Jonathan's less than amiable mood the next afternoon while he scanned the computer printouts placed in front of him.

"Why wasn't I shown this earlier?" he demanded of his young assistant as he whipped off his dark-rimmed reading glasses.

"Th—they wanted to check it a second time in case there was an error, Mr. Lockwood," the young man stammered, shifting from one foot to the other in nervous agitation. "Unfortunately, it isn't wrong."

Jonathan checked his appointment calendar, then flipped the intercom switch on and buzzed his secretary. "Arlene, cancel my appointments for the next two days and get me a seat on this afternoon's flight to Seattle." His dark glower didn't boost his assistant's confidence any.

He then turned back to his assistant. "Naturally, the Bellevue branch isn't to know of my arrival," he drawled, leaving unspoken the threat of what would happen if his orders were disobeyed in any way.

"Yes, sir," he mumbled, glad that he wasn't the one to aggravate Mr. Lockwood's temper.

Jonathan stopped at the house long enough to pack and change his clothes. Since he wouldn't arrive in Seattle until after banking hours, he would have the evening to study the printouts more thoroughly before he appeared on the branch's doorstep first thing in the morning.

After packing and changing into a casual shirt and slacks, he placed his suitcase in the trunk of his car. He glanced toward Holly's front door and vaguely thought of leaving her a note saying he'd be out of town for a few days.

"Help! Help!" A childish voice shrieked just before a tiny figure literally hurled itself at him.

"What the . . . ?" Jonathan looked down at the small girl who tried to burrow her body into his.

"That man," the little girl wailed, pointing at a tall figure standing nearby. "He said I have to go with him and I don't want to."

"Hey, buddy, this has nothing to do with you," the man called over.

"Is that right? Then you won't mind if I contact the police and allow them to decide?" Jonathan's dark eyes captured and held the other man's shifting gaze with unspoken meaning. Muttering explicit curses, the man swiftly moved away and soon, the sound of a car retreating could be heard.

"He scared me!" the small girl sobbed.

"Please, little girl." Jonathan was bewildered and was clearly unable to handle a child on the verge of hysteria. He heaved a sigh of relief when Holly's VW pulled into the adjoining driveway. Holly jumped out of her car and ran over to the pair.

"Heidi, what's wrong?" she asked softly, unable to disengage the girl's arms from their stranglehold around Jonathan's legs.

"A man . . . he wasn't nice . . . I didn't want to go

". . . he made him go away," she explained in her own disjointed way.

Holly glanced to Jonathan for the entire story.

"From what I could gather, a man was trying to coax her to go with him and she came running here," he told Holly in a stiff voice, clearly relieved to be free of his small bundle.

Holly nodded as she rocked the crying girl in her arms to soothe her. She walked to the side gate, unfastened the latch, and called Ralph's name. A moment later the St. Bernard came running out. "Heidi, why don't you ask Ralph to show you where the M&M's are?" she suggested with a loving smile, after unlocking and pushing her front door open.

Heidi's tearstained face turned toward Jonathan. "Are you Holly's daddy?"

For some reason, the innocent question irritated him. "No, I'm not," he replied tersely.

"Go on in, Heidi," Holly urged before further damage could be done. She turned to Jonathan and smiled warmly at him. "Thank you. There's been reports of a child molester in the area and, well, Heidi would be the perfect target because she wanders alone around the neighborhood so much. Most of the children know enough to come here and go in the backyard where Ralph will protect them."

"*He'll* protect them?" Jonathan swept a hand toward the open front door.

"He's a very good watchdog," Holly protested.

"You told me that he flunked obedience school!" he argued.

"That doesn't mean he doesn't know how to bite," she yelled. "He'd protect any one of those children with his life."

"You shouldn't have to worry about those children. That's what their mothers are for," he said harshly.

Holly's hands were planted on her hips as she leaned forward. "Heidi's father died two years ago leaving very little insurance to take care of his family. Her mother has to work in order to support the two of them. There's a babysitter when Heidi gets out of kindergarten, but she doesn't keep a good eye on her. Heidi's a very friendly and loving little girl. If you hadn't been here and if she hadn't been able to get into the backyard in time, that creep might have taken her away and no one would have seen her again. As to her fate, I don't even want to think about that. The day of the stay-at-home mother is just about gone, which leaves children to be watched by a babysitter or, unfortunately, left on their own. She's safe, thanks to you. Right now, that's all that matters. But I would suggest you call the police and report the incident."

Jonathan couldn't help but stand there surprised by the vehemence in Holly's voice. Before responding, he glanced at his watch. "I certainly will do what you suggested and though I would be most interested in continuing this conversation," he mused, "I have a flight to catch. I'll be in Seattle on business for a few days. It's gratifying to know that my belongings will be safe with a guard dog close at hand." He held up a hand to silence Holly's heated retort. "You're an amazing creature, Miss Sutton." He smiled and then took his leave.

Holly stood there, stunned by Jonathan's backhanded compliment, and watched him drive off. "Why don't I feel insulted?" she muttered, watching the dark car move down the street until her attention was drawn elsewhere.

"Holly, Ralph won't share the M&M's with me!"

Heidi's wail of dismay was probably heard all the way onto the next block.

"I'm coming," she said with a sigh, turning and walking up to the house. She would have to call Heidi's house and speak to her mother when she got home from work. And the words she was going to say about that teenage baby-sitter weren't going to be very pretty!

CHAPTER THREE

It was strange that after only knowing him for a few days, Holly found herself missing her arrogant neighbor. But she did miss him, especially the next morning when her usually faithful Beetle gave up the ghost when she was ready to leave for work.

"I really don't need this," Holly grumbled, trudging back into the house to call the service garage. They promised to pick her car up in the next hour or so. Since she didn't care to wait indefinitely, she decided she'd better see about getting a ride to the studio. Luckily, one of the cartoonists lived not too far from her. She called the cartoonist, obtained a ride, then called the garage back and told them she'd leave the ignition key under the car mat. She said she'd contact them later in the day regarding her car.

"Whoof!" Ralph pushed his head into Holly's lap.

"This isn't starting out to be a good day, Ralph," she muttered, scratching the St. Bernard behind his ears.

She got to work and talked to the garage mechanic later that morning. He informed her that while a new alternator couldn't breathe new life into the tired old car, it would give it a little boost. After advising her that she really had better start looking for a new means of transportation as soon as possible, he asked her to go out with him the following week. She thanked him for his advice and politely turned down his invitation.

"Fantastic," Hal pronounced after the group viewed the final stage of Carousel's latest feature-length cartoon. *"The Snow Fairy* is definitely ready for a Christmas release."

"Of course. We of royal blood never do anything by half measures," Holly declared in the high-pitched voice she had used for the fairy in the film.

"She's at it again," Steve said, groaning and rolling his eyes in mock horror. "Lately we haven't been sure what character she's going to decide to be next!"

"With Holly it's more than allowed." Hal smiled warmly at his crew. "I think this is a good time to celebrate, don't you?"

"Par-ty! Par-ty!" Steve chanted, jumping up and raising his arms over his head. The chant was soon taken up by everyone as an impromptu conga line snaked its way out of the screening room and down the hall.

"Come one, come all," Holly shouted over the ruckus. "The celebration begins at seven at my house. Bring your own booze!"

"I'll help with the food," Chris offered, and several others volunteered to bring snacks.

"You've got a lot of guts letting these animals invade your house," Hal told Holly.

She grinned. "Don't worry, Hal. If they tear the place apart, I'll let you buy me my very own house! The only reason I'm willing to have it at my place is because my neighbor is out of town. Now the least you can do is give me a ride home."

"Sure, sweetheart." He gave her an affectionate hug. "Donna and I'll be there on time to help keep the peace.

I'll even bring a few bottles of champagne to make the celebration complete."

After Hal drove her home the only housecleaning Holly did was to pick up the few magazines littering the living room. She saw no reason to clean house when it would be dirty again in a matter of hours.

She changed into a pair of sapphire-blue cotton pants with a drawstring waist and a white cotton sweater with a bright blue and pink abstract design on the front.

By seven thirty, everyone had arrived and the noise level was just below the roar of a crowd cheering a touchdown at the Super Bowl. Holly felt confident that there would be no complaints about the noise since the house sat at the end of the block and the nearest neighbors were away on a cruise.

"Hey, babe, great party." Steve followed Holly into the kitchen and watched her refill a large plastic pail with ice and cans of beer. He stood at her side, blocking her exit. "It's a long drive back to my place," he hinted broadly.

Holly rolled her eyes. Steve certainly wasn't giving up! "I won't hold it against you if you have to leave early, Steve," she drawled, moving away, but only succeeding in getting herself cornered between the refrigerator and Steve.

He leaned forward, placing one hand on either side of her shoulders. "You know, with the right persuasion, I might be willing to stay the night," he whispered, sending beer-tainted breath across her face.

Holly pushed the ice bucket into his stomach and adroitly moved away. "Then I'll have to watch my words carefully, won't I?" she tossed back as she left the kitchen.

"Ah, I see our resident lech has struck again," Chris observed, taking the makeshift ice bucket out of Holly's hands and setting it on the table already laden with bowls of chips and dips and half-empty wine bottles.

"I always pictured a kitchen as a wholesome place until Steve cornered me next to the refrigerator." Holly's lips twisted in a pained grimace. "If he wasn't such a good voice, I'd strangle him!"

"And he's also Hal's dear darling nephew," Chris reminded her.

"How could I forget?" Holly said, laughing.

Holly spent the next hour circulating among the crowd. She smiled, accepting the guests' sincere compliments regarding the spur-of-the-moment party.

"No one else can put together a bash as fast as you can, Holly," Larry, one of the artists, told her as he waved a beer can around and dropped cigarette ashes on the carpet.

"Thanks," Holly replied, wondering how long it would take her to clean the carpet.

It was well after 2 A.M. when the last of the partymakers filtered out the front door. For a while, all that could be heard were the sounds of car, van, and truck engines as they roared down the street.

Holly let out a silent sigh of relief. As much as she enjoyed giving parties, she was always happy when they were over. She turned away from her open front door and absently reached for a filled ashtray sitting on a small table as she closed the door behind her.

"You're not going to clean up now, are you?" A male voice intruded on her blessed silence.

"Oh!" Holly spun around, her eyes wide with surprise. "Don't scare me like that, Steve," she scolded. "I thought you had already left."

He shrugged. "Figured I'd better use the bathroom first since you're gonna make me drive all that way home."

"Good idea. Good night, Steve." Holly spoke in a firm voice, leaving him in no doubt of her decision.

His body wove slightly from side to side. "Why won't you go to bed with me, Holly?" His words were slurred from all the beer he had consumed during the evening, but Holly heard him.

"Steve, we've been through this before." She felt as if she were a broken record. She could also feel a whopper of a headache coming on. "Since you and I work together, it wouldn't be a good idea for us to become lovers."

Steve's reply was short and crude. "What makes you think you're better than me? Hell, I'm great in the sack."

"I don't care to hear references," Holly cut him off abruptly. "Steve, I'm very tired, so I'd appreciate your leaving *now.*" She stood to one side of the front door. She only wished she hadn't closed it.

His grin resembled a sneer. "Come on, doll, why not let me show you how good we can be together?"

She wished that Ralph was inside the house instead of sleeping peacefully in the backyard. The St. Bernard's size alone was intimidating. Holly's stomach churned as Steve continued to give a more graphic description of what he wanted to do to her. Since Jonathan was out of town, she had no one to call for help.

"Steve, you're pretty drunk, so why don't you sleep in your van tonight and go home in the morning?" she suggested, refusing to show her unease at the way the situation was turning out.

"Bull!" he snarled, waving an arm around. "You just think you're too good for me, Holly. You always have." His body swayed as he fumbled with the buttons to his brightly colored Hawaiian shirt. "Hey, you're no different than any other broad, except that you don't have too much where it counts." He eyed her breasts with open scorn. "My thirteen-year-old sister has more up top than you do, although I will say that the rest of you isn't half bad." His eyes moved lewdly over her lower body.

Holly was tense for battle. "Get out." Her voice came across as a deadly calm she didn't feel inside.

The three staccato raps on the door resembled the abrupt sound of gunshots. With eyes blazing and a tiny jaw squared for a fight, Holly flung open the front door. The last person she expected to find on the other side was Jonathan.

"I hope I'm not disturbing you." He kept his gaze trained on Holly. "I saw that your lights were still on and I thought I'd pick up any mail that had come while I was gone." Not once did he look toward the sullen-faced Steve.

Luckily, Holly caught on quickly. "Of course." She turned back to Steve. "Good night, Steve."

He pushed past her and walked swiftly to his van parked on the street a short distance from the house. A moment later, all that was heard was the squeal of rubber as the van tore down the street.

"I gather I ruined your friend's plans," Jonathan said wryly.

"His plans, not mine." Holly offered him a weak smile. "I'm just glad you came to the rescue. I thought you weren't going to be home for another couple days."

He glanced at the coffee table littered with foam cups, paper plates, and empty beer cans. "I'm glad I didn't take the afternoon flight," he murmured, then went on to explain. "I finished my work earlier than I expected."

Holly grimaced as she followed the direction of his gaze. "If you can stand the mess, I can offer you a cup of coffee."

"It's late. Thank you, anyway." He began to turn away, but Holly's hand on his arm hindered his movement.

"Please?" she pleaded softly, then added with a rueful grin, "To be honest, that encounter with Steve has left me a bit shaky and I don't want to be alone just now."

"Did he have cause to believe that he'd share your bed tonight?"

She shook her head. "No way! I've been turning him down for over a year. This time, the beer he drank wasn't allowing him to think clearly." Holly headed for the kitchen and picked up her new teakettle, which was decorated with a strawberry design. She was horrified to find her hand shaking uncontrollably.

"Holly, I don't need any coffee," Jonathan said as he took the kettle out of her hand. Finding her skin like ice, he picked up the other hand and rubbed them both briskly between his own to warm them.

"I know I shouldn't feel this way," Holly babbled. "I mean, I know Steve wouldn't rape me or anything, but he acted so different tonight." She clamped her mouth shut when her teeth began to chatter. She offered no resistance when Jonathan enfolded her in his arms.

"So you're not as tough as you thought you were," he mused, keeping her cheek pressed firmly against his shirt front.

Holly blinked rapidly, but no tears came. At least she would be spared that disgrace. Slowly, hesitantly, she slid her arms around his waist and inhaled the warm, slightly sweaty fragrance of his skin.

Jonathan drew back slightly and looked down at Holly's delicate features. He lifted his hand and traced her jawline with his inquisitive fingertip. Her skin felt like silk.

"No man in his right mind should frighten a woman,"

he whispered. "Someone who values laughter and happiness should be treated with the same." Something I could never give a woman, he thought to himself. Get out, while you still can, vibrated in his brain. But he still couldn't resist ordering his fingers to skim over her cheek and back to the soft area just behind her ear.

Holly held her breath under the light touch. His hazel eyes caught her blue-green ones; caught, held, and mesmerized.

Jonathan's hands lowered and circled Holly's neck. "This is crazy," he muttered, a grim expression accenting his features. Every nerve in his body was screaming for him to step away before it was too late. But he knew that the damage had already been done. Just touching her was exquisite torture.

Stung by his words, Holly attempted to step back, but Jonathan refused to relinquish his hold.

"I don't like to be teased," she whispered with a faint catch in her voice.

"I don't tease." His accent became more pronounced with each word. And, by then, his mouth fully covered hers as his hands slid down along Holly's spine until they reached the intriguing dip and he pressed her up against him.

Holly dimly realized that Jonathan was right. He certainly didn't tease!

The tip of his tongue drew an imaginary line around her lips then slid between them to plunge beyond. He absorbed the honey-sweet taste of her mouth and memorized it.

Holly linked her arms around Jonathan's neck, bringing him closer against her. Her mouth opened even wider under his driving force and a soft moan of satisfaction floated up her throat as her hips thrust delicately against him and she felt the potency of his desire. The warm clean scent of his skin invaded her nostrils, more precious than the air surrounding her. She wanted him! *Oh, God yes!* She wanted this man with every fiber of her being. Holly's small breasts swelled against Jonathan's chest, silently inviting his touch. Yet when one of his hands cupped her soft breast she reacted by withdrawing slightly. Steve's disparaging remarks about her figure still rang in her mind.

"You're very sweet, Holly," Jonathan murmured, drawing her lower lip between his teeth and nibbling the tender skin. "Give to me."

His words broke the sensual spell that had begun to weave about them. Holly slowly came to her senses and just as slowly pulled away from him.

"I—ah—I don't think that was a very good idea," she stammered, stepping back another pace. If she hadn't experienced it, she wouldn't have believed that the British "upper lip" could evoke some very erotic responses!

"Call it an experiment." He smiled, looking oh, so cool, calm, and collected.

"Experiment?"

"I was curious to find out if kissing a woman wearing braces tasted metallic."

Holly's face turned a bright red. "I hope your curiosity is satisfied now," she snapped, adroitly hiding the hurt caused by his casually spoken words.

"My curiosity was about all that was satisfied," Jonathan pointed out calmly.

Holly's eyes couldn't help but look down. The strain on Jonathan's expertly cut slacks explained his remark.

"I didn't realize I was trading one sex maniac for another," she snapped, struggling to dampen the fires his kiss had evoked.

Jonathan's cheekbones turned a dull red. "The only difference this time is that you wanted me to continue whereas that young hoodlum wasn't even allowed to touch you." Each word was clipped in cold anger.

Feeling her headache coming on in full force and tears threatening to erupt, Holly rubbed the heel of her hand over her brow. "Would you please go?" she requested. "I think I've more than adequately shown my gratitude for your rescuing me."

"It's too late to hide, Holly," Jonathan chided, brushing his thumb over her moist lips, which automatically parted at his touch. "You can't always retreat from the world by using children as a shield. The day will come when you'll have to come out and discover just how much of a woman you really are." With that parting advice, he left.

Holly stood silently for a moment, then she locked the front door, went to the back, let a happy Ralph inside, and headed for her bedroom. She left her clothes strewn in an untidy heap on the floor and crawled into bed. For once she didn't care that the dog climbed onto the bed and snuggled close to her. It wasn't the kind of comfort she craved at that moment, but it was enough to help her drift off into an uneasy sleep.

An hour later, Jonathan found it difficult to sleep as he tossed and turned in his bed. The memory of warm lips moving under his and the sensation of a soft breast under his palm, not to mention the sweet scent of her skin, were all too potent to allow him to relax sufficiently to sleep. He cursed softly and fluently. He finally rose from his bed, hoping that a brandy and some television would make him drowsy.

After pouring himself a bit of the amber-colored liquor,

51

he settled in his easy chair and reached for the television remote control box. As it was early morning, he didn't have too much of a choice except for the local cable stations, which broadcast movies twenty-four hours a day. He grimaced when the television screen filled with the bright colors and loud sounds of a science fiction film that had been popular the year before. It was definitely not Jonathan's idea of entertainment. He preferred artsy foreign films himself, but it just might put him to sleep.

All he could figure out was that the man commanding the spaceship was engaging in a verbal battle with his computer, whose ultrafeminine audio control sounded very familiar.

"I knew I should have had you reprogrammed on Alpha-Seti Five." The man groaned in exasperation. "Look, all I want are the coordinates for Canna Two-Seven. Think you can handle that little task?"

"Anything you say, darling." The voice purred, with brightly colored lines squiggling across a computer monitor. "I'm yours to command."

Jonathan frowned. Where had he heard that voice before? He sipped his brandy while racking his brain to recall the identity of the sexy voice.

"Umm, I love it when your fingers move over my circuit boards like that." The computer voice laughed throatily after it had given the man the necessary coordinates. "You have such a masterful touch that my wires tingle when you work my controls."

The laugh tipped Jonathan off and he bolted upright in shock. "It can't be!" he rasped.

"Cut out the seduction routine, One-H-Three, and do your job!" The man on the screen snarled as his fingers flew over a computer console. "We don't have much time left before the Tarians catch up with us."

"All I'm trying to do is make your trip pleasurable, Decker," computer One-H-Three declared in a throaty purr. "I'm here to take care of your *every* need."

Jonathan closed his eyes tightly. It was! There was no doubt in his mind now. The sexy audio of the spaceship computer was none other than Holly Sutton.

With out-of-character haste, he gulped down the remainder of the potent brandy, switched off the television, and returned to bed only to dream of a black-haired nymph with rare gemstone eyes.

Although she had had little sleep, Holly was up earlier than usual the next morning to catch the bus that would take her to the service garage. She dressed quickly in jeans and a cobalt and white striped cotton sweater and had a quick breakfast of an apple and instant coffee before leaving for the bus stop.

Holly made it to there with time to spare. She wasn't surprised to find herself alone since it was just after six o'clock. Settling down on the bench, she opened a book and soon became so engrossed in the plot that she didn't hear the sound of a car stopping in front of her.

"Don't tell me that your dog is now in love with your car and won't allow you to drive it out of the garage?"

Holly stiffened at the voice that had haunted her dreams. "I should be so lucky," she grumbled.

Jonathan frowned as he glanced around the deserted street. "Where are you going now?" he asked crisply.

"My car is at a garage across town," she explained. "I'm going over to pick it up."

He didn't hesitate. "Get in."

"Why?"

Jonathan silently counted to ten. "It isn't safe for you to be here alone. I'll drive you to the garage."

Holly was a bit hesitant. She was still aware of what had passed between them not all that many hours before. Of course, since he was a gentleman, he wouldn't mention it, would he? She gathered up her purse and book, and moved toward the passenger door Jonathan held open for her. How had he gotten out of the car so quickly? Without thinking, she voiced the question aloud after she had given him directions to the garage.

Jonathan's lips twitched in a small smile. "It's part of a gentleman's training. You have to pass the class in how to properly open a door for a lady or you fail the entire course." He discovered that if he breathed deeply, the light floral scent of Holly's cologne invaded his senses. It brought back their kiss with an alarming clarity.

"Did you attend a prep school?" Holly shifted in the seat so that her back rested against the door. His profile was as harshly drawn as his face when he turned to look at her, but there was something there, almost a kind of haunting sorrow in his eyes and face. The more she came to know Jonathan, the more he intrigued her. She could feel a strange warmth stealing up her body and a tingling streak across her abdomen. This is purely a sexual attraction, she reminded herself. It's only because he kisses better than any man you've ever met. Just stay calm and you won't come out of this looking like a fool.

"Lock the door if you prefer sitting that way," he instructed, without taking his eyes off the road. "And, yes, I did."

"Very posh?"

"Very spartan. It was also meant to turn us into men.

Central heating, comfortable beds, and hot water weren't part of the curriculum."

Holly arched a teasing eyebrow. "Do you realize that's almost a joke?"

Jonathan slowed the car as the traffic light turned red. "You seem to consider me a pompous ass."

Holly blinked. She'd almost swear he sounded aggrieved. It was just that he came across so serious all the time that she wondered if he ever smiled or laughed.

"Well—" She paused, choosing her words carefully. As she freely admitted, tact wasn't one of her stronger suits. "You do seem to own the typical British upper lip." She refused to think about what that upper lip could do in closer quarters!

Jonathan muttered several dark words under his breath.

"Why are you out so early?" Holly knew it was time to change the subject. "Most banks aren't open on Saturdays."

"I have some reports to dictate so my secretary can begin typing them first thing Monday morning," he explained, flipping the turn signal. "You're also out quite early, aren't you?"

Holly nodded. "I'm supposed to meet some friends for lunch in Laguna Beach and I wanted to get an early start. I like to wander through the shops down there when I get a chance."

Jonathan pulled into a driveway and stopped the car. "Here you are."

"Thank you for the ride." Holly turned to grasp the door handle. Before she could pull it open, Jonathan's hand covered her fingers, sending tingles up her arm as if she had just hit her funny bone.

"Just stay there," he advised, turning back to open his door and get out of the car.

Holly sat back, enjoying the privilege of having her car door opened for her. The closest she had come to that part of etiquette had been when her date reached across her to open the passenger door for her and that was only because it had a tendency to stick. So this was the pampered life!

"Thank you again for the lift," she told him, stepping out of the car.

"I'll wait until you're sure your car is ready," he assured her.

"Oh, no. I've wasted enough of your time already," Holly protested. "I couldn't put you out any more."

"I will wait."

She flashed him a smile. "It seems you're destined to always come to my rescue," she said flippantly.

Jonathan's eyes were riveted on her slightly parted lips. "Yes."

Holly flushed a bright red and hurried away before her discomfort became known. She couldn't argue that she liked the idea of his waiting until she reclaimed her car. It made her feel wanted.

In no time, Holly wrote out the check for the repairs and endured another lecture on the extremely short life span of her car. She was pleased to hear the engine start at the first turn of the ignition key. She managed to give Jonathan a brief smile and wave as she drove away.

The next afternoon, Holly sat on the front porch with Randy, a little boy who lived down the street.

"I wish I could have a dog." He sighed, rubbing Ralph behind the ears. The dog closed his eyes in bliss at having his favorite area scratched. His large paws landed in the small boy's lap.

"I don't think your wish will come true as long as your mother is allergic to dogs," Holly pointed out logically. "You better not forget to wash your hands and brush Ralph's hairs from your clothing before you go home."

"Uh-huh." He looked up when Jonathan walked out of his front door without glancing toward his neighbor. "Doesn't he ever smile?" the boy asked Holly.

Jonathan's head snapped up as the innocent question reached his ears. His eyes met and snared Holly's across the wide driveway. She couldn't help but remember how warm and inviting his body had felt against hers that night he had kissed her. She recalled the musky taste of his skin, the soft sounds in his throat when their mouths caressed each other, and she found herself wanting to relive that experience.

"Perhaps some people don't know how to smile, Randy," she said huskily, not realizing that Jonathan's keen hearing had picked up her low-voiced reply.

Jonathan pulled his car door open and got in, driving off without a backward glance. He turned on the radio, allowing the soothing strains of classical music to fill the car. His fingers drummed impatiently against the steering wheel. What did it matter what she thought of him? She was nothing more than a free spirit who flitted through life without a care in the world.

No, he reminded himself, there was so much more to Holly. Now there was only one question. Was Jonathan open-minded enough to want to pursue the many layers to her personality?

CHAPTER FOUR

Jonathan sat behind his desk and looked out the window overlooking the backyard. He was able to take care of a great deal of work after hours in the comfort of his home by using the second bedroom as an office.

At that moment, he found it difficult to concentrate on the reports he had meant to read sometime during the weekend. He was too busy watching Holly work in her flower garden that bordered the back fence.

Two weeks had passed since the evening he had discovered she was more woman than he had imagined. The taste of her mouth and the memory of how her body had arched so willingly against his still lingered in his mind.

In deference to the warm fall sun, she wore bright pink cotton shorts and a matching candy-striped crop top. He guessed that she and Ralph were playing some sort of game. While Holly tended her garden, a sly Ralph crept up behind her and attempted to snatch her gardening tools. A laughing Holly would then chase the playful St. Bernard around the yard. During one such exercise, Jonathan laughed out loud then instantly sobered as a small boy's voice echoed in his memory.

"Oh, yes, I can smile," he whispered, turning his chair away from the window and returning to his waiting paperwork.

Over the past couple of weeks, Jonathan had found his mind frequently turning to the subject of Holly Sutton. But he certainly didn't want to think about her when he needed to channel his full concentration on his work to prepare for an important meeting to be held at the bank's corporate headquarters in six weeks. Soon he was engrossed in his work and blocking out Holly's laughter and Ralph's barking in the backyard.

The following Monday, Holly left the house for a much-needed run. Since there was a faint chill in the air, she had topped her emerald athletic shorts with a white sweatshirt.

When she arrived in view of her home, she found an angry Jonathan holding onto Ralph's collar.

"Uh-oh." She sighed, speeding up.

"Your dog seems to have acquired the knack of escaping the backyard," Jonathan informed her coolly.

"The gate must not have been securely latched." She hurried forward to take charge of her dog.

"He climbed into my car."

Holly immediately saw the damage from Ralph's exploration. The back of Jonathan's charcoal three-piece suit now boasted a fine coating of white and brown dog hairs.

"At least he didn't chew your briefcase," she offered feebly. She swiftly returned Ralph to the backyard and checked that the latch was firmly in place.

"I *am* sorry," she apologized, returning to Jonathan. "I guess he hoped he was going for a ride. He likes to go in the car every chance he gets."

His smile was frosty and brief. "I wish I knew why your dog disliked me."

"Actually, I think Ralph likes you or he wouldn't bother with you at all." Holly's voice trailed off when she noticed that Jonathan's attention had shifted. Looking down, she found that the oversized neckline of her top had slipped down one arm to bare her shoulder. She flushed and attempted to cover herself.

"You're leaving me to wonder what could happen next." Jonathan was amused by her discomfort. He wondered how someone could keep ten children in line but seemed to have so much trouble with her own life.

"At this rate, the following act will be my prying my foot from my mouth," Holly muttered, turning away. "I'll take care of the cleaning bill for your suit."

"Holly"—Jonathan grasped her arm to detain her—"would you have dinner with me one evening?"

Her mouth went dry. "Why?" she asked dumbly, feeling a strange tingling along her arm from his touch.

His smile warmed his harsh features. "Because I would feel safer if I could get you on my side."

Holly's own smile was a shade embarrassed. "I—ah—if you like."

"Friday evening at seven." Jonathan released her arm and returned to the house to change his clothes.

Holly entered her side of the house and went into her bedroom to change. As she was undressing, the full impact of their conversation hit her. "Oh, my," she said faintly, once the realization hit her. "He asked me for a date."

That afternoon Holly was running late. She had promised to meet Liza for lunch at one o'clock and it was twenty after by the time she reached their favorite sidewalk café.

"Don't tell me your watch stopped?" Liza teased when a breathless Holly dropped into the chair opposite hers.

"More like I lost track of the time," she admitted sheepishly. "Sorry."

"No problem." Liza smiled brightly. "I had an excellent view of the scenery."

Holly couldn't help but notice the many good-looking men who frequented the café. She wouldn't be surprised if many were in search of wealthy women looking for "escorts." "Poor Harry!" Holly laughed.

"Sweetie, I'm married, not dead." Liza motioned to the waiter and requested a wine spritzer for Holly before the two women turned their attention to the menus and chose their food.

"How do you like your new neighbor?" Liza waited until their food was served before dropping the loaded question.

Holly shrugged, praying she looked indifferent. "No problem."

"You have to admit Jon's a sexy devil." Liza's sea-green eyes twinkled merrily.

Holly ducked her head, pretending a great interest in the colorful quilted placemat before her. "If you like the stuffy type." She then gasped in horror, realizing that at one time Liza certainly had! "Liza, I'm so sorry!"

"No offense taken," she said, and laughed. "Jon can be a pompous ass at times, but he was able to make magic in ways some women only dream about." She spoke softly, obviously lost in the past.

Holly could feel the burning heat caress her cheeks. Erotic images of a naked Jonathan reclining in bed danced before her eyes. Since she had no idea what he looked like with his shirt off, she had to fill in the important areas with her imagination. If her mother knew what turns her mind was taking, she would wash it out with soap!

"As far as he's concerned, I'm nothing more than an incorrigible hippie." Holly forced a nonchalance into her voice.

Liza finished the last bite of her Caesar salad. "Jonathan needs to be around someone like you, Holly. He tends to forget that he has emotions like anyone else."

Holly's grin was mischievous. "I guess a man who hates children and dogs can't be all bad."

Liza shook her head. "Jonathan tends to hide his feelings so no one knows the hurt he's endured," she answered, looking a little sad. "He's a good man, Holly. His loyalties are strong, he's an excellent lover, and he's a man a woman would kill for."

"Then why did the two of you get divorced?" Holly blurted out, then flushed at the audacity of her question.

"It was best for both of us," Liza replied, tactfully closing the subject.

With a smile, Holly suggested ordering dessert and, over Liza's protests, chose black forest cake for each of them.

"I'll have to walk miles to work all these calories off," Liza said, groaning, as they waited for the parking valets to bring their cars to them.

"You only had a salad for lunch," Holly reminded her.

"And three of those delicious buttery rolls." Liza looked down at her slender body as if she was afraid it had suddenly blown up.

"At least you have some curves to worry about." Holly couldn't help but compare her boyish form to Liza's voluptuous figure.

"You're too hard on yourself, Holly," the other woman chided, stepping back a pace when her white Lincoln Continental rolled to a stop in front of her. "Perhaps I should make you my next project instead of Joe Royce's new apartment complex. With the right clothes and makeup, you'd be a woman no man could forget."

Holly looked skeptical. "He asked me out to dinner," she blurted out without thinking. "And don't look so dratted smug about it either! I doubt I'll even go," she muttered.

"Go. At least you'll have a decent meal," Liza urged, aware of Holly's culinary ineptitude.

"I can't believe this! The ex-wife is urging another woman to date her ex-husband!" she explained.

"Why not? Jon is an excellent dinner companion, and he won't feed you hamburger either!"

Holly would have questioned Liza's not-so-subtle matchmaking further, but her attention was caught by the sight of her little VW pulling up behind Liza's Lincoln and the somewhat embarrassed valet who climbed out of the car.

"I can imagine the comments Jonathan has to offer regarding your car." Liza shook her head, baffled by Holly's all-too-thrifty nature.

"At least it doesn't guzzle gas like that tank you drive," she tossed back flippantly, walking to her car. "I'll talk to you later."

"Holly." She looked back. "Remember what I said. Jonathan needs someone like you." Liza's perfectly arched eyebrows lifted as she smiled. "You'll see that I'm right."

Holly shook her head. "No, thanks. I can't see him sitting down with a can of beer and a bowl of popcorn to watch the Super Bowl and I'm certainly not the type to attend the opera or a classical music concert. Don't worry, Liza, I'm fine on my own." She grinned and turned to tip the valet before getting into her car.

"Are you?" Liza murmured aloud to herself as she settled in behind the steering wheel. "We'll see."

When Friday came, Holly wished many times that she had given Jonathan an excuse to get out of her dinner date.

"Perhaps I could catch a quick case of the measles," she muttered, pawing through her closet to the corner where her few fancier dresses were stored. "Why am I so worried?" she demanded, spinning around to face Ralph who lolled in the middle of her bed. "You'd think this was my first date."

In a burst of curiosity, she wondered if Jonathan would show up wearing his typically conservative dark suit, white shirt, and dark tie. Her solution was to add some color. She held up one dress with bold splashes of pink and purple along the bodice and skirt. It would certainly add color, but she couldn't imagine walking into a nice restaurant looking like a flower garden! She had never needed to bother with dressy clothing before and she had only one outfit that would be appropriate for her evening out.

Holly noted the color of the silky dress—a deep raspberry. She knew that the style would look better on a taller woman, but the dress was the most suitable one in her meager wardrobe.

Much to her chagrin, the doorbell rang promptly at seven.

"Now I can understand the meaning of sweaty palms," she said under her breath as she walked across the living room to open the front door. She was right; Jonathan was immaculately attired in a dark-gray suit, white shirt, and deep-gray tie.

"Hello." She suddenly felt very shy.

"You look lovely." Jonathan offered her a brief smile.

Holly was prepared to dispute that fact but her early teachings were too strong. Her mother had instilled in her at an early age that she must always act the part of a lady, no matter how difficult it might be.

"Thank you," she murmured. "Would you care to come in for a drink?"

He shook his head. "I made reservations for seven thirty," he explained.

Jonathan assisted her inside his dark-blue sedan and walked around to the driver's side, wondering why Holly appeared nervous. He couldn't imagine anyone or anything affecting her. She had certainly stood up to him enough times!

"I haven't seen too many of the neighborhood children in the yard lately," he brought up casually.

"I haven't been home very much," Holly replied. "We've been busy at work with a new idea for a feature-length cartoon."

"I thought you just supplied the voices."

"Some of them, yes. But Hal, the head of Carousel Productions, likes input from all his people," she explained. "He feels a group effort puts together a better show."

Dinner was a luxurious treat for Holly. The quiet, dimly lit restaurant that featured Continental cuisine was a new and pleasurable experience for her.

"Very nice." She smiled slightly, looking around.

"But you don't like it?" Jonathan was too attuned to her thoughts.

"It's not that," she hastily reassured him.

"Why do you persist in acting like a misfit?"

Holly's head snapped up at his abrupt question. She silently damned him for being too perceptive. "When I know you better, perhaps I'll tell you," she replied quietly, studying her glass of Chardonnay.

"Why don't you tell me more about your work?" Jonathan proceeded to smooth over the tense moment. "How long have you been a—what is it you call it—a voice?"

Holly nodded. "I've been doing it since college . . . about seven years."

"What did you study in college?"

"Psychology," Holly explained, unaware of a shadow briefly passing over her face. "As for my work, it's decided ahead of time who will read what voice. We work in a recording studio and the cartoon characters' mouths are drawn to match our words."

"Do you ever feel as if you're any of the characters you've given voice to?" he asked curiously.

Holly thought about it for a moment. "Lucretia Margolia."

"I beg your pardon?" He wasn't sure he had heard correctly.

"Lucretia was the villainous witch in a medieval cartoon program," she explained with a smile. Suddenly her voice deepened to a husky purr that sent shivers down Jonathan's spine. "She was such a lovely creature. She was always very sure of herself and knew exactly how to use people. What a wonderful dark and dank castle she lived in. The kind of home only a sorceress could love." Just as suddenly, her voice became breathy and slightly high-pitched. "Of course, Tanya was just the opposite. She lived in a magnificent castle made of ice. One came from the darkness, the other composed of light."

"Lucretia must have been the one with a strong hunger," Jonathan murmured.

Holly had an idea that he wasn't referring to food. "Her

hunger was power," she adroitly informed him. "She wanted to rule the world."

"And did she? Rule the world, that is?"

She tsked. "Surely you know only the honorable people win in the end," she reprimanded him mildly.

"Sometimes I wonder," Jonathan murmured almost to himself, then quickly changed the subject.

Over sole broiled with herbs, Holly learned more about Jonathan's profession as a banking auditor. With skillful questioning, she found out that his father had been a well-known name in international banking until his retirement five years ago. Jonathan's parents resided in a country house outside of London where his father raised roses and his mother continued with her many charity functions. He had no brothers or sisters, and was in his mid-thirties.

Holly confessed that she had two older brothers, one sister, and both her parents were still living. Other than that, she didn't discuss her family background any further.

For dessert, she chose a chocolate and brandy mousse and enjoyed every calorie-laden spoonful.

"It's nice to watch a woman who enjoys her food," Jonathan commented, not taking his eyes off the tip of Holly's tongue, which was retrieving the last speck of mousse from a corner of her mouth. He was positive that her sensual love for food could easily match another more physically active appetite if he cared to pursue that side of her personality.

"If you're trying to say I eat a lot, I'm not offended."

Jonathan smiled at Holly's cheeky answer. "You believe laughter is better than medicine, don't you?"

"Yes, because a lot of people have to laugh so that they won't cry." Holly's eyes wandered over the large dining room with its carefully placed tables covered in white linen tablecloths with floral centerpieces. She wanted to look anywhere but at his face.

Why do I feel that she's talking about herself? Jonathan mused to himself as he paid the check and they left the restaurant.

The ride back to the house was silent, with both of them lost in their own thoughts.

Holly kept wondering if an evening had ever been spent so uncomfortably. "Would you care to come in for coffee?" she offered tentatively after Jonathan parked his car in the driveway.

"That sounds very good, thank you." He got out of the car, then helped her out.

"Ralph is out in the backyard so you won't have to worry about him jumping on you," Holly told him, walking inside and allowing the faint glow of the kitchen light to guide her to one of the lamps in the living room. "I'll get the coffee."

Holly entered the kitchen and looked around with glazed eyes. Did she honestly ask him in for coffee? Even her instant coffee tasted like mud!

"Is anything wrong?" Jonathan followed her into the kitchen.

"I—ah—I'm out of coffee," she stammered.

Jonathan glanced toward one partially opened cabinet and spied a familiar can. "Is there something wrong with this?" He plucked the can from the cabinet interior and held it up.

"Oh, what's the use?" Holly moaned. "Basically, I'm no good at making percolated coffee. Kitchens and I don't agree. I can boil water as long as I can remember to keep an eye on it and can do a few other simple tasks, but most normal cooking tasks turn into disasters for me."

Jonathan continued to hunt through the white painted cabinets with their red lacquered handles until he found filters to go with the coffeemaker on the counter.

"I gather you didn't purchase this?" He measured coffee grounds and poured them into the coffee filter. A moment later, they only had to wait for the water to drip through.

"It was a Christmas gift from my parents." Bitterness tainted Holly's voice. "As far as my mother is concerned, there's no reason why I can't function adequately in the kitchen since she and my sister are excellent cooks."

Jonathan noted that there was a strain not only in Holly's voice but on her face when she mentioned her family. He was curious about her relationship with them, but he wasn't the kind of man to probe.

"I can understand exactly what you mean. My father grows award-winning roses while I can't keep the simplest plant alive. He keeps insisting that it's just a matter of the proper care and feeding, but I only have to look at a green leaf to watch it wither," he explained. "When someone is an expert in one area, it's difficult for them to understand that everyone isn't as proficient."

She glanced up out of the corner of her eye and couldn't help focusing on his mouth. For just a brief moment, her breathing became constricted as she imagined those lips again tasting hers.

"You have that questioning look again," Jonathan told her.

She treated him to a wary frown. "What am I questioning?"

"This." Jonathan's fingers tangled in her dark curls and with gentle pressure he drew her mouth up to his.

The outer edges of Holly's mind acknowledged that he didn't know how to kiss in just one way. This time, his firm mouth set about to seduce. His lips passed over hers once, twice, then retreated to the corner of her mouth to nibble lightly.

Her lips were bathed with the moisture from his kiss and parted in invitation for further exploration. She lifted her hands and manacled his wrists with her fingers. The heat of his skin seared her, but she was afraid that if she let go, she'd fall to the floor.

Jonathan's tongue plunged into Holly's open mouth, trading her taste for his. He'd swear that the rich flavor of the mousse she had eaten was still there. She was swiftly becoming a narcotic in his blood. The more he tried, the more he wanted. Jonathan wrapped his arms around Holly and pulled her up hard against him until air couldn't have moved between their bodies. She linked her arms around his neck and waited for the rollercoaster effect of their kiss to hit the plunge. Her tongue flicked inside his mouth and curled around the end of his tongue. Small moans gathered in the back of her throat and were swallowed up within his own. She was as hungry for him as he was for her.

Now Jonathan knew what drowning felt like. He needed air to survive, but he didn't feel suffocated. He only knew that the feel of Holly's body pressed against his was enough to arouse him almost painfully. It would have been very easy for him to pick her up and carry her into her bedroom to discover the extent of her response. It already appeared that it took little to ignite the passion between them.

Suddenly Holly tensed, dampening her desire. She had never responded to a man so strongly and it frightened her. Even Rob hadn't left her in such a wrung-out state.

Jonathan could immediately sense her withdrawal and

gradually eased his mouth away. "It appears our coffee is ready," he murmured.

"Yes." Holly was still dazed from the past few moments. It took another moment before she fully returned to the present. With a great deal of self-control, she forced herself to pour the hot coffee carefully into two mugs.

"Your kitchen looks like you," Jonathan observed, noting the strawberry theme in the ruffled curtains and on the quilted placemats on the small round table in one corner. "Bright and cheerful." He silently wondered how she could have such good sense in decorating her house yet obviously she couldn't choose suitable clothing for herself. This was the first time he had seen her in a dress that showed her slender figure off in the best possible way.

In an effort to escape the close confines of the kitchen, they carried their steaming cups into the living room. Sensing that Holly was still rattled from their explosive kiss, Jonathan chose the chair closest to the couch.

"You can't deny that there's something between us," Jonathan began, wanting to get it out in the open.

Holly winced when the hot liquid burned her slightly swollen lips. "No, I can't." Her answer was barely audible.

"I'm a very direct person, Holly. I want to know you better."

She set her cup carefully on the table in front of her, and hesitated before speaking. "You mean getting to know me in the physical sense, don't you?"

"Yes." Jonathan saw no reason to beat around the bush.

A brief smile curved Holly's lips. "And here I thought you were cold as ice," she murmured.

He was stung by her remark. "Hopefully you've found out differently," he clipped.

"I think you see me as some kind of fool. That you think

that I'm a woman who offers her body easily. Let me assure you right away that I'm not."

"I saw you with that surfer, remember? You certainly weren't asking him to spend the night with you, and your actions alone that night told me that you're not promiscuous."

"We're oil and water, Jonathan." He liked the way she said his name. "Besides, you disapprove of me."

He searched his mind for the right words. "I know I'm not the kind of man you've been used to." He spoke slowly. "Still, there is that attraction between us. Why not see how far it leads?"

Because I'm afraid of what would eventually happen, her mind screamed. She sensed that Jonathan was the kind of man to take a woman over body and soul.

Jonathan set his coffee cup down and rose from the chair.

"I'm a stubborn man, Holly," he warned her. "I don't understand this any more than you do. I only know that if we both try to ignore what is going on, we'll never know the outcome." He grasped her forearms and pulled her gently to her feet, brushing a light kiss over her lips, before he left.

Afterward Holly felt numb as she let Ralph into the house and went into the bedroom. Even a long, hot shower failed to restore her sense of feeling. Jonathan wasn't the right kind of man for her and she certainly wasn't for him. Yet even as she later drifted off to sleep, one thought kept tickling her mind. What kind of lover would Jonathan be?

All through the next week, Jonathan would have sworn Holly was deliberately avoiding him. When they were at home at the same time, either children were visiting Holly or she was out jogging. It appeared that she ensured there was no free time for her to accidentally run into him, and Jonathan's free evenings were limited as he was preparing an important report for discussion at the executive meeting at the corporate headquarters the following month. On the weekend, he sat at his desk in his office and, behind partially drawn drapes through which no one could see him, watched Holly run and laugh with boys and girls of various ages. Finally he closed his ears against the raucous noise filtering in from outside and attempted to apply himself to his paperwork.

Though Holly was busy refereeing an energetic game of tag, she still kept her eyes on the window she thought was in Jonathan's office. She had been tempted to ask him if he'd like to come outside for a while, but she guessed he'd probably refuse. She grimaced as she looked down at her grubby jeans and sweatshirt. Holly knew that Jonathan would never be caught looking so disreputable. Her speculation was shortlived when the children called her back into the game.

By midafternoon, the children were gone and the yard was again quiet.

Holly hunted through her refrigerator for dinner makings, but found nothing that interested her. That was when she came up with a better idea. Before her courage could desert her, she let herself out the front door and strode to Jonathan's door. She could hear the peal of the doorbell echo through the house.

Holly was ready to back away from her impulsive idea when the door opened.

"Hello, Holly." Jonathan quickly masked his surprise at his unexpected visitor.

"I hope I'm not interrupting anything." She ventured a bright smile.

"No." He was puzzled by her surprise visit.

Holly took a deep breath and rubbed her damp palms over the front of her jeans. "Basically I'm in no mood to fix dinner just for myself and I thought that you might like to go out for a hamburger. My treat," she added hastily.

Jonathan's hesitation warned her that his answer was to be a negative one. But before he could open his mouth, the telephone rang.

"Excuse me for a moment," he murmured. "Come in." He turned and swiftly walked into the kitchen.

Holly entered the living room and looked around with open curiosity. The couch was upholstered in an oatmeal nubby fabric and a black leather reclining chair flanked it. She walked toward a bookcase against one wall and studied the titles of the many hardcover books. It appeared that Jonathan's reading habits were divided between economics and politics. There wasn't one fiction book on the three shelves.

"Hello, Patricia." Jonathan's low voice sounded almost caressing.

Holly picked up a magazine and flipped pages, pretending not to hear his side of the conversation.

"I've been busy preparing my report for Corporate. Yes, I know it's been a while." His husky chuckle was equally disturbing.

"She's probably tall," Holly muttered to herself. "A woman named Patricia could only be tall."

"I'm sorry," Jonathan apologized, entering the room a few moments later after he had finished his call.

"No problem." Holly smiled, laying the magazine down on the coffee table. She waited expectantly.

"I'm not in the mood for cooking my own dinner either," he informed her. "Your suggestion of going out for a hamburger sounds fine with me."

"Let's go then."

Jonathan didn't look pleased when Holly escorted him out to the little VW.

"Are you sure it's safe?" he murmured, folding himself into the bucket seat.

"She's still in her prime." Holly patted the cracked dashboard lovingly.

"Ready for the junkyard is more like it," he said derisively.

"Volkswagens are like a fine wine. They get better with age," she corrected him, pumping the clutch several times before switching the engine on.

Much to Holly's relief, the little Bug behaved itself during the short drive to her favorite fast food restaurant.

Sammie's Burgers and Dogs had been a popular drive-in restaurant for the high-school set during the late fifties and early sixties. It still specialized in the biggest burgers and greasiest fries north of Los Angeles.

"Hi, Hank," Holly greeted the teenager behind the counter. "Isn't Sammie working the grill?"

Before the boy could answer a booming voice rang out. "He sure is, darlin'."

Jonathan was astounded to see a large man of about fifty pick Holly up and give her a bear hug that threatened to break her ribs. After he put her down, he looked at Jonathan, not missing the neatly pressed slacks and cotton shirt compared to Holly's dusty jeans and fisherman's knit sweater.

"Sammie, this is Jonathan Lockwood, my new neighbor." Holly smiled brightly. "And Jonathan, this is Sammie, ex-Marine, ex-bouncer, ex-martial arts expert, ex-you name it, and a very good friend."

"Lockwood." Sammie offered his hand. "I suppose the two of you are here for my specials."

Jonathan looked puzzled but Holly nodded. "Two double cheeseburgers with the works, two large orders of fries, and two chocolate shakes," she announced.

"Make mine coffee," Jonathan interrupted hastily, still enthralled with the tattoo of a sailing ship on Sammie's massive, hairy chest.

"Got it." Sammie grinned.

A few minutes later, Holly led the way outside to find an empty table. On the way, she stopped to exchange greetings several times.

"You look as if you've never been to a fast food restaurant before," she commented, eyeing her cheeseburger with pleasure.

"No, I haven't."

She was stunned. "How long have you been in the States?"

"Since college."

Holly shook her head in astonishment. She picked up her hamburger carefully and peeled back each part of the paper that wrapped it. "Then you are going to be in for a treat. One thing you have to watch out for is that these can get"—she gulped when a spot of catsup appeared on Jonathan's shirt—"messy."

He looked down at the red glob on the white cotton and sighed deeply, as if wondering what would happen next while in Holly's company. "Why do you enjoy food that is one step away from heartburn?" Jonathan asked, sipping coffee that resembled mud.

"Because it tastes better than anything I'd cook." She laughed and went on to assure him when she saw the skepticism in his eyes, "Believe me, the culinary arts and I just don't agree."

"What you're saying is that you can't cook?"

Holly dipped a French fry in a small pool of catsup and brought it to her lips. "When I try to cook anything, the kitchen turns into some horrible monster determined to shoot me down. I used to try simple meals, but they were either overcooked or caught fire. . . ."

"What about frozen dinners?" Jonathan asked her, inwardly wondering if his stomach would be able to digest the greasy hamburger.

"I seem to have a bad habit of forgetting they're in the oven. I use a timer and then never notice when it goes off until the smell of food burning alerts me," she explained. "It's just easier to fix a salad or steam vegetables or just go out to eat. It's not that I'm a klutz in the kitchen. I guess that other things just take priority."

"Didn't you ever help your mother with meals?"

Holly concentrated on sipping the last of her milkshake. "She always preferred doing everything herself," she muttered. "I wasn't allowed in the kitchen."

Jonathan could have sworn that he saw a trace of pain cross Holly's face. He was so used to seeing her lips stretched in a bright smile that her signs of bitterness affected him in a way he didn't expect. He sensed that his concern and interest went beyond normal friendship.

"Thank you for keeping me company," Holly said, once she had parked her car in the driveway. "I usually end up going by myself so having someone along was a nice change."

They got out of the car and walked up to Holly's front door.

"Then I'm glad you asked me to go with you." Jonathan turned to study her face back lit by the nearby streetlight. "We haven't been able to see each other very much lately."

She wrinkled her nose. "Neither of us seem to have a regular nine-to-five schedule."

"And I'll be going out of town again next week on business," he told her.

"I'm going away for a mini-vacation that weekend," she murmured, and smiled. "Good night, neighbor." She quickly raised her head and brushed a brief kiss across his lips. Then she hurriedly unlocked and opened her front door. Before Jonathan could blink, Holly was inside the house.

Jonathan couldn't help smiling. A woman asking him to dinner wasn't necessarily a novelty, but being taken to a hamburger joint was something entirely new for him! As he entered his front door, he silently hoped that a bottle of antacid would protect his stomach from the greasy hamburger he had consumed.

CHAPTER FIVE

Jonathan didn't see much of his neighbor over the next few days. He was too busy working long hours at work preparing his report and using his computer terminal to doublecheck all his figures. His goal was to make vice-president before he turned thirty-five. If his new project was accepted by the board, he would be well on his way to promotion.

One evening, he pushed his chair away from the terminal and rubbed eyes that were tired from looking at the screen for the past two hours. He laid his glasses aside and closed his eyes to give them a brief rest. It was moments like this when thoughts of Holly intruded on his peace and quiet.

And he thought of her as he drove home, wondering if he was going through some kind of emotional crisis, although his disciplined mind couldn't imagine allowing such a thing to happen. Holly, with her zest for life and infectious laughter, had touched something deep inside of him.

Holly was sitting on the front step of her house with Ralph sleeping peacefully at her feet. The late-afternoon air was cool but not uncomfortable. She rubbed the St. Bernard's back and haunches easily with her foot as she concentrated on the pile of stapled papers in her hands.

She didn't look up from her reading when Jonathan pulled into his driveway. At the same time, there was a funny little lurch in her stomach as she listened to the sounds of the car stopping, the faint squeak of the parking brake being pulled back, and the door opening.

"Where's your brood?" he asked, reaching back inside to across the front seat for his briefcase.

Holly could again detect an abrasive note in his voice that appeared whenever he mentioned the children. She wondered, as she had several times before, what had happened to turn him off kids.

"They're home probably giving excuses why they don't have to do their homework."

"Interesting reading material?" He gestured to the papers she held.

Holly nodded. "A new script. I'm Lulu Belle, a white Persian cat," she explained, turning the pages and indicating the lines highlighted with a blue marker.

"Why do you study it? After all, it's not as if you have to memorize your lines ahead of time. There isn't an audience watching your performance, is there?"

"If I want Lulu Belle to sound authentic, I have to think her character through first. I decided that her name warranted a syrupy Southern accent. She's a friend to everyone, even if they're Yankees." She spoke in the gentle dialect she had chosen for the languorous feline. "She's even got a full bushy tail every cat in the county envies."

Jonathan had to admit that Holly sounded just the way he would imagine a seductive Persian cat's speech pattern. In fact, he was curious to see the feline who made a big production of twitching her plumed tail!

"Your watchdog certainly takes his time waking up,"

Jonathan commented, fending off Ralph who had his own way of greeting his friends.

"He knows you belong here, so he wasn't all that worried." She shrugged, then brought up a question she had been thinking about for some time. "Why are you wary of me, Jonathan?"

"Because you don't play by any of the rules I'm familiar with." As if he didn't wish to clarify his statement, he turned and walked to his front door.

Holly listened to the click of the door closing. "I guess we're even then because your games are a bit out of my depth too," she murmured, getting up and going into the house to answer a persistently ringing telephone.

"What do you mean you can't go to San Francisco?" Holly wailed into the telephone receiver. "Chris, we've had this trip planned for six months! You can't do this to me!"

"I'm not the one doing this to you, my sinuses are," Chris replied in a nasal voice. "Holly, I only get a cold every few years and when I do, it's always bad enough to turn me into a complete invalid. I'm really sorry." There was no mistaking her regret.

Holly then realized that she was sounding inconsiderate when Chris was so ill. "No, I'm the one who should apologize. You're sick and I act as if it's your fault you came down with a cold. Why don't I call the hotel and see if I can change our reservations for a few weeks from now when you're feeling well enough to go?"

"If we change the reservations we won't be able to get the special rate Jay got for us." Chris was referring to her boyfriend who managed a travel agency. "Look, there's no use in losing our deposit. Why don't you see if you can find someone else to go in my place? I bet Steve would jump at the chance to spend the weekend with you," she teased.

"Give me a break!" Holly groaned, twirling the telephone cord between her fingers.

"Then fly up there on your own," Chris urged. "You've been looking forward to this for a long time and there's no reason why you should miss the trip. Who knows, you might meet some gorgeous guy on the plane and end up having a wild affair!" she joked.

"Sure." Holly was suspicious about such a thing happening. She was well aware that she wasn't the kind of woman to fall into some handsome man's lap and allow him take her away from it all. All she seemed to attract were creeps like Steve who thought only with their libido. "I'll see if I can find someone to go with me. A *female* someone," she stressed. "You see a doctor about that cold and I'll talk to you later."

During the next week, Holly checked with many of her friends and discovered that no one was available that particular weekend. When Steve learned about Holly's predicament, he volunteered to help her out only to receive a very firm "no!"

As the departure date grew closer, the more Holly was tempted to fly north on her own. After all, the room was already paid for, as was her plane fare. She had been looking forward to going with Chris since this was her first visit to San Francisco and she wanted to be with someone who was familiar with the sights. But she still wanted to go and the more she thought about it, the more decisive she became about going on her own.

The day of Holly's departure was also the date of a long awaited dental appointment to have her braces removed

For that she wasn't about to be late. Her orthodontist, who was usually prompt, was running behind schedule, and she ended up spending an anxious forty-five minutes in the waiting room before seeing him.

On the way home, her car acted up again and she had to coax the little Beetle to its destination. Holly called an airport express van to pick her up and packed quickly. She had little time to freshen up—and all she had time to do was leave her key with a neighborhood boy so he could look after Ralph.

Holly watched the time all during the ride to the airport. Once dropped off in front of her terminal, she ran inside to the check-in counter and checked her luggage. From there, she had another race to the boarding gate.

Holly kept a tight grip on her small tote bag as she pushed her way through the people sauntering down the tiled hallway. She encountered another setback at the metal detector; she had to walk through it twice because of her keys and loose coins in her jacket pocket.

"The way my day is going I'll probably miss the plane," she muttered, running up the stairs instead of bothering with the escalator. "Gate seventy-two, gate seventy-two." She scanned the overhead signs and ran toward the appropriate area.

Holly was one of the last passengers to board the jet. She walked down the aisle, looking for an empty seat. She sighed with relief to see a window seat in the nonsmoking section. A dark-haired man was seated on the aisle, studying a sheaf of papers in his hands.

Holly was just beginning to ask if the seat was taken when someone from behind jostled her, causing her to lose her balance and topple into the man's lap.

Her embarrassed apology died on her lips when the expression in the man's dark eyes turned from exasperation to stunned recognition.

"Uh-oh." She lifted trembling fingertips and rested them against her slightly parted lips.

Jonathan's smile reflected mild amusement. "This is quite a surprise, Holly. Are you here to see me off or were you planning on sabotaging the jet?"

"Of course not," she retorted crossly, trying to wiggle her way out of his lap until she realized that all she was doing was arousing him. "Don't worry, I'll find another seat," she said as she finally eased her way out of an embarrassing situation.

Jonathan took hold of her wrist and guided her in front of him to the empty seat. "I think you better sit where I can keep an eye on you. Someone else might not be as understanding."

"Will you stop treating me like a child?" Holly demanded under her breath. She looked down at her fingers fumbling with the buckle of her seat belt. Jonathan saw her problem, reached across, and calmly clipped the two pieces together.

"I wouldn't dream of treating you like a child, Holly," he replied. "In fact, I believe I have just revealed that I don't visualize you as some precocious teenager."

Holly could feel the heat steal into her cheeks at Jonathan's subtle reminder of what her movements had caused when she tried to extricate herself from his lap.

"You hadn't mentioned that your vacation would be in San Francisco," he commented. "Weren't you going with a friend?"

She nodded. "Unfortunately, Chris came down with a bad cold and wasn't able to come," she explained. "She talked me into going by myself."

"Is this your first trip there?"

"Yes, and I intend to see as much of the city as I can," she vowed.

Jonathan frowned. He wondered if it was a good idea for Holly to run loose in an unfamiliar city. Especially one as large as San Francisco. Oh yes, he was more than fully aware that she was an adult, but he had been raised to look after the so-called weaker sex and Holly's petite figure, overly large eyes, and delicate features made one think she was much younger until she spoke. And that smoky voice told any man that she was certainly all woman. On second thought, perhaps he should worry about the city instead!

Holly could already feel the tension building as she listened to the jet engines warm up. She was trying to decide if she was better off sitting next to someone she knew rather than a stranger. She barely listened to the flight attendant's speech regarding oxygen masks and emergency exits. She was too busy freezing up as the jet slowly backed away from the terminal and began its short journey down the runway. That was when she knew she definitely felt more confident sitting next to someone she knew.

"Jonathan," Holly whispered, reaching blindly in his direction.

"Are you now going to tell me that you get airsick?" He took in her distressed expression. "We haven't even taken off."

Laughing softly, she shook her head. "I just hate take-offs and landings," she explained, gripping his hand tightly. "Even flying in a storm doesn't upset me as much as a take-off." Holly kept her eyes boring straight into Jonathan's. He has such beautiful eyes, she decided. She only wished they'd look warmer more often. Feeling more relaxed, she flashed him a broad grin.

Jonathan blinked, unable to believe his eyes.

"Jonathan, you're staring," Holly urged gently. A teasing light glittered in her eyes; she knew the reason for his stunned expression.

"Your braces are gone," he stated.

"As of this morning," she announced happily. "That's why I was late. My dentist was running behind schedule and I didn't intend to take a vacation still wearing my braces."

Jonathan was perplexed. Every time he thought he was beginning to figure Holly out, she surprised him again. The absence of braces seemed to elongate her facial bones and add the necessary maturity to her features. Now the face most certainly went with her bedroom voice.

"Why did you go to so much trouble at this time in your life?" Jonathan found himself fascinated by the way the afternoon light played over Holly's animated features. She was so different from any of the other women he had known. He couldn't imagine Holly acting blasé about anything life had to offer.

There was a darkness in her eyes that resembled pain. "I believe I told you before that my parents didn't believe in braces because they considered them cosmetic." She spoke softly. "I didn't consider them cosmetic since I had enough of an overbite that my nickname in school was Holly Chipmunk. I decided that I would have it corrected as soon as I could afford it. So for the past two years I've been wearing some not very pretty hardware. But it was worth it." She flashed him a broad grin that revealed two rows of even, white teeth.

"And here I thought you weren't self-conscious about anything," Jonathan teased lightly.

Holly shrugged. "When you're barely over five feet tall

and look as if you still belong in high school, braces are even more of a hindrance. I decided I'd better get them before I hit thirty or for all I knew I could be a little gray-haired lady wearing braces! Although getting asked for my ID when I order a drink has been kind of fun."

"I'm sure you did give the bartenders quite a jolt," he replied dryly.

The pained expression on Holly's face told Jonathan that she didn't like to remember the jokes she had suffered from many of the less than tactful people she'd encountered in the last two years. "You had mentioned that you're flying up there on business," she commented, preferring to change the subject.

Jonathan nodded, comprehending her reason for not pursuing the subject. "I'm meeting with the bank's corporate heads to discuss a new computer system."

"Does this have to do with that project you've been working on?"

He was surprised that she had remembered. Of course she had, since he had shouted at her enough times that either her dog or the children screaming through her yard was upsetting his concentration—and he needed to concentrate on the special project he was involved in.

"Yes, I've come up with a new computer system that will send all statements and reports from individual branches to the corporate offices in a matter of moments," he explained. "For the past year, reports have been delayed up to three days because our regular computer system can't handle the heavier workload since we've expanded our operations. The system I've looked into will save the bank a great deal of time and money."

"This meeting is very important to you, isn't it?" she

asked quietly, discerning the tension in his features when he spoke.

"Every meeting with the corporate heads is important." He didn't like the way she could delve into the core of the matter. This meeting could mean a promotion for him, and he wasn't about to make even the smallest of mistakes.

Holly looked down at the briefcase in front of Jonathan's feet. "Then I won't feel guilty reading since I'm sure you would prefer to get back to your work."

The appearance of the flight attendant taking drink requests was their only interruption, at which time Holly eagerly asked for a glass of soda.

"I used to live on this stuff," she confided to Jonathan after savoring her first sip of the carbonated beverage. "That and popcorn were the hardest to do without."

For the next forty-five minutes, Holly read her book, but she found it hard to concentrate when Jonathan sat so close to her that their arms occasionally brushed. She decided that she liked the aftershave he used, a subtle scent, just like the man. Several times, little frissons of alarm scattered through her body. What did her guardian angel have in mind in throwing Jonathan and her together?

Holly had to remind herself to remain calm. She knew that once they landed, she'd be on her own for the weekend. In a city as large as San Francisco, there was little chance of her seeing him again until they were back in L.A. having the same old battles. The trouble was, she wasn't sure she wanted to resume their skirmishes!

At the same time, Jonathan was thinking that he wouldn't feel right leaving Holly entirely on her own. He decided that he'd volunteer to take her to lunch over the weekend or, perhaps, to dinner.

"Thank you so much for your help," she told Jonathan

after they had retrieved their luggage from the baggage carousel. "I hate to admit it, but I get nervous around a lot of people when there isn't anyone I know. You've really made it so much easier for me." She draped her tote bag over her shoulder as they walked outside.

"What hotel are you staying at?" he asked abruptly, not missing the slight confusion in Holly's eyes as she looked around at the unfamiliar surroundings.

Holly named an inn on Lombard Street. Jonathan reached into his jacket pocket and withdrew a pen and business card case. Extracting one of the cards, he jotted something on the back.

"This is where I'll be staying." He handed her the card. "If you need anything, call me. Also, I'd like to take you to dinner tomorrow evening if it would be convenient for you."

Holly smothered a smile. Jonathan was so damned polite at times! As she didn't know anyone else in the city, she couldn't imagine making any kind of definite plans. But he always insisted on doing everything by the book—etiquette book, that is. The times he lost control were rare and usually attributed to one thing. A sneaky voice in her mind told her this was not the time to lay a lip lock on him!

Instead, Holly murmured a polite thank you and tucked the card into her jeans' pocket. "That sounds very nice." Her acceptance sounded just as stiff and polite!

"Don't become too effusive," Jonathan said dryly, enjoying the sight of hot color rushing into Holly's cheeks. "I'll call you to set up a time."

"Fine." She picked up her small suitcase and tote bag. "Thank you for your help, Jonathan. I'll see you tomorrow evening." Holly didn't want Jonathan to think that she would try to be a millstone around his neck. He was in the city on business and she was there for pleasure. She edged away and took the first taxi she came to. As the taxi took off, Holly dared a brief glance in the rear window to watch Jonathan getting into another one.

Her lips twitched with mirth as she remembered the stunned expression on his face when she fell into his lap! Chris's teasing words came to mind. Well, Holly did fall into a handsome man's lap, but there wouldn't be any more than that to it. She doubted that Jonathan had ever had anything close to a wild affair. She refused to remember that the kisses and caresses he had given her were nothing like those of a cold-blooded man.

She gave in to the warmth stealing into her body as she remembered his dinner invitation. This time, she was determined to show him she was very definitely a woman.

Holly discovered that she liked everything about San Francisco. She liked the way the old blended in with the new, the fresh, almost briny smell of the sea in the air, the big-city sophistication on one street and the shopworn exterior on the next block that all seemed to belong.

Once settled in her room, Holly set her suitcase on the second bed and quickly unpacked her jeans and sweaters. She hadn't anticipated going out to dinner to anywhere requiring more than casual dress and had brought only sportswear. She instinctively knew Jonathan wasn't going to take her out for a hamburger and decided a shopping trip the next morning was definitely on her agenda.

She had dinner at a nearby pizza parlor and took a short walk before returning to the hotel. While she would have preferred exploring further, she could see a few men eyeing her speculatively and knew enough to avoid any trouble.

Holly decided to laze her way through the balance of the evening with a leisurely hot bath and curling up with her book. The only problem was that every time she read a love scene in the celebrated spicy novel, she couldn't help but superimpose Jonathan's face over the writer's image of the hero.

She kept telling herself that she was crazy. She knew she had to stop thinking about sex and concentrate on the book. It wasn't long before she realized how much of a mistake that was as each love scene grew more explicit and her uneasiness rose with each word.

Jonathan was agitated for many reasons that evening. He sipped from his glass of whiskey and wandered restlessly through the company hotel suite. Luckily the bar in the suite carried his favorite brand of whiskey. The trouble was, he was drinking more than usual that evening.

Jonathan crossed the sitting room to stand at the window. The city's skyline was brightly lit and appeared almost unreal to him. He idly wondered what kind of view Holly's room afforded her.

He chuckled softly. He hadn't expected her to appear on the plane that afternoon and he had rather found it a pleasant surprise. He'd have to call her in the morning to arrange a time to pick her up for dinner. If all went as hoped at the meeting, it would be a celebration in many ways.

Holly discovered the luxury of sleeping past dawn without Ralph jumping onto her bed barking for breakfast. When Jonathan called her not long after seven in the morning, she was feeling pleasantly lazy.

"I remembered that you're also an early riser so I

doubted that I'd disturb you," he explained. "If it's all right with you, I'll pick you up at seven thirty."

"That's fine." She couldn't ignore the rush of pleasure at the sound of his voice.

"I'll make sure to give you a taste of the city," he went on. "I have to go since I'm meeting someone for breakfast. Have a good day."

"Jonathan"—for a moment her voice faltered—"I hope all goes well for you today."

She could sense that he smiled, although she couldn't see the change in his expression. "Thank you, Holly, so do I."

Holly spent the first part of her day exploring the embarcadero. She grew fascinated with the Cannery with its many unusual shops and cafés tucked away in odd corners. Once a seafood canning plant, the multistory building was now an experience in shopping for items not found anywhere else. Along a nearby street, she found a perfect shop to buy a dress for that night.

Holly had first been enchanted with the store's name— the Petit Chalet—when she passed the two-story Victorian-style house. Seeing a lovely dress in the window, she couldn't help but enter and discovered that it was the kind of shop she had been looking for for years.

"May I help you?" A brown-haired woman about Holly's age and only an inch or so taller approached her.

"I have an idea that this is my kind of store," Holly replied with a smile. "I'm looking for a dress."

The woman looked her over with a practiced eye. "I'd say you're a size three." She led Holly over to a rack. "I'm sure we could find something for you among these and I doubt you'll have to worry about alterations."

Holly studied each dress, finding it difficult to choose from such a large selection. "I'm not usually so lucky to find so much in my size," she murmured with a laugh. She spun around looking at the additional racks of pants, blouses, suits, evening wear, and even an alcove displaying shoes. "I don't think that will be a problem here."

"No, far from it." The woman smiled. "In fact, that's why I opened my store. Like you, I had trouble finding clothes to fit me and finally decided the one way to get around that was to own a boutique catering to petite women. I also carry clothing from local designers that are one of a kind, and the shoes I have are in the smaller hard-to-find sizes. Please feel free to take all the time you need." She began to move away.

"No!" Holly almost shouted, then lowered her voice. "I'm afraid that I've lived in jeans for so long that I've forgotten what it's like to look at anything vaguely formal. I really would appreciate your help."

"Then I'll give you any assistance you'll require," she said graciously.

A couple hours later, Holly left the shop a great deal poorer in money and richer in clothes. She couldn't remember ever buying so many clothes at one time. She hadn't stopped with a dress for her dinner date with Jonathan. She had also purchased slacks and blouses, several pairs of shoes, and even lingerie that was geared to the petite figure. For once, she could wear a teddy that didn't hang on her small frame. She was also pleased to hear the owner say that she was opening a second shop in Los Angeles and would send Holly a card to announce the opening date.

Holly returned to the hotel to put away her new clothing and then left again to do some additional shopping. She realized that her new clothes required a heavier application of makeup than her occasional bit of lip gloss so she purchased the extra cosmetics that she needed.

The woman at the makeup counter applied some special eye shadows and lipstick, and when Holly caught a glimpse of herself in the store mirror she couldn't help smiling. She still wasn't used to looking at herself without the silver flash of braces glaring back at her. And with all her new makeup on, she definitely liked what she saw!

CHAPTER SIX

Holly prepared for her evening with great care. She started out with a leisurely bubble bath and shampooed her hair. She used more makeup than usual and stroked on a perfume the salesclerk guaranteed would drive a man wild.

As she stepped back and examined the blush-pink strapless teddy, she could only hope all her preparations were not in vain. Ordinarily Holly would have shunned anything strapless because her lack of proper bustline meant the item would immediately fall to her waist. But this garment was specifically cut for the smaller figure and left the wearer feeling totally secure, not to mention very sexy.

Holly's dress was cut along simple lines with narrow straps, a low-draped neckline, and an A-lined skirt. The watermelon-color silk was a perfect foil for her dark hair and creamy skin.

"Sutton, when you do something, you certainly do it with style." Holly preened in front of the mirror before slipping on her black high-heeled sandals.

The hour hand of the clock had barely hit seven-thirty when a knock sounded at the door.

Holly took a deep breath, stepped across the room and turned the knob.

"Hello, Jonathan," she greeted him with a calm her stomach didn't feel. "Won't you come in?"

Jonathan froze once the door had opened. His eyes turned so dark, the gold flecks stood out.

"Thank you." He finally found his voice. He entered and watched Holly cross the room to gather up her purse and a silvery-gray velvet jacket.

"I heard that there's a chance of rain tonight." Holly glanced out the window at the overcast sky. "Do you think I should take a heavier wrap?"

"I'm sure you'll be all right," he assured her, unable to keep his eyes off the lissome figure before him. Why had she hidden all those delectable curves in jeans and sweater? "The last weather report I heard stated that the rain wasn't due until early morning."

Holly raised her head just in time to see the intense expression on Jonathan's face. She felt a heat sear her body under his vibrant gaze. She was as securely trapped under his gaze as if she were a statue. Except that statue's nipples didn't peak in reaction and a strange heat didn't invade the lower regions of their bodies. She was afraid to look down to see if her arousal was apparent to Jonathan.

"You look lovely, Holly," Jonathan said, finally breaking the thick silence between them. He was sorely tempted to circle his suddenly tight shirt collar with his fingers. Was there no air conditioning in there? The room seemed stifling.

"Jonathan?" Holly looked at him curiously. She couldn't remember ever seeing him with such a haunted look on his face. "Is something wrong?" Was something showing that shouldn't be and he was too much of a gentleman to tell her?

"No, nothing. Shall we go?" He had regained his poise. Holly turned away to hide the look of concern in her eyes. She stood quietly as Jonathan took her jacket from her and assisted her with putting it on.

She wasn't sure exactly what was happening between them, but she knew that their previous personal encounters were kindergarten exercises compared to what was happening at that moment.

The restaurant Jonathan took Holly to specialized in French Creole recipes with music and decor that allowed diners to believe they were in New Orleans.

Holly looked around the large room with its many alcoves designated for private dining. A black wrought-iron railing circled a balcony where the musicians resided out of sight, while their soft sounds drifted through the air. She turned back to Jonathan with a dazzling smile on her lips.

"This is wonderful," she announced. "I've never been to New Orleans, but right now I feel as if I could walk out the front door, wander down a few blocks and find Bourbon Street."

"I'm glad you like it." He smiled, sipping the wine the sommelier had poured for his inspection. He looked up. "Yes, this is fine."

"What do you recommend?" Holly asked, after studying the menu.

"Jambalaya is their specialty," he replied. "It's a spicy fish stew served over rice."

"I think I'll try that." Holly watched Jonathan under the safety of her lowered lashes. Tonight he wore a dark-blue suit, a blue and silver striped tie, and the inevitable white shirt. She wondered how many white shirts he owned. Of course, then there was no problem in choosing what shirt to wear each day, she told herself.

Some women might consider Jonathan's harsh features unattractive, but Holly was positive that they would be few, judging from the number of interested looks he received from the female diners. He exuded a male sensuality the way a woman wore perfume. She noticed his hands holding the menu, the fingers lean with nails clipped neatly. Holly remembered their heated touch on her skin and longed to feel it again.

Jonathan was doing a bit of studying on his own. He had received quite a surprise when he picked Holly up at her hotel and found her waiting for him wearing a subtle yet very sexy dress. He gazed at the creamy expanse of skin above the low neckline and wanted to taste every inch. He could tell she was nervous by the pulse beating erratically at her throat.

"How did your meeting go?" Holly asked softly, breaking into his thoughts.

Jonathan's features relaxed. "Very well. They're seriously considering my proposal."

"Jonathan, that's wonderful." She reached across the table and impulsively squeezed his hand. "We should be drinking champagne to celebrate."

"They're only considering my idea, Holly," he corrected gently. "It will be a while before I'll know if they will go ahead with it."

"They'll accept it," Holly said confidently.

"What makes you think so?" Jonathan couldn't help but feel amused by her positive attitude.

She captured his gaze even as her fingers lightly stroked his. "Because you wouldn't have presented an inferior proposal to them in the first place. I'm sure that you've been with the bank enough years for them to know your worth." Her smile was pure sunlight. "You'll get it all, Jonathan. I know you will."

"I wouldn't argue with that," he replied emphatically.

All of a sudden, Holly felt a new and much stronger surge of electricity between them. The current ran up her arm and radiated throughout her body to rest in the lower regions. She experienced a heaviness in her abdomen that was far from lethargic. Slowly she withdrew her hand and hid the trembling appendage in her lap.

Jonathan began to speak, but the waiter appeared with their meal, and Jonathan did not resume whatever he had been about to say. They ate in silence, all the while unable to keep their eyes off each other.

Holly looked down at the brandy mousse pie she had been toying with for the past few moments. She raised her eyes and gazed directly at Jonathan. As usual, he gave no indication of his thoughts. Slowly and deliberately, she used the tip of her tongue to moisten her bottom lip. She glanced down at the table and studied her fingertip idly circling her wineglass.

"Are you ready to leave?" There was a faint rasp in Jonathan's throat as if he found it difficult to speak.

Holly nodded, keeping her eyes on the enticing movements of his mouth.

The check was dispatched speedily. There was no question that they would return to Jonathan's hotel.

During the drive to the hotel, Jonathan wanted nothing more than to take Holly into his arms, but his inborn reserve refused to let go for even a moment. He had always prided himself on his self-control, but now it seemed more a nuisance than a help. He kept remembering the vision of Holly's tongue against her lips and wanted to feel the tiny pink tip against his own mouth. In the airless confines of the taxi, the scent of her perfume threatened to consume him. He barely listened to the mindless chatter of the cab driver talking about the upcoming storm. Sharp streaks of lightning across the sky already heralded the coming storm with the air close and suffocating.

Holly wished that she could move her leg comfortably without coming into contact with Jonathan's thigh. The atmosphere between them was more electric than any act of nature. She could swear she heard the air around them crackling when the cab slowed to a stop in front of the sumptuous hotel. The doorman stepped forward to assist Holly out of the taxi and she turned to watch Jonathan exit. She wondered if anyone else could see the sparks fly between them as they walked beneath the canopy and into the ornate lobby.

She wasn't surprised to find Jonathan's hotel one of the more exclusive ones with curved stairs, chandeliers, and furniture from another era. She walked beside him across the lobby as if it were her natural right.

By the blessing of the gods, Holly and Jonathan were alone in the elevator. She felt as if her body were nothing more than a mass of raw nerves as the car rose silently and swiftly to the proper floor. Holly was in no doubt as to what was to happen, but that didn't make her any less apprehensive about the man standing beside her. She wasn't frightened of Jonathan, she only hoped she would be all he could want from a woman.

Jonathan was silent as he unlocked the door to his suite and ushered Holly inside the dark room. She half turned to speak to him as he closed the door behind him, leaving the room in total darkness.

Jonathan silently reached out to Holly and pulled her into his arms. His mouth was hot and demanding on hers, his tongue penetrating her lips and teeth to explore the brandy taste of her mouth as he turned her around until her back rested against the cool wood of the door.

She lifted her arms, which he shackled by the wrists and pinned against the door on either side of her head. Holly could feel the carved wood panels imprinting their design on her back, but she was beyond protesting. Jonathan may have kissed her before, but it was nothing like the way he made love to her mouth at that moment.

She moaned softly under his sensuous invasion and arched her body, seeking his masculine heat. Her tongue skimmed against his and darted into his open mouth to search out every crevice. She twisted her hands within their human shackles, wanting to touch him. Her unspoken wish was granted when he released her hands.

Jonathan ran his palms along Holly's spine, lightly touched the indentation at the end, and reached lower to cup her rounded buttocks, pressing her up against his swollen arousal.

Holly tipped her head back to gasp for air. Her lips tingled and glistened from the moisture of their kiss. Her body tingled with awareness. There was no turning back now. She wanted him too much!

"Jona—" Her whisper was swallowed under a fresh onslaught of his mouth.

Jonathan pulled Holly up hard against him. His mouth traveled over her face, branding her with fierce kisses and flicks of the tongue over her closed eyelids, along the pert nose, each corner of her lips and the delicate shape of both ears. Holly trembled when Jonathan's tongue slipped inside the shell-shaped orifice. He next concentrated on the slim line of her throat, bathing the delicate skin with his tongue. Oh, yes, her pulse most certainly did increase when he concentrated on that area! He roughly pulled the straps of her dress down her arms and nibbled along her bare shoulders.

For the first time in his life, Jonathan lost control. His brain wasn't functioning properly although his body certainly seemed to know what to do!

What happened to the preseduction brandy, the small talk, the sharing of light kisses that led into intimate caresses and then the short walk to the bedroom? All Jonathan knew was that his hunger for Holly was increasing and he wondered if he could wait long enough to take her into the bedroom. His kisses and hand movements took on a savagery unknown to the calm Jonathan Lockwood the world knew.

Instead of feeling repulsed by this primitive side of Jonathan, Holly reveled in it. She unwound her arms from around his neck and smoothed her hands under his jacket and down his side to his slim hips. Her hand brushed lovingly over the swollen bulge of his trousers and felt his body jerk in reaction. She returned to boldly caress him through the thick material. She could feel her own body turn to liquid fire. Her breasts swelled until they hurt and her thighs tingled with anticipation.

The room flashed white for a brief second and thunder rumbled off in the distance as Jonathan lifted Holly in his arms.

She hooked her toe over the strap of her shoe, slid it off, and repeated the procedure with the other shoe. They made no sound when they hit the carpet.

Jonathan needed no guidance to find his way across the darkened room to his bedroom. When he reached his destination, he gently placed Holly on her feet next to the bed and proceeded to undress her.

The dress may have faithfully followed her curves, but the strapless teddy gave them an even more seductive meaning. He leaned over and nibbled on the flesh rising over the semisheer fabric. His teeth grasped the material and pulled it down to her waist, pausing to drop a kiss along the soft skin. He dipped his tongue into the tiny crevice while she vainly tried to reach down to loosen his tie and unfasten his shirt buttons.

Jonathan preferred to continue his pleasurable task. Holly's sheer black hose ripped as he tore them off her. He lost several shirt buttons when he pulled his own clothing off.

There was no reason to close the draperies. Only a curious bird, brave enough to battle the elements, would have seen the entwined bodies on the king-sized bed with its covers pushed haphazardly to the floor.

Jonathan's body already gleamed dark with sweat. He lay on his side so that he could fully observe Holly as he ran his hand from her shoulder to knee. He felt as if his body were clenched in a tight fist as he silently called on every ounce of willpower he owned. He wanted to take his time exploring every centimeter of her body before making her his, while fearing his senses wouldn't allow him to. Intermittent flashes of lightning bathed them with white light. It added a primeval touch to their lovemaking.

Jonathan's lips found the ultrasoft skin behind Holly's ear and laved it with the moisture from his mouth. He learned that one eyebrow arched just a bit more than the other. He discovered an intriguing curl near her temple that refused to mingle with the others and perused the slight uptilt of her button nose.

"Yes," Holly breathed, when the tip of Jonathan's tongue lapped at the smooth surface of her teeth. She returned the gesture, delighted to find one slightly crooked molar. So he wasn't so perfect after all!

Holly couldn't believe that Jonathan still hadn't uttered one word. His worship of her body was conducted in silence, but it didn't unnerve her or cause her to wonder if her body didn't please him, because she could tell exactly how much she did please him!

Jonathan was a man who would worship the right woman from his soul. He sipped at the corners of her lips before delving back into the sweetness of her mouth. His tongue curled around hers and drew it back into his own mouth.

Holly ran her palms over his chest, enjoying the crisp feel of his hair curling around her fingers. She draped her leg over his thigh and rubbed her pelvis against his in seductive circles. His faint groan of pleasure was music to her ears. She flattened her hands against his firm buttocks, feeling the muscles clench under her touch. Lightning flashed again. Nature's primitive ways were on both sides of the building's walls.

Jonathan's mouth continued over Holly's shoulders and down to her breasts. The heat of her body intensified the fragrance of the lotion she had used earlier. The faint scent of almond blended with her femininity brought to mind harems and hot desert nights. Her husky murmurings were a rich honey mixed with cognac, if there could be such a combination. Now all that mattered was to pleasure her to the best of his ability.

At first, when he caressed her breasts, she drew back, but he refused to allow her to escape his touch. He gave equal attention to each dusky rose-tipped nipple, which puckered under the suckling motion of his lips. Even the delicate underside of her breasts knew the liquid heat of his mouth. He caressed the juncture of her legs and cupped her warmth. Her legs drifted apart at the sure touch of his hands and probing fingers. She was warm, moist, and ready for him. Still he continued. He wanted to wait until they both were turned inside out with desire.

In return, Holly was determined to explore the lean lines of Jonathan's body with the same attention he paid to her. She tongued his nipples into tiny brown nubs, and her teeth grazed over them leaving him in an exquisite pleasure-pain. She traced the dark silky hair that narrowed down to his navel with her lips then dipped her tongue in the tiny well. She ran her lips over a faint appendectomy scar and sent feathery kisses along his hip and thigh. She caressed the velvety skin with tenderness and felt the ever-growing surge of power at her delicate touch.

Jonathan drew in huge gulps of air as her lips moved back up his chest while her fingers moved downward. Before he lost himself completely, he twisted out of her hold and pushed her back against the sheets.

He sat back gazing down at the damp body silvered by the occasional flashes of lightning. Holly's eyes were half closed, her parted lips full and glistening with the moisture from his mouth. He grasped her hips and drew her up to the searing brand of his mouth.

Holly's eyes widened with shocked surprise. This was a form of loving she was unfamiliar with even though her own primitive instincts had urged her to caress him further with her mouth. She gasped as the lightning from the sky entered the center of her body through his lips.

"Jon-a-than!" Holly's plea was wrung out between clenched teeth. She gripped his shoulders pressing her fingertips against the resilient skin. She arched her head back against the pillow, the tendons of her neck standing out.

Jonathan's mouth was a fiery seal against the part of her that ached and burned for more. Her body jerked upward, but he merely tightened his hold on her hips. She wasn't sure if the roaring in her ears was due to the thunder overhead or the lack of air reaching her brain. He nibbled his way from thigh to knee and back up again. There was little time for her to find her senses.

Holly cried out for Jonathan's full possession, she pleaded and she demanded, but he paid her no heed. He drove her to her limit, backed off for the space of a breath, and drove her again and again before he allowed her to reach her release.

Holly exploded into a million fragments. She clawed at the sheets in an attempt to keep her body from splintering into tiny shards.

She had barely recovered before Jonathan moved up and entered her in one strong thrust. Holly sobbed with relief, blindly reaching out to hold him to her.

He lay still for a moment, allowing her body to accommodate his larger one. Only his concern of hurting her held him in check from the fierce hunger coursing through his veins. He felt her flow around him and he knew he had never felt such strong emotions with any other woman.

"Jonathan, please," Holly pleaded, wrapping her arms and legs around him. She murmured to him how good he felt to her and exactly how much she wanted him. She had never spoken so wantonly before, but her soul whispered that this time she must because Jonathan was important to her.

A tiny corner of Jonathan's mind enjoyed Holly's frank response to his touch. He had always been a silent lover and preferred his women to be the same. He believed in showing his feelings in a physical sense only and left emotion out of it.

Holly tasted the salty moisture on his face and eagerly mated with his mouth. The thunderstorm outside was the perfect accompaniment to their fevered loving. Jonathan's lovemaking was as primitive as the unleashed forces outside. Holly lifted her hips upward to meet him in perfect tempo. She was vibrantly aware of every thrust and withdrawal of his velvety masculinity.

Holly's body grew hotter with each passing second. Her skin was on fire and she felt consumed by Jonathan's lovemaking. Normally thunderstorms badly frightened her, but this time primeval forces were uncoiling themselves in her body. She desired all he would give her and would lovingly return the favor.

Holly gasped. She was smothered by a heat no amount of water could cool.

Jonathan increased their rhythm. He was as lost in the flames of their loving as Holly was.

They were soon caught up in the ultimate completion of the sexes. Holly's cries were muffled by Jonathan's open mouth even as she swung high into the multicolor heavens. She breathed his name and gripped him tighter for fear of spinning out into space alone.

Jonathan's body tensed then shuddered as he shared his hot sensuality with Holly.

Breathing raggedly, he propped himself up on his elbows to keep most of his weight off Holly. His tongue blotted the tears glistening in the corners of her eyes.

"Jonathan?" Holly questioned softly, reaching up to caress the damp skin of his cheek.

Jonathan was a silent lover by choice. He refused to say anything that could be construed as a commitment he would never be able to keep. He relied on body language to let his partner know how much he desired her. He smiled and placed a light kiss on her tender lips. Then he rolled off to one side and pulled her against him. Jonathan continued pressing his palms over the tousled black curls and down along her bare shoulder to her breast.

Holly's murmured words were unintelligible as she snuggled up to him. She burrowed her face against his shoulder, breathing in the warm scent of his skin blended with the musk of their lovemaking.

"You are so beautiful," she mumbled as she curled her arm over his chest. Scant seconds passed before she fell into a deep sleep.

Jonathan lay awake, holding Holly in a protective embrace. How had he been so lucky to have a woman who responded so naturally to him? He couldn't remember ever feeling as drained after lovemaking as he did then. Holly had taken everything from him, but she had also given it all back.

He sighed wearily. He was tired but just holding Holly drew his weariness from his veins. He was careful not to disturb her as he reached down to pull a blanket up over their rapidly cooling bodies.

It was as if the end of their lovemaking signified the end of the thunderstorm. Now a gentle rain fell, meant to lull lovers to sleep. He brushed a light kiss across her forehead. She didn't stir from his caress.

Jonathan knew that Holly lived by expressing her feelings. She gave of her heart only to those who deserved it, and he knew far too well that he did not deserve such a woman. What would happen if the moment of truth ever came about? he wondered. He prayed that it wouldn't happen for a long time.

"You're the beautiful one, Holly." He spoke softly, so as not to awaken her. "In so many ways you have a beauty that cannot be seen, but is so much more significant."

He carefully adjusted their positions and closed his eyes. He was soon asleep.

Sometime, just before dawn while the rain still dropped gently to earth, the lovers awoke.

Jonathan's dark eyes studied Holly's face and her eyes reached out to him. He took her into his arms and proceeded to make slow and easy love to her.

Time stood still for them. Soft, delicate touches brought about the same responses as the night before, but this time the fulfillment was more soul glorifying than before.

Their love flight rose until they could fly no higher. Holly lay half sprawled across Jonathan's body when she fell asleep. The smile on her lips spoke volumes.

CHAPTER SEVEN

When Jonathan woke up midmorning, he lay still for a moment savoring the sleeping bundle of femininity in his arms. Finally he carefully slipped his arms away from Holly in order to ease himself out of bed.

Holly murmured something unintelligible in her sleep and curled up into a ball in the spot Jonathan had just vacated.

He quietly picked out clean clothes and used the shower in the second bedroom so that he wouldn't disturb her. As he spread shaving lather over his face, he couldn't miss the lack of tension in his features. He also couldn't ignore the reason behind his feeling of relaxation.

"Damn," he muttered, carefully stroking the razor over his jaw.

Jonathan knew that he was in trouble. Last night his instincts told him that Holly wasn't the kind of woman to indulge in a casual affair. And that was all he was looking for. So why did just thinking about last night and knowing that she was lying naked in his bed tempt him to return to the bedroom and wake her up in a most satisfying way for both of them? Typical male reaction? No, he knew better than that because he was adult enough to realize that if he wasn't careful, this could turn into more than just an ordinary coupling.

Jonathan sensed that Holly was the kind of woman who needed love and affection, two emotions he would never give to a woman because he just didn't have them to give.

Meanwhile in the bedroom, Holly stirred and stretched her arms over her head. She smiled sleepily, remembering exactly why her body ached and felt so good. She opened her eyes, prepared to cuddle up to Jonathan, but found herself alone in the large bed. She had to content herself with hugging his pillow, which still carried his scent.

She wondered where he was until she heard sounds in the sitting room. She got out of bed and pulled her teddy on. When she walked into the other room, she found Jonathan looking out the window.

"Good morning." Holly's voice was still husky with sleep. Her cheerful smile faded when Jonathan turned around. There was nothing in his face to hint that they had been lovers the night before. "I didn't hear you get up," she said finally. "I hope I haven't slept too long."

"I used the other bathroom so I wouldn't disturb you," he explained quietly. "I thought I'd wait until you awakened to see if you preferred eating a late breakfast here, or I can take you back to your hotel to change and we can go out if that would appeal to you more."

It was on the tip of Holly's tongue to suggest they call room service and request breakfast in bed, but she didn't think her idea would be accepted. What happened to the warm and loving man from last night? Her mind raced madly with questions.

"Please don't feel that you have to continue to look out for me," she said with quiet dignity. "I'm sure that you were planning on returning to L.A. today."

"I'm staying until tomorrow," he informed her. "If

you'd like we can have an early lunch at Fisherman's Wharf."

Holly couldn't hide the spark of pleasure that shone in her eyes. "I'd like that. I'll finish dressing." She returned to the bedroom bewildered by the almost formal conversation that had taken place. All she knew was that she wanted her passionate lover of the night before back.

She dressed quickly, all the while wondering what had changed Jonathan so abruptly, and when she was ready they left together.

Holly felt uneasy crossing the lobby in a dress obviously meant for evening wear, but she had no choice. Jonathan seemed oblivious to her discomfort and she didn't mention it.

He had arranged for a rental car and they silently got in. During the short ride to her hotel, they were both lost in their own thoughts, and Holly didn't even try to make conversation.

He went upstairs with her, and she quickly showered and changed her clothes.

Jonathan offered her a brief smile when she reentered her room.

"Would you mind if we stopped somewhere for coffee before we go to Fisherman's Wharf?" she asked, grabbing her shoulder bag and transferring her wallet and personal articles from her evening purse.

"Of course not." Jonathan waited as she grabbed her short jacket. Then they left the room and walked to a nearby coffee shop.

The shop provided them with cups of strong brew and cinnamon rolls, and their conversation was sporadic, mainly dealing with the weather.

An hour later, Jonathan left the car in a parking garage

across the street from Pier 39, a conglomeration of shops and restaurants built of weathered wood to give the appearance of being years old instead of having been built recently.

"I like to window shop," Holly cautioned, gazing avidly at the two-level minivillage.

She wasn't joking, Jonathan realized as they wandered around. Holly was entranced with the shops displaying rare crystal figurines, another selling music boxes from all over the world, and another filled with movie memorabilia.

Holly wandered through the shop specializing in Christmas decorations and succumbed to purchase several expensive teddy bear ornaments.

"It isn't all that far off," she explained to Jonathan who questioned her about buying Christmas decorations in September.

"Were you born at Christmastime?" Jonathan asked, taking the bag out of her hands. "Is that how you got your name?"

Holly shook her head. "Actually, my birthday is on Halloween." She stopped to inspect the window of a fudge parlor. "Mm, chocolate–peanut butter fudge." She ducked inside and soon came out with a white paper bag. "I bought two pounds," she announced cheerfully. "We can have a fudge orgy tonight." She burst out laughing at Jonathan's slightly lifted eyebrow. "How do you do it?"

"Do what?"

"Express your opinion with just your eyebrow." Holly's attention was diverted to a shop filled with kites of every size, color, and shape.

"I didn't realize that I had such a rare talent." He then switched back to their previous topic. "Why is someone born on Halloween named Holly?"

"At least I wasn't named Goblin or Spook." A hard note entered her voice. "The nurse told my mother that I was red and round like a holly berry, hence the name." She forced a false gaiety into her voice as she swiftly changed the subject. "Didn't you say something about dinner?"

We're both people with secrets who can't let go of the past, Jonathan thought. It wasn't difficult for him to see that Holly preferred not to talk about her family, even though she was more than ready to discuss any other subject.

They decided to walk the short distance from Pier 39 to Fisherman's Wharf, even though the wind blowing in from the bay made it a cold trek. Holly was glad she was wearing her heavy jacket to keep the chill out. Jonathan had worn a dark-gray wool jacket over a pewter wool sweater and dark-gray slacks.

Holly looked across the bay at a remote island with its austere buildings. "How sad it must have been," she murmured.

"Only the most hardened of criminals resided at Alcatraz," Jonathan reminded her.

"It's still sad to think that people had to live there knowing they'd never leave." Holly sighed, moving closer to Jonathan in a silent plea for comfort.

"They deserved a harsh punishment, Holly," he replied coolly, not wanting to admit that she was tugging at his heart again with her empathy for men who, in his judgment, didn't deserve it. He found his only defense was in withdrawing from her. "There's no reason to be upset. It isn't even inhabited any longer."

She continued staring out over the gray water topped with whitecaps. "Their spirits will always be there." Her husky voice was barely audible.

Jonathan's logical mind wanted to point out that such a thing didn't happen except in the cartoons she worked in.

As they ate a late lunch at the Fisherman's Grotto with their table overlooking the water, Holly gestured to a harbor seal swimming near some of the incoming fishing boats and two pelicans floating on the water a short distance away.

"This must be a routine for them," she observed, unable to take her eyes from the graceful seal.

Jonathan sat back in his chair, feeling sorely tempted to drink his whiskey down in one gulp. What was there about Holly that fascinated him? What made her so different than the other women he had made love to? Simple: She was a woman who didn't necessarily take life at face value. He had a good idea that she wouldn't think twice about probing a man's subconscious until she learned all his secrets. He knew he would have to ensure that she wouldn't have that chance with him.

"I want to thank you for giving me such a lovely day." Her sensuous voice broke into his thoughts.

"You're easily pleased, aren't you?" His cool, indifferent manner was a well-constructed shield Holly didn't miss.

"In some ways, yes." She injected a proper touch of frost into her words. "Of course, I was also taught to be appreciative."

This barb hit Jonathan where it hurt the most. He leaned across the table and asked, "Is that what you were last night, appreciative?"

Holly reared back. "I have never repaid a dinner with sex," she replied, stung by his accusation. "As far as I'm concerned, that would make me no better than a prostitute. I know I'm not like the other women you've known, but I can't believe that you would forget your very proper upbringing to say something so rude."

Jonathan's smile was more of a grimace. "You certainly have a way with the verbal knife. I hope the blood won't ruin your meal."

"I have a strong stomach." Luckily, their food arrived before any further barbs came her way. Holly had been surprised that Jonathan would say such a thing to her and was beginning to think that he seemed to strike out whenever he was afraid of being hurt himself.

Holly enjoyed scallops in wine sauce while Jonathan had swordfish. At least their lunch gave them a reason not to engage in further warfare, but the tension hung heavily over them.

"I could probably make this a meal of its own," Holly told Jonathan as she buttered a large slice of warm sourdough bread.

"Since that's your fourth slice, I assumed that's exactly what you're doing." Amusement warmed his earlier coolness.

"I saw you sneaking a third piece," she teased.

"I couldn't allow you to eat it all," he retorted.

She looked up when the waiter approached them and asked if they'd care for dessert.

"I think I'll take the cheesecake," Holly decided, catching the amazed expression on Jonathan's face.

"Would you care for strawberries or blueberries on top?" the waiter asked.

She shook her head. "I'm watching my weight," she confided, with a straight face.

Jonathan almost choked out his request for coffee only.

"Did you see the look on his face?" she asked laughing,

after the waiter glided away. "I think I baffled him by telling him I was watching my weight."

"I doubt he's had too many customers ask for cheesecake and turn down the fruit, which is certainly less fattening," Jonathan threw back. "I think we better go for a *long* walk after we finish here."

"As long as it isn't up any hills," she requested.

Under Jonathan's bemused gaze, Holly did full justice to her dessert. He wondered how such a small package of femininity could eat so much food and not blow up into a tiny dirigible!

After lunch, they strolled up one street and down another. Holly breathed in the pungent aroma of the sea air mixed with the odors of fish cooking in large pots on the sidewalk. She couldn't help but stop and examine the large quantities of crabs and fish filets lying decoratively on crushed ice. She chatted companionably to the men who explained to her why their seafood was the best while Jonathan stood back and watched every man who came into contact with her charmed under her spell. Her voice belonged in the bedroom, her diminutive form evoked a man's protective instincts, and her friendly personality fascinated any man alive.

Their leisurely walk took them up the steep street where the large sign of Ghiradelli Square beckoned to them.

Holly's eyes lit up at the sight of the old-fashioned chocolate factory, which was now a several-storied building housing many shops, restaurants, and an old-fashoned ice cream parlor.

She couldn't resist exploring each shop, until she realized that she was dragging Jonathan behind her without any regard for his feelings.

"I'm sorry," she apologized when she realized what she

was doing. "I tend to forget time and people when I'm window shopping. You must be bored silly."

"I haven't been bored once," Jonathan assured her, startled because he spoke the truth. Accompanying a woman on a shopping trip had never been one of his favorite pastimes, but with Holly he found the excursion enjoyable. "Although I'm surprised you're not buying out the stores."

Holly shook her head. "I did most of my shopping yesterday," she murmured, remembering all the bags she had carried out of the Petit Chalet.

An hour later, they stopped to relax and enjoy a cup of coffee. Holly sat in her chair wondering if she would ever be able to take another step again. The lack of sleep the night before and their walking had finally caught up with her.

"Would you mind taking me back to my hotel?" she asked, looking weary for the first time that day. "I've finally discovered how much my legs disliked walking up these hilly streets. I don't think they'll ever be the same again."

"Not at all." Jonathan was feeling tired himself and the idea of a long hot shower was sounding more appealing by the minute.

He later dropped her off at her hotel, informing her that he would pick her up later to take her out to dinner.

"I don't want you to feel that you have to spend all your time with me," she protested, nevertheless pleased that he wanted to.

"This restaurant is a bit more casual," he explained, ignoring her argument as he escorted her into the lobby. "I'll see you at eight."

Holly took the elevator up to her room and decided to

shower before she took a much-needed nap. Feeling more refreshed, she wrapped herself into her robe and pulled the bed covers back, sliding between the cool sheets.

Twenty minutes later, she was still awake. The feel of the sheets on her bare skin was too potent a reminder of another bed and set of sheets caressing her back. It also generated a reminder of the warm body covering her, moving over her and possessing her. . . .

"No!" She leaped out of bed and headed for the closet to decide on her wardrobe for the evening.

Holly was ready when Jonathan arrived. In view of his advice, she wore burgundy and navy muted plaid culottes and a burgundy pullover sweater.

"I think you'll enjoy this restaurant," Jonathan murmured as he led Holly out to his car.

His observation was an understatement. The restaurant was named The Grey Horse and was a perfect reproduction of an English pub. One half was a tavern complete with a polished oak bar, a player piano in one corner, and dart boards in another. The other side was furnished for the diners. A buxom young woman led them into the dining room.

"Our steak and kidney pie is excellent tonight," she informed them with a broad smile in Jonathan's direction.

Holly mentally compared the woman's measurements to her own and found herself sadly lacking.

"Does steak and kidney pie taste as awful as it sounds?" She leaned across the table to whisper her question.

Jonathan smiled. "No, it's very tasty," he assured her.

"As tasty as me?" she couldn't resist asking.

His face flushed.

"You're not shocked, are you?" she pressed. Her eyes

sparkled with amusement at the idea of ruffling his feathers.

By then Jonathan was able to school his features into an unemotional mask. "I found you more delectable than any dessert and I wouldn't think twice about sampling you again," he reassured her in a rough voice.

This time, Holly was taken off guard. "I think I'll have the lamb chops," she muttered, pretending a great interest in the menu. She knew this was the time for her to back down.

"Would you care for a drink first?" he asked her, inwardly pleased to see that he could ruffle her feathers as much as she disconcerted him.

"Bourbon and water." She needed something good and strong at that moment.

Holly didn't miss the telltale arch of Jonathan's eyebrow.

"It happens to be what I usually drink," she defended her choice.

"You don't have to act defensive with me, Holly," Jonathan reminded her. "You may not believe me, but I'm on your side." He glanced up when the waitress appeared to take their order.

Holly couldn't help but think that if she needed someone on her side, Jonathan was certainly the person she would want. No matter what, she instinctively knew that he was a man a woman could count on in the darkest of times.

As the evening wore on, Jonathan seemed to relax more. After dinner, they sat in the tavern part of the pub where Holly discovered that stout was not at all like the beer she had drunk a few times during parties. She laughed at the bawdy songs the patrons sang and soon sang along in her slightly off-key voice. She couldn't remember having ever so much uninhibited fun and told Jonathan so.

It was just past closing time when they left the pub and Jonathan drove Holly back to her hotel. He parked and locked the car before accompanying her to her room.

From the moment they stepped into the hotel lobby, Holly could feel the pressure building up between them.

They entered her room in silence, Jonathan remaining near the door as Holly walked over to the table to lay her purse down. She spun around and faced him. Their eyes spoke the words they were reluctant to voice out loud.

Jonathan remained in the same spot, remembering the feel of Holly beneath him and her response to him. His mouth had already memorized the taste and shape of her lips and now he wanted to revive his memory. A prickling sensation traveled over his hands with the remembrance of her breasts fitting perfectly in his palms. He wanted her again!

Holly faced him, wondering what was going through his mind. The tension between them pushed down and around her so thickly that she felt as if she would end up in a small box the size of a Rubik's Cube. If such a thing happened, would he slip her into his pocket and take her with him? she wondered wildly.

A muscle twitched in the corner of Jonathan's mouth. I wish she didn't affect me so strongly, he kept telling himself. In the flash of a second, he knew he would be better off acting instead of speaking.

He broke his frozen stance and swiftly crossed the room to pull Holly into his arms. For a brief moment, her hands lay on his forearms and her face upturned to catch the hunger in eyes the shade of cool, polished wood. Jonathan drew her even closer and lowered his mouth to hers.

Holly whimpered with delight as Jonathan's tongue searched out the secrets of her mouth and then tempted her tongue into his mouth to conduct her own exploration. She wrapped her arms around his neck and pressed herself even closer to his warmth. His arousal burned through his clothing, making them aware that even a kiss would light the fire between them. There was no going back.

Jonathan abandoned Holly's lips for the enticing curve of her neck. He listened to her breathy moans as he nibbled the soft skin. Needing more, he pulled the neckline of her sweater aside to reach the hollow that still carried a faint hint of her perfume mixed with the natural scent of her skin. For the first time in his adult life, he was tempted to tear a woman's clothes off, pull her down to the carpet, and make fierce love to her. He found the urge almost frightening. At the same time, it didn't diminish his ardor. His hands found the curve of her breasts and kneaded them through the wool. In an effort to feel more of her body against him, he slipped her jacket off.

Holly dug her fingertips into Jonathan's neck and moved upward to the silky hair. She wanted to discover him in the same way he had learned her body the night before. She rubbed her palms against him in tiny erotic movements, centering on the masculine heat that beckoned to her. Jonathan's ragged breathing against her skin told her she was accomplishing her purpose.

"Take me to bed, Jonathan," she pleaded softly. "Show me a glimpse of heaven again." Her hand stroked him in a gentle, but insistent, action.

Jonathan needed no further encouragement. He kneeled down, slipped her boots off, and reached for the zipper to her culottes. They were easily pulled down over her hips and tossed to the floor. His eyes locked with hers as he slowly reached for the hem of her sweater and carefully drew it up over her head. Now Holly only wore lacy bits of froth on her breasts and across her hips with the moonlight adding a magical silver cast to her skin. Jonathan picked up Holly's hands and placed them on his hips in a silent question.

Holly kneeled on the bed and ran her palms over the waistband of his slacks before unbuckling his belt and working on the fastener and zipper. Once loosened, his slacks needed little assistance to drop to his feet. She raised herself up to take his sweater off then realized he was still wearing his briefs.

"You'll have to sit down if I'm to take your shoes and socks off," she breathed in the voice that skittered across his nerves.

Jonathan stepped away from his slacks and sat on the edge of the chair while Holly took off his half boots and socks. Then she held out her hand to lead him to the bed.

Once they lay down on the cool sheets, Jonathan grasped Holly's waist and pulled her over him. They kissed hungrily as if afraid this was their last time together.

Holly grazed her teeth over Jonathan's lower lip and sucked it into her mouth. She kept her eyes open, wanting to see every speck of emotion on his face. This was one time when she wouldn't allow him to hide from her. She slid her hands over the damp skin of his back and slipped them under the soft cotton covering his buttocks. She could feel his muscles tense with need.

Jonathan's head dipped toward her breast to find the puckered nipple through the filmy material of her bra. He covered it with his lips and his tongue bathed the nub to an acute pleasure Holly could feel racing through her body even as she wondered fleetingly if her breasts were too small for his taste.

Jonathan's fingers tangled in her hair and gently kneaded her scalp. From there, they traveled down the sides of her throat, over her shoulders, and pushed down her bra straps. He easily unfastened the clip at the back and carefully peeled away the semisheer material. The lace triangle at her hips was also easily discarded.

Holly mimicked his action by sliding her hands under his briefs and sliding them down over his hair-roughened legs. She took delight in exploring his body again. She ran her hands over his chest and down to lightly score each rib with her nails.

"You're too thin," she whispered, burrowing her lips in the hollow of his shoulder. She nipped the taut skin before lifting her head and smiling. "Perhaps you should have eaten my cheesecake."

Jonathan shifted his weight, lifted Holly up, and placed her over him.

"This is my dessert," he rasped, arching upward.

Holly gasped as he filled her to her very depths. Jonathan was again consuming her as he continued thrusting her into a storm-filled sea of forgetfulness. There was nothing for her but the man filling her with such heat.

Jonathan felt as if he were surrounded by liquid fire. A fire that wouldn't harm but heal him. He wrapped one hand around Holly's neck and drew her face down to his. Their tongues merged together as their bodies moved toward that final culmination. Holly cried out when everything momentarily went black and Jonathan tensed, now with both hands digging into her hips. As they both went limp, he kept his arms around her with their bodies still joined.

Holly rested her cheek against the damp hair on Jonathan's chest. She closed her eyes wishing she could hold that moment forever. She could hear Jonathan's erratic heartbeat slowly return to normal.

"Don't shut me out, Jonathan," she whispered. "We all have our fears. The problem is that they're usually not real. Let me be your friend as well as your lover and I'll help you fight them." She rubbed her cheek over the damp surface, unable to keep her sigh back. She felt as if her muscles had turned to gelatin. She began to slide off Jonathan to relieve him of her weight.

His arms tightened, preventing her move. "Stay," he ordered huskily.

She curled her arms around his neck and was soon asleep.

Sleep wasn't as easy for Jonathan. He had surprised himself during the past hour. He had revealed his hunger for Holly. What rule would he break next because of the dark-haired witch lying so trustfully in his arms? As for her remark that most fears weren't real, she didn't know his and she wouldn't either. Not only was his fear real but it was one that could never be cured.

Holly wasn't sure exactly what awakened her in the early-morning hours unless it was the lack of Jonathan's body warmth against her. She turned over and saw him standing at the window looking out as she had seen him the previous morning.

All she could think of was how sad and lonely he looked. While she wanted nothing more than to go to him and offer comfort, she stayed under the covers, knowing he'd prefer his privacy at that moment. She pretended to be asleep when he later returned to bed.

CHAPTER EIGHT

It was barely eight o'clock in the morning when Jonathan stood near the gate at San Francisco's airport preparing to board the waiting jet.

He kept telling his conscience that he hadn't wanted to hurt Holly by leaving so abruptly. But he knew it was for the best. He was fully aware that the cruel way he had left was his only way to be kind.

Jonathan knew that if anyone could penetrate his well-built defenses, Holly could, and all that would do in the end is hurt both of them even more. He realized that it wouldn't take long for someone as free and open as she was to delve into the inner regions of his soul, and he couldn't allow that to happen. Therefore he decided that his safest recourse was to get away. He moved forward when his flight was announced. He was more than ready to return to Los Angeles.

Five hours later, Holly sat on the slightly worn leather seat of the airport express van and stared out the window as the vehicle worked its way through the crowded streets to the freeway. She couldn't remember ever feeling so relieved to be home.

Couldn't anything ever go right for her? Last night she felt as if her chance for that "elusive something" was in her grasp, but Jonathan had abruptly jerked it out of her reach.

How could the same man make such beautiful love to her one moment and totally shut himself off from her the next? What was he so afraid of? How could he have left her the way he had? The question kept hammering in her brain, but she was still no closer to an answer.

When Holly had awakened that morning, she had been alone. A note, propped up against her purse on the table, had stated that Jonathan had taken the first flight back to Los Angeles and would see her there. It was merely signed with the letter *J*.

She had only stared at the note, unable to believe that a man could so cold-bloodedly leave a woman's bed to catch a plane. His leavetaking was obviously an escape from her.

From the moment Holly had read the note to the time she boarded a plane to L.A., she had cushioned herself in a very safe, very numb coccoon. By shutting out the rest of the world, she was able to make the return trip without embarrassing herself with a deluge of tears.

Holly couldn't remember her little home ever looking so good. She got out of the van and turned to take the suitcases from the driver. The smile on her face disappeared when two hands appeared to take the cases out of her hands. She hadn't heard him approach her.

"I'll take those for you," Jonathan said quietly.

"Since I've carried them quite easily through two airports, I doubt I'd have any problem now," she said coldly. "You certainly didn't worry about me earlier while you were in such a hurry to get away from me. I don't need your help, Jonathan." When she tried to retrieve her luggage from him, he refused to loosen his grip.

"I will take them inside for you," he insisted.

Holly turned away and walked up to her front door. She was so angry with Jonathan that she was afraid she would explode if she didn't get away from him within the next few minutes. She hunted through her purse for her door key until she found the brass-colored metal and unlocked the door, stepping inside. She quickly opened the living-room drapes and switched her answering machine off.

"Thank you." She mouthed the words merely out of courtesy. As far as she was concerned, they held no meaning.

"I'm sorry, Holly," he surprised himself by saying. "And not just for leaving you so abruptly. You're a lovely woman, but . . ."

"Don't do this to me!" she lashed out, slicing the air with her hand. "I'm not like you, Jonathan. I can't shut my feelings on and off like a light switch." She only prayed that she wouldn't break down in tears until she was alone. "You're not even normal. No man nowadays wears nothing but white shirts." Her voice wobbled. Why had she brought up something so ridiculous? She rubbed the back of her neck with her hand to relieve some of the tension eating her up. "Don't be concerned that there might be complications. I make sure to take my little blue birth control pill every morning. There won't be any worries," she finished defiantly.

Jonathan's face turned a pale gray at her pronouncement. "Yes, no worries," he repeated woodenly. He walked out the door, closing it after him.

That was when Holly sank down onto the couch and indulged herself in a good cry. When she finally lapsed into hiccups and sniffles, her eyes were swollen and itchy, and she felt a whopping headache coming on. She took two aspirin before going outside to greet Ralph, who had been barking eagerly since he first heard his mistress's voice. She kneeled on the grass and wrapped her arms around his neck.

"I missed you too, boy," she said softly, burying her face in his soft fur.

Jonathan stood back from the bedroom window and watched the forlorn figure still seated on the grass. He cursed softly at the knot in his stomach. "Damn it all." He turned away to finish his unpacking.

That night, he found it difficult to sleep as he remembered Holly snuggling up to him and sleeping half draped over his chest as naturally as if she had done it for years. He cursed and thought about getting up and watching some television until he remembered the last time he had tried that remedy. He was better off lying in bed and counting sheep.

Holly was having just as much difficulty sleeping. She lay under the covers with the electric blanket on high, and Ralph lay sprawled at her feet. She finally resorted to one of her sleep-inducing tricks by thinking up new voices for general characters. As a test of will, she even tried out a haughty British accent. Ironically, all she got out of her plan was a bad case of the hiccups. A disturbed Ralph finally lumbered off the bed and curled up on the carpet.

"Fine—*hic!*—friend—*hic!*—you are," Holly muttered, punching her pillow and putting it over her face for a few moments. Just before she dozed off, she moodily wondered if a chronic case of the hiccups could be terminal.

Jonathan sighed and finally broke down and took another two aspirin. Funny, he couldn't remember suffering through this many headaches during his life as he had in the past two weeks—the same amount of time since he and Holly had returned from San Francisco.

He had seen little of her in the last fifteen days. And during that time he had all the peace and quiet he could desire. Now it didn't seem to matter as much.

What had also been running through his mind was something Liza had said to him when she was on one of her rampages to get him to mix more socially. His retort had been to mildly question her as to what she thought Patricia was, whom he had been seeing about twice a month. Liza's remark about Patricia's cool patrician beauty was unladylike.

"You're barely thirty-four, Jonathan, and you act as if you're coated with some kind of impenetrable steel," she had told him. "You won't allow anyone to touch the inner you because you're so afraid of being hurt. The trouble is no one can hurt you because you don't have any feelings!"

Jonathan certainly wasn't about to admit that perhaps a part of what Liza had accused him of was true. It was bad enough to realize that he missed Holly's smiles and laughter. Patricia had become a thing of past.

He gazed blindly at the reports on his desk. He even missed the noise the kids running through the yard made. They had seemed to make themselves scarce lately. The only thing he didn't miss was Ralph's early-morning canine concert.

Jonathan sighed wearily. He was beginning to wish that he had moved into an apartment. He had a good idea that his life would have been a great deal simpler.

"Okay, cut," Ron, the sound engineer, ordered into the microphone with a frustrated sigh. "Again."

A thoroughly miserable Holly edged off her stool. "I'm —*hic!*—sorry." She hiccuped again.

"What is your problem, Holly?" Steve erupted. "We're running almost two hours late because of you, lady."

"I—*hic!*—can't say—*hic!*—any more than that!" she cried.

"Cut it out, Steve," Chris ordered, setting her headphones aside. She placed an arm around Holly's shoulders. "Come on, let's see if we can find a permanent cure this time."

"Try putting her head in a paper bag for a while," Ron advised.

Chris shot him an icy glare. "Since Holly's the one who has a way with words, I'll let her tell you off," she threatened, leading Holly out of the recording studio.

"Her constant attacks of hiccups will kind of take away the effect if she does," Ron called after them.

"They're all such idiots," Chris muttered, leading Holly down the hall to the bathroom. She filled a paper cup with water and handed it to Holly. "Drink it all down without taking a breath."

"It—*hic!*—didn't work the other time," Holly protested, even as her body jerked with another air explosion in her lungs.

Chris pushed the cup at her and waited until it was emptied. "Then I suggest you find out what's causing them," she advised, slipping her fingers into her jeans pockets and leaning against the counter.

Holly nodded and laughed, which was choked off by another hiccup. "Whoever thought a man would be the cause of anything so ridiculous," she muttered. She had purposely stayed away from even the slightest contact with

Jonathan and she had had hiccups since the day she had returned from San Francisco.

Chris watched her. "We only have five more lines before we're finished with the script," she said. "Afterward, I'm taking you out for pizza and I'll make you eat more than your share."

Holly smiled faintly. She knew the last thing she wanted to do was go home and spend the evening alone again. "No anchovies?"

Chris made a face. "Definitely no anchovies! Come on, let's finish up so we can get away from Steve's ugly face."

"You just found the perfect cure for my hiccups." Holly laughed, sounding like her old self for the first time in weeks.

Jonathan sat in his easy chair studying the fat envelope in his hands. If he didn't know better he'd swear Fate was using the U.S. Postal Service to make a point.

In his hands was a large envelope, obviously a bank statement, that was addressed to Holly but had been placed in his mailbox by mistake. He pondered his choices; he could just slip it in her mailbox since he'd noticed she hadn't returned home yet or he could wait and hand it to her personally.

He tapped the envelope against his open palm. There was no rush in his decision. Holly hadn't come home yet.

Holly entered her house with one destination in mind. All she wanted was something to settle her overly full stomach. Chris had kept her promise in making sure Holly ate more than her share of a large sausage and cheese pizza.

She rummaged through her bathroom cabinet for the

blue foil packets of tablets that would ease her upset stomach.

"I feel like a stuffed turkey at Thanksgiving," she muttered, walking back out into the kitchen to pour herself a large glass of water. "Not now!" she moaned, after the sound of the doorbell faded away then rang again. "All right, all right." Still carrying her glass of water in one hand and the two white tablets in the other, she went to the front door. Her eyes doubled in size when she found Jonathan standing on the other side. "Ah—*hic!*" Oh, no, not now!

Jonathan looked down at Holly's red face and the tiny sounds from her throat that she vainly tried to smother. "The postman left this in my mailbox by mistake." He held up the envelope.

"Oh—*hic!*" Still flushing, she stood back. "Would you like to come in?"

Jonathan stepped inside and began to hand Holly the envelope until he realized that her hands were already full.

She quickly dropped the tablets into the water, and the fizzing sound was loud in the silent room.

"Too much pizza," she muttered, hastily drinking the contents and setting the glass down.

"Is that what caused your hiccups?" Jonathan asked, handing the envelope over when Holly held her hand out.

"No." She glanced at the bank address printed in the corner of the large envelope. She opened a drawer in her small desk and tossed it inside.

Jonathan couldn't help but see a small pile of identical envelopes crammed into the drawer. "I'm not meaning to pry, but aren't those bank statements?" he inquired incredulously.

Holly nodded. She was afraid to look at him too much or her hunger for him might appear in her eyes.

The banker in Jonathan couldn't help but inspect the envelopes to discover them still sealed. "These are from the first of the year." He was amazed.

"My accountant balances them at tax time." Why did he want to talk about stupid bank statements? If he wanted nothing to do with her, why didn't he just drop the envelope in her mailbox? And why didn't he just go away since his task was done? Her body jerked with her hiccups.

"Holly, it isn't a good idea to ignore these for so long," he said gently. "Haven't you ever been overdrawn? For all you know even the bank, God forbid, could have made an error with your account."

"I thought bankers never made mistakes," she whispered, looking up slowly and drinking in the lean planes of his face.

"Sometimes they do."

Holly could only hiccup.

Jonathan watched Holly whom he gauged looked thoroughly miserable. His motions were tentative as he placed his hands on her shoulders. "How long have you had those hiccups?" he asked.

"About two weeks—*hic!*"

Jonathan's fingertips found the tender center of her nape. "Have you tried holding your breath and counting to ten?"

"Yes."

"Drinking water from the wrong side of the glass?" He probed the back of her shoulders and found the muscles tense under his touch.

"Yes—*hic!*"

"What about blowing into a paper bag?" he questioned.

"I thought that was used for hyperventilation."

"I think I have a sure-fire cure," Jonathan told her. He could see that she had lost weight and looked much too weary for just experiencing a bad day at work. "Permanent cure." He lowered his head.

"No." Holly moaned, shaking her head almost violently. She couldn't endure the hurt again. "Don't torment me any more, Jonathan."

"The torment worked both ways." His lips feathered over her forehead, along her cheekbones, and over her jaw before searching her lips. Even those were treated to the lightest of caresses. That was all he had meant to do until her lips just barely parted. Groaning her name, Jonathan tightened his hold on her body and deepened a kiss that made Holly's head swim.

Holly told herself to recoil from Jonathan's probing kiss. She reminded herself of the cold rejection that would follow as it had before. That same tiny bit of sanity informed her that while she might be good for a few nights when they were spending time in a different city, she wasn't good enough to speak to on their home ground. But her body wasn't about to listen, because it remembered the joy Jonathan had given her during those two nights. She could feel the heat of his skin through his clothes and snuggled even closer before she regained her senses enough to resist him.

"No!" Holly pushed against his chest until he released her. She stepped back several paces, needing a stiff objectivity to get through the next few moments. "I'm not someone who can be used on a whim!"

"I never thought of you that way," he argued.

Holly pressed trembling fingertips against her temples. She looked down, squeezed her eyes shut and wished Jonathan would just go away.

"I can't go away, Holly." It wasn't until then that she realized she had spoken her wish aloud. "I think we should talk."

"I don't," she replied in clipped tones. "I got your message loud and clear the last time."

Jonathan winced. He wasn't used to explaining his actions, but he did want to ease the tension between them. He wasn't conceited enough to think that Holly had lost weight because of him or that her eyes were shadowed and the pinched look around her mouth was because of his earlier behavior. If he was the cause for her lack of usual boundless energy, then he couldn't believe that he'd ever feel any worse than he did.

"I can't say that I'm not physically attracted to you," he began hesitantly. "At the same time, we appear to be on opposite ends of the sphere and I find you difficult to comprehend."

"Take me out from under your microscope, professor," Holly advised, spearing him with an icy glare. "This microbe is running free."

"For once, would you be quiet and listen to what I have to say!" he snapped, clenching his fists at his sides. "I'm trying to tell you that I knew I was also a new experience for you. Once we had gone out together in San Francisco, it was inevitable we would make love." Holly choked. "Then once we were back here, we would see it as nothing more than a holiday romance and we'd part."

Holly frowned at Jonathan's pronouncement and shook her head. "The way I see it is that you decided to reject me before I rejected you," she said slowly. "You've always seemed to visualize me as some kind of kook who goes to bed with any man who asks her, and you probably just wanted to test out your theory. And I hope you were pleased with your research," she added bitterly.

"I never thought that!" he argued.

She was past stopping now and continued ruthlessly. "I'm not on a continual lookout for a stud!" Holly knew she was going too far, but she was past caring. Tears gathered in her eyes but she was too angry to let them flow. "I don't believe in sex as a release from tension or as some kind of crazy prescription to clear the skin. I was raised very strictly. My parents may have thought I was a lost cause, but they still hammered morals into my head." She collapsed into a chair and rested her aching head back. "You're right, we are different," she whispered, wishing the postman hadn't misplaced her bank statement. She was beginning to recover and would have been fine soon. At least, that was what she kept telling herself. "But don't worry, I'll make sure not to disturb you for the balance of your stay here. Who knows? Perhaps your house will be finished ahead of schedule and you'll be back to your nice safe and sane world."

Jonathan turned away and studied the collection of cartoon cells on the wall. "What's wrong with us trying to be friends for the next few months?" he asked quietly, not wanting to hear her wipe away the memory of their weekend with a few harsh words.

Holly digested his question. "We were lovers too soon."

Jonathan ran his fingers through his hair in a rare show of agitation. "Lovers can be friends also."

"Maybe your other lovers can, but I'm not that sophisticated." She turned her face away, willing her despair not to show in her voice. "I can't be friends with a man who obviously doesn't respect me."

Jonathan only had one ace up his sleeve and he knew

now was the time to use it. Ordinarily, he would have been relieved that a woman wasn't about to turn possessive, but then, he hadn't felt this way about a woman before either.

"You once told me that you wanted to be more than my lover," he reminded her with a touch of his arrogant streak. "Where's that compassion for my soul now?"

Holly closed her eyes. "You really know how to play dirty, don't you?" she murmured, feeling the sorrow rise up and overtake her.

"When it's necessary."

It seemed an eternity before she turned her head and faced him. "Well, Mr. Banker, what is your brilliant plan that will turn us into old buddies and keep that nasty old physical attraction at bay?"

"I don't have one. We'll just have to take each day as it comes."

CHAPTER NINE

Holly's eyes went blank for a moment as she searched her heart for an answer. Not finding one, she looked at Jonathan.

"Would you like some coffee?" Her voice was so low that it barely reached his ears. "I can promise it won't kill you."

"If it wouldn't be too much trouble," he replied, glad that she hadn't thrown him out.

Holly stood up and gestured toward the couch as she hurried out to the kitchen.

Jonathan took a seat and listened to the sounds of water running and cabinet doors opening and closing. He also soon heard sounds of Ralph being let into the house and the whirr of a can opener running along with Holly's soft-pitched words to the dog.

Ten minutes later, Holly entered the living room carrying two mugs. She handed one to Jonathan and sat gingerly in the blue chair near the couch. "Have you heard anything on your presentation yet?" she asked, sipping the steaming brew.

"Not yet." Jonathan smiled wryly. "The wheels at the top always turn slow."

"Hurry up and wait," she murmured, smiling to herself.

"I can't count how many times I've heard that over the years."

"I think all of us have at one time or another," he agreed. "You're not originally from California, are you?"

"Iowa. A small town that you didn't dare blink while driving through or you'd miss it." She shot him a sharp glance. "What gave me away?"

"A faint accent," he observed. "Nothing very noticeable, but something that appeared occasionally. What would you be doing if you had stayed there?"

Holly's smile thinned. "Well, I guess I probably would have celebrated my tenth wedding anniversary with Herman Tolliver. We would have gotten married the day after we graduated from high school." She was oblivious to her audience. "Herman's mother would run the house so I could help Herman with the farm, and she'd be reminding me every day how lucky I was that Herman had married me instead of Sarah Rush. And twice a week, I'd be enduring Herman's mechanical lovemaking while all he would talk about is our having another son to help him around the farm." Her vividly colored eyes were looking into another time frame and didn't see Jonathan flinch.

"Did Herman marry Sarah after all?" Jonathan strove to ease the tension evident in Holly's face.

A tiny smile curved her lips as she nodded. "They have six girls."

Jonathan chuckled. "Why does that sound fitting?"

Holly slipped her shoes off and curled up more comfortably into the chair. "Turnabout is fair play. What would you be doing if you had stayed in England?"

"I probably would have worked for the same bank as my father and married the daughter of one of my mother's friends."

"Yet neither of us did what we were expected to do," she mused. "You can't be all that stuffy after all."

"I'm surprised you haven't given me a complex," Jonathan told her with a touch of asperity in his tone.

Holly shrugged. "Men who are stuffy are also very methodical. People with that kind of personality don't travel to another country to go to school and then travel another thirty-five hundred miles to begin a job. A methodical man tends to remain strictly on the path forged him by his ancestors." She ran a hand through her curls as she remembered Liza filling her on all the details about Jonathan. "So you can't be stuffy."

"I'm glad to see I passed your test." He didn't appreciate everyone seeing him as a prim and proper, bad-tempered individual. Liza had complained about his temper and he knew without a doubt that she had supplied Holly with his personal history and now Holly had seen him as stuffy. If this was the way people continually saw him, Jonathan wanted to break out of the mold fast. Perhaps his interest in Holly was a part of that rebellion.

Holly set her coffee mug down and leaned against the arm of the chair, her chin propped in her hand. "You don't like having people see you that way, do you?"

"It appears that I have no choice," he grumbled.

"It isn't derogatory, Jonathan," she protested softly. "You're just the proper image of an English gentleman, that's all. There's certainly nothing wrong with that." She wrinkled her nose, reminding him of a whimsical rabbit. "In fact, I think it's kind of cute," she confided.

"I thought cute was used to describe you?" Jonathan countered.

Holly groaned. "You just found my weak spot! I hate being called cute!"

"Why?"

She seemed to look off to one side. "I look younger, I have a face that wouldn't sink a ship, much less launch a thousand ships, I have no figure to speak of, and hair that has to be kept short or the curls resemble Medusa's hairstyle. I prefer not discussing my lack of height."

What Jonathan heard was only a portion of Holly's insecurities. While she could deal admirably with anyone else's problems, hers were always pushed back into her subconscious.

"You're too hard on yourself, Holly," he disagreed. "A woman isn't always judged by what's on the outside."

"I didn't realize the *Playboy* sales figures were dropping so drastically," she said sarcastically.

"Then may a stuffy Englishman ask a short Medusa to attend a foreign film with him this Friday evening?" Jonathan asked, setting his mug on the table in front of the couch.

Holly felt a warmth spread through her body. "I'd like that very much," she murmured.

Jonathan stood up and looked down at her looking so comfortable in the soft chair. "I don't think it's going to be an easy path for us," he observed.

Holly's grin was teasing. "Too much for you, am I?"

She could barely catch her breath before Jonathan pulled her out of her chair and into his arms. The kiss was over as soon as it had begun.

A stunned Holly watched Jonathan walk out the front door. As she touched her still-tingling lips with her fingertips, she wondered how he could continually surprise her.

Jonathan's choice in films was a shock to Holly. They had decided beforehand to eat dinner after the movie; therefore they were able to make the early show.

"What movie are we seeing?" Holly asked softly once they were seated in the theater.

Jonathan's reply made absolutely no sense.

"I beg your pardon?" She gave him a confused look.

Jonathan repeated the title then translated it for her. "It's Turkish," he explained.

Holly nodded slowly. It's going to be a long evening! she warned herself. Luckily, the theater lights dimmed before Jonathan saw the blank expression on her face.

If Holly had one failing, it was that she grew sleepy when she got bored. A film with subtitles and a man bemoaning the loss of his favorite horse was enough to send anyone into a catatonic state.

She settled back in the cushioned seat and fought the yawns that kept rising in her throat. Holly blinked rapidly as her eyelids grew heavier and heavier. She even bit the inside of her cheek in an attempt to remain alert, but she was fighting a losing battle.

Holly rested her head against the top of the seat, her eyes slowly closing until the loud sound of a gunshot from the film startled her. She sneaked a glance at her watch and was dismayed to find that only a half hour had passed.

How can he watch this? she silently wondered. Having seen her share of foreign films, she couldn't remember any as boring as this one. She shifted her position in the seat and stifled another yawn.

At one point during the movie, Jonathan glanced toward Holly and did a doubletake. She was asleep! He turned back to the screen with a tiny smile on his face.

Luckily, Holly roused just before the film ended. She

would have hated for Jonathan to know she had slept through most of it.

"Do you like Mexican food?" Jonathan asked as they left the theater.

"Love it," she pronounced.

"The restaurant is a short walk from here," he explained, gesturing down the street.

As they walked, Holly racked her brain to find something complimentary to say about the film. "The cinematography was excellent," she finally ventured.

"But you didn't like the film." There was no censure in his tone.

"Oh, boy," Holly muttered under her breath. He had noticed her inattention after all! "I slept badly last night."

"Holly, I don't want you to feel defensive," Jonathan chided gently.

"It's not that I don't like foreign films," she went on. "That one was just a little dull."

"A lot dull," he corrected, opening the door to the restaurant.

Holly shot him a sly grin. "But you didn't fall asleep." She looked around the restaurant's South of the Border decor with interest.

A young woman dressed in a white cotton peasant blouse and gaily patterned skirt approached them and led the way to a table.

"If you've sat through as many managerial meetings as I have, you learn to look interested despite how dry the subject matter is," Jonathan told Holly, sitting across from her.

She shook her head in disagreement. "I can't imagine you ever getting bored with anything. Sometimes I feel as if I have one of the shortest attention spans in history."

"It's not a short attention span. It's your enjoyment in learning new things," he replied, lacing his fingers together on the table in front of him.

"It's part of my inquisitive nature." She smiled warmly. "I have an insatiable curiosity."

Jonathan stopped listening after the word insatiable. The waitress had brought their drinks and he found himself engrossed with the way the tip of Holly's tongue delicately licked the salt off the rim of her Margarita glass. He silently cursed his body's reaction to the small gesture. Perhaps this getting to know each other better wasn't such a good idea if all he wanted to do at that moment was take her to bed.

Luckily the waitress appeared to take their food order before Jonathan could indulge in another impulsive gesture. They first shared an order of nachos, corn chips covered with melted cheese with guacamole on the side.

Holly laughed as she tried to loop a string of melted cheese around her chip. "What is your new house like?" she asked conversationally.

Jonathan dipped a chip into the guacamole and ate it before replying. "It's a ranch style with three bedrooms and two baths and a stone fireplace. There's quite a bit of open space around it."

She shook her head in mock disgust. "Never ask a man about a house unless you want vital statistics. What does your kitchen look like?"

Jonathan shrugged. "It has a stove, double oven, a sink, dishwasher, trash compactor, and garbage disposal. Just what is this intense interest in a kitchen when you freely admit you can't cook?"

"It doesn't mean that I can't like kitchens," she defended herself. "What's your color scheme?"

"I haven't decided yet." Jonathan leaned back when the waitress placed a plate of chile verde in front of him and shredded beef enchiladas in front of Holly. "Would you care for another Margarita?" he asked.

"All right." She dipped her fork into the spicy Spanish rice that accompanied her dish. Holly suddenly didn't want to think about the house or the day when Jonathan would be gone. It was an ironic feeling since after their first encounter she had been eager for him to move out.

"What made you choose to attend college in California?" Jonathan asked her.

"I received a partial scholarship to UCLA," Holly replied, emitting a small breath when the hot, spicy food slid down her throat. "I worked in a bookstore to pay the rest of my expenses."

"And you majored in psychology?" He found himself wondering how many sides there were to Holly and how long it would take him to learn them.

"Yes." Holly glanced up when the waitress set her drink in front of her.

"No wonder you figured me out so quickly," he mused, surprised that someone so lighthearted would engage in such a heavy subject.

"I know, it doesn't sound like me." She easily read his mind. "I had wanted to work with disturbed children."

"That's quite a change from working in cartoons," Jonathan remarked.

Holly's features turned somber. "I worked in a clinic during my third summer of school and discovered that my emotions tended to overrule my head. That's when I knew I had better find myself a new career. A friend who knew about my gift for mimicry suggested I apply at Carousel Productions since they were looking for new voices. After

I was hired, I quit school and I enjoy my work immensely."

Jonathan didn't doubt Holly's words but he also sensed the faint hint of regret that she felt over leaving her studies.

Holly hadn't thought about her years in college for some time. She remembered that summer when she had looked forward to working at the clinic in the San Fernando Valley which specialized in disturbed children. For the first few days she had been able to hide her dismay at the blank faces of boys and girls and her inability to evoke any kind of reaction from them. But by the end of the first week, Holly couldn't sleep because of the many children who were unable to respond to her smallest gesture.

Holly's college advisor had called on her the following week. She hadn't needed to be told that she wasn't right for that kind of work.

That was when she had learned about the job at Carousel and found a new way to work with children that wouldn't affect her emotions so strongly.

They left the restaurant and Holly was quiet during the drive back to the house.

"Would you care to come in for a cup of coffee?" she asked when Jonathan stopped the car. She had been so lost in the past that for a moment she had almost forgotten her manners.

"I'm afraid I'll have to decline since I have an early appointment with the contractor working on my house," he explained.

"Then perhaps you'd be willing to attend a rock concert with me next Saturday?" Holly asked impulsively. "A friend works for the band and gave me two tickets. I assure you that you won't get bored."

Jonathan hesitated for a moment. A rock concert wasn't his idea of a pleasant evening, but he knew the best way for them to understand each other was to learn about the other's interests.

"Are you recommending that I take ear plugs with me?" he inquired.

Holly laughed. "They would only lessen the sound, not deaden it."

Jonathan got out of the car and walked around to open the passenger door. They walked up to Holly's front door and Jonathan waited as she hunted for her keys.

"It was a lovely evening, Jonathan," she assured him.

"I think I'll always question the wisdom of the critics who praised that film." Jonathan's fingers found their way under the collar of Holly's navy and green striped blouse. He discovered that the delicate skin was as soft as he remembered.

She looked up to get a better view of his face darkened by the evening shadows. "Jonathan?" Her throaty whisper revealed her ache of remembrance. She reached up and grasped his wrist. Her forefinger pressed lightly against his pulse and found it beating erratically.

He lifted his other hand and used his palms to form a living frame for her face. His lips feathered across her cheek and down to her mouth. They tasted the faint hint of salt on the corner of her lips before he dipped his tongue into the cavern of her mouth to find the sweetness he craved. Desiring further contact, he slid his hands around her head and down her back to press her closer to him.

Holly's moan of delight was reason for Jonathan to cup her buttocks and lift her up into the cradle of his hips.

"I remember all of you, Holly," he rasped, before outlining her lips with the moist heat of his tongue. "How the taste of your skin only left me wanting more, how you welcomed me so joyously into your body and your cries of ecstasy when we tumbled into oblivion together. Do you know how soft and inviting you are? Do you remember how you moved under me so wildly?"

"I only remember one thing." She gasped when his hand kneaded the aching fullness of her breast. "I remember your strength tempered with gentleness, Jonathan. I remember you filling me with rapture." She ran her hands over his shirt front feeling the heat of his skin through the fine cotton.

Jonathan slowly eased back. He drew in several deep breaths to slow the fire racing through his veins.

"What we have here is a combustible combination." He still found it difficult to speak coherently.

"It seems so." Holly deliberately lowered her voice to a seductive murmur. "But I'm sure we could come to a mutual solution on how to effectively quench the fire."

"No," he said gruffly. "That's how we made our first mistake."

"Is that how you see it, a mistake?" she asked softly.

Jonathan shook his head, cursing his unfortunate choice of words. "No, but people should try to get to know each other better before embarking on an affair."

Holly closed her eyes. She knew Jonathan was right, but she had always lived by her emotions. The last word she would have used to describe her relationship with him would have been "affair." To her, an affair was between two people who *didn't* want to get to know each other.

"Good night, Jonathan." She adroitly twisted out of his loose grasp and slipped into the house.

Holly's body was still shaking as she prepared for bed.

Her only consolation was that she knew Jonathan's night wouldn't be any easier.

"You've set a new record, Holly," Chris told her the following Wednesday as they relaxed with cups of coffee and doughnuts.

"For what?" She delicately licked raspberry jelly from her fingertips.

"It's been almost two weeks and you haven't had one case of the hiccups." Chris leaned forward to select another doughnut from the white box. "I can't believe I've eaten three of these things. How many calories are in one of these?"

"You don't want to know. Mmm, this one has a fluffy chocolate frosting filling." Holly's eyes lit up. "What did you say was the name of the doughnut shop?"

Chris choked back a laugh. "Would you believe Dilly's Delights?"

Holly looked at her friend with disbelief. "That sounds more like a massage parlor than a doughnut shop."

"Maybe there was one in the back," she quipped.

"No matter what the name is, Dilly makes great doughnuts." Holly got up to pour herself another cup of coffee.

"You still haven't said what your hiccup cure was," Chris queried.

Holly's shrug was deliberately noncommittal. "Tickling the roof of my mouth with a cotton swab works great."

Chris looked highly skeptical. "Men can be such a pain in the rear, can't they?" She sighed, flicking a speck of powdered sugar from her jeans. "Jay has the bad habit of assuming I enjoy watching the boxing matches on TV. Last night was finally the last straw. I told him if he wants to watch them so badly he can do it at home."

Holly smiled, knowing that just because Chris appeared to change the subject didn't mean anything. She would still find out what she wanted to know in the first place. "What did he say to that?"

Chris grimaced. "He reminded me that he only has a small black-and-white TV while mine is color."

"The better to see the blood, I guess." Holly finished the last of her doughnut.

"This time must be serious," Chris guessed, reverting back to her former source of conversation.

"Are we playing Madame Zelda now with her crystal ball?" Holly inquired sweetly.

"I don't need one." Chris set her coffee cup to one side. "I'd wager a guess you've met a man, perhaps in San Francisco." She tactfully ignored the red in Holly's cheeks. "Obviously the two of you clicked and just as obviously the two of you clashed. Instead of indulging in a good long crying jag, you got a terminal case of the hiccups. Lately not even the slightest hic has left your lips, so you must have gotten back with the mysterious gentleman."

"Hic left my lips," Holly repeated, wrinkling her nose. "Chris, you've been here too long."

"I'd like to see how you'd talk after thinking like a cocker spaniel puppy all week," Chris grumbled, reclaiming her coffee cup.

"I'll trade you roles," Holly offered. "It's much easier than a snake with a lisp. You can't hiss with a lisp!"

Chris choked on her coffee while Holly politely slapped her on the back.

"I cannot wait to see that cartoon," Chris said once she had recovered her voice.

"I asked Hank if he would give me big brown eyes," Holly told her, mentioning one of the artists. "He told me

151

they'll be black and beady." She grimaced. "A sneaky snake with a lisp. Oh, well, I guess it could be worse. They could have wanted him to have a foreign accent!"

"Holly?" A young man stood in the doorway of the coffee room. "They got that short in the wiring fixed now."

"Okay, thanks, Ron." She wadded her napkin into a ball and tossed it into the wastebasket before turning to Chris. "The next time Jay wants to watch the boxing matches on your TV, give me a call and we'll go out to a movie."

"Better yet, I'll tell him that I'll spend the evening at Chippendales. Mmm, all those gorgeous hunks of men on stage stripping to reveal equally gorgeous bodies." Chris's dark eyes sparkled merrily. "He'll lose interest in boxing in a big hurry when I let him in on those particular plans!" She quickly finished her coffee and threw the foam cup in the wastebasket.

"Don't tell him what you're going to do, just call *me* to go with you!" Holly laughed as she left the room.

Holly again had to nurse her ornery car home.

"If I had any brains, I'd turn you over to a junkyard," she muttered, giving the front tire a vicious kick on her way to the front door.

"Hi, Holly." A girl of about six stood on the sidewalk.

"Hi, Jenny," she greeted the girl who lived across the street. "Does your mother know you're out so late?"

"Mom had to work late and I locked myself out of the house." Jenny looked at her with pleading eyes.

"Come on in and we'll fix ourselves some hot chocolate," Holly invited, holding an arm out.

The girl ran up to her and hugged her tightly around her waist.

"Why hadn't you gone around back to stay with

Ralph?" Holly asked her, keeping an arm around Jenny's shoulders as they stopped at the front door.

"I forgot," she admitted.

"Jenny, you know that Ralph is back there for your protection also," Holly scolded, unlocking the door and ushering her inside.

"I was careful." Jenny ran into the kitchen and flicked the light on.

"Would you let Ralph in, please?" Holly stopped at her bedroom first to put down her purse and jacket. She smiled when she heard Jenny's squeals and Ralph's barks of greeting.

During the next hour, Holly and Jenny fixed hot chocolate complete with marshmallows on top.

"Your mother is going to kill me for ruining your dinner," Holly said, taking several M&M's from the candy dish and handing one to Ralph. "That's all you get, fella," she informed the dog. "The last thing I need is a fat St. Bernard."

"He's already fat," Jenny declared.

"Um." Holly squinted her eyes and studied the waiting animal. "Well loved is more like it."

"The man next door is awful sad," Jenny said suddenly, changing the subject as children are wont to do.

That really caught Holly's attention. "Sad?" She was puzzled by the girl's choice of words. "Jenny, why do you think he's sad?"

"Because when he watches us play sometimes, he looks like my daddy does when he brings me home on Sunday night." Jenny stuck her finger into her drink and licked the sticky substance off. The product of a broken home for two years, she acted blasé about seeing her father only on the weekends.

Holly sat back, digesting this new piece of information. She didn't doubt Jenny's comment because the small girl's perception was stronger than that of most children her age. Holly could only wonder why Jenny thought Jonathan looked sad and if he did, why.

CHAPTER TEN

As Jonathan stepped out of the shower and pulled a towel from the nearby rack, he could only question his sanity in agreeing to go to a rock concert—especially since he hated rock music. As he quickly dried himself off, then draped the towel around his hips and prepared to shave, he reminded himself that she had attended that horrible movie with him and that the blending of their two lifestyles had been his idea. As he dressed in navy slacks and a deep-gold pullover sweater, he recalled how she had acted a little nervous when she'd asked him to go with her, as if she feared he'd refuse.

He still puzzled over Holly's unusual behavior when she had stopped by an hour ago to verify the time. She had looked at him as if searching for something. He would have sworn that the expression in her eyes resembled compassion, but why would she feel that toward him? He froze just before his brush touched his hair.

No! Then his common sense took over. Relax, she doesn't know, he told himself, but he still found it difficult to relax and slow his accelerated breathing.

Two hours later, they arrived at the amphitheater, which was already crowded with people. Jonathan couldn't believe the crowd, much less the bizarre appearance of many of them.

"What is the name of this band?" he echoed a variation of the question Holly had asked about the movie.

She wrinkled her nose. "Silver Gas. They're new to the scene, but their first two albums went gold in a short period of time. This performance marks the end of their first concert tour," she explained.

"Silver Gas," Jonathan repeated, watching one teenage girl walk past him wearing vivid pink jeans and a poison-green shirt that did nothing but draw attention to her dark-purple hair. He shuddered at the violent color combination.

They joined the hordes of people entering the building, although their progress was severely hindered due to the crush of people around them. At one point, Jonathan felt a caressing hand pat his buttocks. He frowned and glanced around, hoping the gesture was an accident in the large crowd.

Holly noticed his wandering gaze and hid a smile. She doubted she had attended one concert without getting pinched or patted on the rear.

"Don't try to figure out who," she advised softly. "You're better off not knowing."

This could be a long evening, he warned himself, unaware he had repeated Holly's words from their evening at the movie.

After they found their seats, Jonathan looked around at the audience, stunned by the colorful clothing, strange hairstyles, not to mention hair colors, and wondered how Holly could feel comfortable around people who looked as if they belonged in a science fiction movie.

The yelling, whistling, and other varied noise rose to a

deafening level as the time for the concert to begin arrived. Jonathan winced, wondering when this assault on his eardrums would end. Obviously no one heard his prayer.

Holly felt a little guilty dragging Jonathan to the concert, but she thought it wouldn't hurt for him to discover one side of her life. She had forgotten that this wasn't at all like attending one of Barry Manilow's concerts! She turned away before he could see the smile that hovered on her lips. He looked shell-shocked!

I sincerely doubt he'll get bored here, she thought, listening as the announcer introduced Silver Gas. She had an idea their music would be another shock to Jonathan's nervous system.

Jonathan found it difficult to believe that listening to seven people of indeterminate sex jump and scream was a form of entertainment. Each time he doubted the decibel level could get any higher, it did just that. The howling from the audience only blended in with the band until he couldn't tell them apart.

When the concert finally ended, Jonathan was only too happy to fight the crowd to reach his car. He didn't think that even a bottle of extra-strength aspirin would cure his pounding headache and bring his hearing back. At one point, Holly had grabbed hold of his hand in fear of being separated from the crowd. With her petite stature, she could have easily been trampled if it hadn't been for the security of hanging on to Jonathan's hand.

"They must be getting more popular than I thought," Holly decided when they finally reached the car. "The place was packed. Although their music seems to have changed a lot since I last heard them."

"How could you tell?" he muttered, reaching for his

keys. The expression on Jonathan's face changed from bewilderment to anger as he hunted through his pockets.

"What's wrong?" She noticed his alarmed motions.

"My wallet's been stolen," he informed her in a gritty voice.

"Oh, no!" Holly breathed, reaching out to grip his hand. "Are you sure you didn't just leave it at home?"

"I'm positive."

She looked around. "We better go find a security guard."

For the next few hours, Jonathan filled out reports and answered questions. He cursed silently, remembering the magnetic key cards in his wallet that would have to be reported to the bank's security office on Monday. He was glad that the cards didn't carry the bank's name.

Holly was silent during their walk back to the car.

Before Jonathan switched on the engine, he hunted around inside the glove compartment and withdrew a small notebook.

"What are you writing?" Holly asked.

"A reminder to make an appointment with my audiologist," he said curtly, wondering if the ringing in his ears would ever stop.

"Save your money. Your full hearing will return soon." She laid her hand on his arm. "Jonathan, I'm so sorry this happened."

"I'll have to return to the house and call the credit card protection service. It shouldn't take me long; we can go to dinner afterward." He shook his head, wondering why he felt like laughing. "How can you stand that kind of music?"

"I only attend a few concerts a year." She still felt contrite. "Jonathan, I feel as if this were my fault."

He shook his head. "It's something that can happen

158

anywhere, Holly. I'll be honest with you. I'm acting a lot more calm about this than I thought I would be." He switched on the engine.

"Let me treat you to dinner, Jonathan," Holly offered, unaware that her hand was still on his arm and gently rubbing the wool fabric between two fingers. "There's a restaurant near the house that serves great food," she coaxed, smiling up at him.

"All right," he conceded, hoping that she didn't mean to feed him hamburgers again. His stomach hadn't forgotten the last time Holly had taken him out to dinner.

It didn't take Jonathan long to leaf through his private telephone book at home and find the number for the credit card protection agency. A telephone call left him secure in the fact that his cards would be cancelled immediately.

The restaurant was just a few blocks from the house. Its western motif was carried through the many dining rooms.

They both declined predinner drinks and ordered their meal right away. Holly smiled at the napkin-covered basket holding warm sourdough bread.

"I wonder how many baskets we can go through?" she questioned with a sly wink.

"Two, one basket each," he replied, unable to resist her teasing. "Unless you're afraid a full order of barbecued ribs won't fill you up."

"And steak fries," she added, buttering a slice of bread.

For the first time in the past few hours, Jonathan smiled. "You're not going to let me feel sorry for myself, are you?"

"Nope." She broke off a piece of bread and popped it into her mouth.

Holly kept up her teasing banter and asked how his proposal was received at the bank in hopes that Jonathan would forget his misfortune for a few hours. Her interest in his work did seem to take his mind off his stolen wallet, as he informed her that the new program would be implemented in the next few weeks. Then he sank back into silence again.

"Here you give me a bad time about my order of ribs and they practically give you a kettle of stew," she accused playfully, wanting to make him laugh.

"A small kettle," Jonathan corrected, dipping the soup spoon into the thick stew.

"I'm sure they had to use an entire cow to fill that pot up with beef."

"Holly, concentrate on your own food."

"Probably a bushel of carrots and potatoes."

"Holly." His voice held a warning.

"And plenty of other vegetables."

"If you don't care to walk to your house, I'd suggest you be quiet."

Even after her large meal, Holly's sweet tooth succumbed to a velvety chocolate mousse baked in a chocolate cookie crust.

Halfway through her blissful appreciation of dessert, she stared across the table at Jonathan who sat back in his chair, one hand circling his coffee cup. With an ancient message written in the shimmering depths, aquamarine eyes held hazel ones. Jonathan's fingers tightened their hold on the cup.

"Are you finished?" he asked in a strangled voice.

Holly nodded. The lump in her throat didn't allow her to reply. They left the restaurant as quickly as possible.

Holly could feel the familiar tension swirling around them like a fog. No matter what Jonathan said about their taking it slow and easy, their bodies had other ideas. She fingered the cold metal of the seat belt buckle.

"Jonathan?" Her soft request floated in the air between them. "For once, would you please exceed the speed limit, even a little bit?"

Jonathan kept the speedometer needle wavering between sixty and sixty-five miles an hour during the return trip home.

By unspoken agreement, they entered Holly's half of the house. Jonathan crossed the length of the bedroom to switch on the bedside lamp. He looked around the room, noticing the colorful patchwork quilt on the double bed, ruffled curtains in a solid color to complement the quilt, and a pale-green easy chair in one corner. He turned back to Holly who stood uncertainly in the doorway. Little did he know that her thoughts centered on her relief that she had picked up her dirty clothes before she had left.

With an anguished cry, Holly literally flew into Jonathan's embrace, almost strangling him from her fierce hug.

"Please." Her breath was warm and moist against his throat. "Please don't leave me afterward. Don't reject me in the morning. I couldn't stand it."

Jonathan wrapped his arms around her in a tight squeeze. He inhaled the subtle lemony scent in her hair and couldn't imagine anything so seductive. He widened his stance until she stood pressed intimately against him.

Jonathan couldn't imagine desire could be as exquisite as the heat flowing through his body. He brushed the back of his knuckles over the soft skin of her abdomen through the material of her top.

Not to be outdone, Holly pushed her hands under the hem of Jonathan's sweater and sought the smooth surface of his back. She traced the rippling muscles with inquisitive fingers and teased the sensitive skin just under the waistband of his slacks. She nuzzled his throat and ran her tongue over the taut surface and tasted the salty skin.

Jonathan combed his hands through her hair and pulled her head back for his kiss. As before, it revealed a turbulence the public Jonathan never displayed.

His tongue plunged into her open mouth and found remembered pleasures. He circled her tongue and caught the faint hint of chocolate. With each move of his mouth, Holly imitated his gestures and opened her mouth even wider under his driving force.

Holly was delirious with joy. She inhaled the subtle tang of Jonathan's aftershave mixed with his skin and moved up on her toes to align her body more perfectly with his.

Before she realized it, her sweater was pulled over her head. Jonathan's sweater was similarly peeled off before their bare torsos met then drifted apart as they finished undressing.

As Holly made ready to turn back the quilt, a horrifying thought occurred to her.

Jonathan frowned and cupped her chin, tilting it upward. "What's wrong?" He was past allowing her any doubts now!

"I—ah—they were given to me as a joke," she murmured, finally pulling the quilt back.

Jonathan stared at the sheets festooned with cartoon animals frolicking in a forest of multicolored trees. "Quite a mood breaker, aren't they?" he murmured.

Holly looked crestfallen. "That's what I was afraid you'd say." She sighed.

Jonathan reached his arm around her and snapped off the light. "Now we can't see them." He gently pushed her onto the bed.

As with the first time, they lay on their sides content

with deep kisses and fleeting caresses that would only heighten their anticipation. No words were needed to tell the other they wanted to draw it out as long as possible. As always, their bodies were in perfect tune with each other.

Jonathan marveled at the silky feel of Holly's skin under his exploring fingertips. Her breaths deepened when he traced an imaginary line along the underside of her breasts and then followed it with his lips. He found the rosy nipple, gently grazed his teeth over the tiny nub, and drew it back into his mouth. Holly whimpered at the sharp pleasure-pain in the center of her body. In return, she edged her foot up his leg to his thigh and felt the muscles tense.

"My, you're sensitive there, aren't you?" she whispered, dropping a moist kiss on his chest and tasting the tart flavor of his skin. She edged her foot a fraction higher.

Jonathan jumped under her teasing caress then reciprocated with one of his own. His hand traveled over her midriff and along the quivering skin of the abdomen.

"Jonathan!" Holly cried out, holding onto his shoulders even as her body moved up against his probing fingers. She needed him so badly! She lifted her mouth to his, her tongue flicking into his mouth, and reached down to lightly caress his velvety manhood.

A deep groan vibrated in Jonathan's throat as he lay back and pulled Holly over him. With a shifting of their weights, they melded into a rhythm that increased with each breath they took and shared.

Jonathan ran his hands freely over the damp surface of Holly's body. He reached up to nuzzle each breast with his lips before moving up to her lips.

Holly was beyond knowing who paced their loving. The fire that burned within her raged into an inferno no amount of water could quench. She murmured words of desire as Jonathan thrust her into the flames that eventually consumed them both.

Holly cried out as sparks flashed before her eyes and Jonathan shared her ecstasy. For long moments afterward, they lay close together, their bodies still trembling with the aftershocks.

Holly pressed her cheek into the hollow of Jonathan's shoulder. "I feel as if I'm on a cloud," she murmured, just before she fell asleep.

Jonathan's arms never left her as he slept deeply.

Sometime in the night, Holly stirred sleepily only to wiggle closer to his comforting warmth.

This time when Holly awoke, she was not alone. She lay quietly enjoying the feel of Jonathan's arms around her. She was also free to study him at length. She was happy to see his features relaxed and his body free of tension. She smiled, remembering something he had once said. Oh, yes, they were very combustible!

She crept out of bed and first stopped at the bathroom to freshen up before going into the kitchen and letting Ralph into the house. She was planning a special surprise for Jonathan.

Jonathan woke up slowly and blindly reached out for Holly.

"What the—?" He jumped as a cold nose nuzzled his hand and a large tongue lapped his palm. Jonathan discovered his sexy bed partner had turned into a St. Bernard. A yelp of pain from the kitchen caught his attention next. He leaped out of bed and ran out of the bedroom.

He found Holly, dressed in an oversized T-shirt, staring morosely at a charred mess in a frying pan. She held her hand with the fingers curled protectively inward.

"What happened?" he asked.

"I burned my finger." She held up her forefinger. "I wanted to surprise you with scrambled eggs for breakfast and everything went wrong." Tears glistened in her eyes.

Jonathan moved forward and picked up Holly's injured hand. He drew the wounded finger into his mouth and suckled it gently, wrapping his tongue around the raw and reddened tip. All the time he soothed the burn, his eyes remained on her.

"Does anything else hurt?" he asked.

Holly used her other hand to touch her lips. They burned all right; they burned for his kiss. Jonathan used the same extreme care in bathing her mouth with his tongue.

"Why don't I let Ralph out while you go back into the bedroom and wait for me?" he suggested. "We'll go out to breakfast . . . later."

Instead of breakfast, Holly and Jonathan finally settled for a late lunch. During their meal, Holly reflected back on the two sides of Jonathan. Whenever they were completely alone, he always seemed to touch her. And that morning, he had even showed her new ways of seduction that left her breathless. She hadn't realized that taking a shower could turn out to be so erotic.

The public side of Jonathan was too circumspect, to Holly's way of thinking. Even dressed casually, he projected the image of the successful bank executive. That was when she decided to work on dissolving the barrier and allowing the two sides to mix.

When they returned to Holly's house, the answering machine's blinking light beckoned to her. She played the message back and listened to a woman's voice that was as arid as the desert.

"Good afternoon, Holly. I certainly hope you attended church this morning instead of frolicking with your friends. As it is, I suppose I'll have to talk to that infernal machine of yours. I would appreciate hearing from my daughter once in a while." The machine clicked off.

Jonathan watched Holly stiffen at the first sound of what must have been her mother's voice. "Would you excuse me for a moment?" she murmured, walking into the bedroom.

Jonathan sat down on the blue couch and reached down to rub Ralph's head when he pushed against his leg. Holly spoke softly, but he could hear every word clearly.

"Hello, Mother. I—ah—I was out with a friend."

"Yes, I know when Thanksgiving is, but I don't think I'll be able to come back then."

"For Christmas?" He could hear the strong hesitation in her expressive voice and then guilt surfacing. "Yes, I'm aware I wasn't there last year. You hadn't told me you were having a family reunion then." There was silence as if she were listening to her mother speaking. "All right, I'll be there this Christmas. I'll call you when I know the date I'll be flying back." She sighed heavily. "Good-bye."

A moment later, a subdued Holly entered the living room. "I'm sorry, I had to return the call to my mother since she and my father go to bed early." She managed a feeble smile. She wandered aimlessly around the room, picking up a vase here, a ceramic figurine there. Without any warning, a loud *hic!* escaped her lips. She jumped, pressing her fingertips against her lips.

"Holly, go into the kitchen and get yourself a glass of water," Jonathan instructed. "Then come back in here and while you're drinking your water, you can tell me what is upsetting you."

Holly went into the kitchen and did as ordered. She returned with the glass of water and sat on the carpet near Jonathan's leg. She sipped the water slowly even as another hiccup sneaked its way past her lips.

"Are your parents the reason you left home?" he asked quietly.

She shrugged. "Yes and no. There were plenty of reasons why I left and no one main motive. Some people called me a bonus baby, others referred to me as a change-of-life baby. What my mother thought was menopause turned out to be the early stages of pregnancy. She was forty-four and involved in her new career as secretary to the town's only attorney when I was born. She had decided that she wasn't about to give up her job to change diapers and heat formulas when her other children were in high school. I was basically raised by my brothers and sister, who grumbled about being unpaid babysitters," she finished bitterly.

Jonathan looked down at the silky black curls nestled near his knee. "A lot of mothers have to work, Holly," he reminded her. "At least you had siblings to look after you."

"Only until I was old enough to take care of myself." Unconsciously she rested her cheek on his knee. "It wasn't my fault that I was born so late in her life," Holly whispered more to herself.

The hard layer surrounding Jonathan's heart began to soften when he heard the wistful note in Holly's voice. His mother may not have been overly affectionate to him when he was home on school holidays, but she was always available when he needed her. It sounded as if Holly missed out on a mother's love during her growing-up years. Was that why she sounded so hesitant over spending Christmas with her family and disliked talking about them? And was that the reason for her spreading her love over every child in the neighborhood?

His hand rested on her head, the fingers tangling in the dark curls. "If you could have anything in the world what would it be?"

There was no hesitation in her reply. "A chance to produce my own program."

"Cartoons?" This time there was no derision in his voice as he said the word.

Holly nodded, her curls curving lovingly around Jonathan's fingers. "But they'd also be geared for children with emotional problems. A human being might not be able to reach disturbed children while a pet or cartoon character could get them to respond."

Jonathan slid his hands over Holly's shoulders and down under her arms to lift her gently up onto his lap.

"There's not one ounce of fluff in your head, is there?" Now his hands cupped her face in a warm embrace.

"Maybe a quarter of an ounce," she murmured, turning her head to kiss the slightly rough skin and tickle his palm with the tip of her tongue. "That allows me those impulsive moments of mine."

His voice came across rough with barely suppressed desire. "Such as now?"

Her eyes were cloudy with answering passion. "This isn't impulsive, Jonathan," she whispered against his skin. "If it were, I would have merely pulled you down onto the carpet and ripped your clothes off."

Jonathan's thumb rubbed over the moist silk of her lower lip. "I think I like your idea of impulsive behavior," he said thickly. "Do you think you could pretend to be impulsive right now?"

Holly's gaze fixed on Jonathan's face, which was dark with the same heat that raced through her body. She gripped his wrist and nudged her lips over his thumb. Her tongue swirled over the pad and her teeth grazed the nail.

"Like this?"

"Yes," he groaned.

"What about this?" She traced a small pattern along his throat and felt the racing pulse.

Jonathan knew that Holly was testing out her feminine powers, and he allowed her liberties that no woman had ever taken with him. He stared down at her passion-flushed face with a searing gaze.

"Is this what you prefer?" Holly whispered, fingering the buttons of his shirt and slipping inside to caress the warm skin.

"Try again." The words were torn from his throat.

"This?" She moved her hand down to smooth lightly over the taut material covering his straining manhood.

Jonathan stood up so suddenly, Holly would have fallen to the carpet if he hadn't held her so possessively. He picked her up and walked into her bedroom. He didn't bother turning on a light since the lamplight filtering in from the living room was more than enough.

He wasted no time in tearing Holly's clothing off and made short work of his own.

"Don't wait, Jonathan," she pleaded, reaching up to pull him down to her. "Please, I need you." The throbbing in the center of her body had steadily increased until she could feel her arousal building to a pleasure so acute it sent shafts of pain through her.

He hesitated for a moment, worrying that he might hurt her. He placed his hand over the downy skin of her belly.

"Now!" Holly demanded, arching up and teasing his pulsating need with her fingers and guiding him into her welcoming warmth.

Jonathan couldn't wait then. He plunged into her moist sheath, relieved that she was more than ready for him. Each thrust was deep and part of a rhythm that could not be kept up for long. The uncertain ties of the past few weeks, the memories of a hot lusty loving, and the knowledge of their attuned sensuality sent them spinning out to deepest space. They were two primitive beings reaching out to each other in the most elemental of ways. For one brief moment, Jonathan almost threw his head back and roared his completion.

They lay spent, gasping for air as if it would be their last.

Jonathan had thought he had lost his self-control before where Holly was concerned. He was wrong. Even as he pondered his unusual lack of composure, he could feel his body hardening in anticipation. He silently turned on his side and proceeded to kiss Holly into eager submission. Even after a repeat of their previous loving, the hunger still hadn't been appeased.

CHAPTER ELEVEN

Click-click-click-brrrrt. Click-click-brrrrt. Click-click-click-brrrrt. Click-click-

"Damn!" Holly glared at her calculator as if it purposely gave her the wrong answer each time she hit the total button.

She sat in the middle of the living room with piles of calculator tape surrounding her like many white paper serpents. So far, she had gone through three rolls of tape and finally decided that her self-appointed task was a major disaster. Ralph jumped in and attacked the spiraling paper.

"Whooof!" He rolled over onto his back.

"You are not any help," Holly scolded, staring at the final figure again. Now she knew why people doctored their books when the same answer never came up twice. She leaned over, propping her chin on her curled palm. Ten months' worth of bank statements were scattered around her and the cancelled checks were many colored strips of paper littering the area.

Holly was beginning to wonder if she'd be better off just piling it all into a grocery bag and sending it to Ted, her accountant.

But she knew he wouldn't thank her for bringing in such a mess. She hadn't forgotten his previous grumblings about her refusing to balance her checkbook. She also remembered Jonathan's look of horror when he had seen the many statements littering her desk drawer. Well, she'd show him!

With renewed vigor, Holly rummaged through the mess to find the statement from the past January. She hoped she wouldn't have to make another trip to the stationery store for more calculator tape.

When the doorbell rang a half hour later, Holly saw it as a sign of salvation. "Coming!" she trilled, jumping up and running to the door. She threw it open, offering her visitor a beaming smile.

"I know that smile wasn't intended for me, but I'll accept it," Jonathan greeted her, surprised by her exuberant salutation.

"I wouldn't have cared if it had been someone selling magazines," Holly confided blithely, grabbing his arm and pulling him inside. "Would you like a soda or some coffee?"

"Perhaps a new arm," he said dryly, looking down at her death grip on his wrist.

"Sorry," Holly apologized, pulling her hand away.

Jonathan looked over Holly's head at the many white streamers layered over the living-room carpet along with a St. Bernard snoozing in the middle.

"I didn't realize you were working." Now it was his turn to apologize. "I can come back later."

"No!" she all but shouted.

Jonathan took another look at the living room. He moved around Holly. "It appears you've been doing a bit of reconciling," he observed, leaning down to pick up part of the miles of calculator tape.

"Actually, it's called the sure way to go crazy," Holly grumbled.

"How are you doing?"

She made a rude noise. "Either I have fifteen thousand dollars more in the account than the bank says I do or I'm two hundred thousand overdrawn, which would really be a joke." She slapped her hands at her sides. "Would you believe that they charged me ten dollars and forty cents for new checks?"

Jonathan hid a smile. "Would you like me to give you a hand with this?" he asked casually.

Holly's eyes widened. "Would you?" She held out her hand, palm up. "Don't go away, I'll get you some new pencils. I've chewed the erasers off the ones I've been using."

Two hours later, Jonathan began to regret his offer of assistance. The first thing he had done was gather up the used calculator tape and drop it into the wastebasket before embarking on a mission any self-respecting banker would blanch at.

Holly sat cross-legged on the cream-color carpet and carefully arranged the cancelled checks into numerical order as Jonathan had instructed her to do. She looked up and watched his fingers fly over the calculator keys while his eyes were glued to the figures printed on the statements.

He never looks at the keys! she thought with amazement. If I did that, I'd have an even bigger mess.

"You don't list your deposits," Jonathan accused, not looking up from his work.

"I know how much money I put in the bank every two weeks and I don't write out all that many checks. I'll have you know I've never received an overdrawn notice," she defended herself. "Obviously I'm doing something right."

He sighed heavily. "I hope you have the courtesy to give

your accountant fair warning before you appear." Jonathan spoke more sternly than she had heard him in quite a while.

Holly grinned. "And scare him off? I'm not that crazy." She reached up and coiled her arms around his neck. "Too bad he's sixty and balding, otherwise I'd probably be on his doorstep the day my statements arrive," she cooed.

Holly never knew the inner strength it took for Jonathan to grasp her wrists and lower her arms.

"I intend to finish your bank statements," he said firmly. "Are the checks in order?"

Holly nodded, chagrined that her attempt at seduction didn't work.

"How far along are you?"

"I'm just finishing up June."

Jonathan shook his head, amazed that someone could so blithely ignore her financial situation.

"Would you care for some coffee?" she offered.

"Two scoops in the pot, not four," he said absently, as he continued punching figures into the calculator.

"If a person listened to him, you'd think I didn't know how to make coffee properly," Holly complained to Ralph as she filled the coffeemaker with water. She took a dog biscuit out of a box and tossed it to the waiting St. Bernard.

It was true that her last attempt at making coffee had ended up with the hot drink resembling mud with darkbrown granules floating in it. But that was because she had been too aware of the intense man seated at the small round table in the kitchen and she had lost count as she scooped the coffee into the filter.

"I'll show him." She carefully measured the coffee and dumped it into the basket set over the glass pot. She flipped the switch to brew and rummaged through the cabinets for a snack. Her search revealed chocolate-covered graham crackers and toffee-covered peanuts.

"Not exactly filling." She poured the peanuts into a small white bowl decorated with a strawberry design.

"Is the coffee ready?" Jonathan appeared in the doorway.

"It certainly is." She poured the coffee into two mugs and handed one to him.

Jonathan cautiously sipped the dark brew then took a longer drink. "Very good," he complimented.

"Naturally," she declared haughtily, as if there should be any question regarding her culinary ability. But she couldn't hold her disdainful pose for long and soon dissolved in giggles. "Actually, this is probably the first time I've fixed coffee that's drinkable. Is the reconciling getting any easier?"

"Does your accountant receive combat pay for balancing your statements?" He carried his mug back into the living room.

"No, but he mutters a lot," she quipped, following him.

"I'm surprised he still works with you." Jonathan stacked the statements into a neat pile.

Holly curled up into her favorite chair. "This may be a bit late, but you hadn't said why you stopped by."

He smiled. "I wondered when you'd think to ask. I have to go out of town Monday on business and I hoped you'd pick my mail up for me."

"Of course," she agreed readily. She sipped her coffee and watched Jonathan surreptitiously under lowered lashes. There was just the faintest hint of a change in his demeanor. It wasn't anything earthshattering, but there was a decided lack of tension in his harsh features and a bit more relaxation in the lines of his body. A tiny corner of her heart wondered if she just might be the reason. "Do you have any idea how long you might be gone?" She hoped she sounded casual enough with her question.

"A week to ten days." Jonathan penciled in an entry in Holly's checkbook and closed the cover. "I doubt you'd have a problem in reconciling your account next month," he informed her.

Holly wrinkled her nose. "I'll be sure to lay in a big supply of calculator tape first." She set her cup down and braced her elbow on the chair's arm, her chin propped in her palm. "Jonathan, I'd like to thank you for helping me with this mess. All I ended up doing was getting more frustrated."

He leaned over to help himself to some of the peanuts. "I once heard someone discuss people like you," he said by way of conversation.

She lifted an eyebrow. "You're making me sound like a disease."

Jonathan shook his head, impatient with her good-natured quips. "You have a very creative mind, Holly," he acknowledged. "As a result, you cannot be bothered with mundane details."

"Such as cooking and balancing bank statements," she brought up.

"Or looking after your car," he added. "I have a hunch that it has developed an oil leak."

"Ugh!" Holly groaned, throwing her head back.

"Why don't you just buy a new car?" Jonathan suggested.

"Because I hate car salesmen," she confessed. "They're too pushy and I usually end up getting mad and walking off the lot."

"Perhaps you should try a troll's voice out on the next one you meet," Jonathan recommended. "Or even the voice you used in the space age film. I'm sure you'd receive excellent service then."

Holly laughed. "Careful, Jonathan, or I just may think you're developing a sense of humor."

He shook his head as he rose to his feet. "I have an idea I'll always be thought of as some kind of ogre," he rumbled. "I should leave so I can begin my packing."

Holly also stood up. "Thank you again." She followed him to the front door while whimsically wondering what he would look like in a pair of tight jeans.

"I'll let you know if I happen to be delayed." Jonathan opened the door only to find a small boy standing on the other side.

"Hi, Bobby," Holly greeted the boy.

"Hi, Holly." He looked curiously at the tall man standing beside her. "Hi."

"Hello." Jonathan remembered him as the boy who had once erroneously delivered a bunch of balloons for Holly to him, giving him his first chance to speak to her.

"My cat threw up on the rug in my bedroom," Bobby announced.

Holly bit the inside of her cheek to keep from laughing. "I'm sorry Seymour is sick, Bobby," she said gravely.

"He isn't sick. I think it was cause he ate my goldfish," the boy explained.

"How did he get your goldfish?" Holly couldn't resist finding out.

"I let Seymour play with it, but he ate it instead."

Holly sneaked a glance at Jonathan and for a brief moment, she could have sworn that his dark eyes looked haunted before the mask of indifference passed over them.

"I have an early-morning flight," Jonathan murmured, stepping outside. "I'm sure I'll see you when I return."

Holly looked after his departing figure, disappointment reflecting in her eyes. She was tempted to stop him and lay a toe-curling kiss on him, but she knew he would only withdraw from her again.

Oh, Jonathan, when are you going to realize that two people can be affectionate in public and won't get arrested? she silently implored.

"Have a good trip," she said, but her thoughts were still centered on more intimate ramblings.

Jonathan nodded and let himself into his side of the house.

"I asked Mom if I could have another fish." Bobby spoke up, bringing Holly back to earth. "She said no."

"I don't blame her. You'd probably just give it to Seymour." She opened the door wider, allowing him to enter. "I suppose you're here while your mother cools off about Seymour getting sick?"

He nodded, slipping inside. "Can I have some milk?"

"Please," Holly prompted.

"Please?" Bobby parroted with an angelic smile, looking far from the type of boy who would give his cat a goldfish to play with.

That night, Holly lay sleepless in her bed. For the first time, she felt desperately alone. The bed felt too wide and empty although until recently she had never shared it with anyone. She shivered, rolled over on her side, and reached out to turn the control knob up a notch on her electric blanket.

She stared at the curtains and decided they needed to be

changed. In fact, a lot of changes needed to be made and what better timing than during the coming week.

Jonathan was still gone ten days later and Holly had a small, neat stack of envelopes addressed to him on a corner of her desk. For the past few days, she had been wandering around the house feeling abandoned, even though Jonathan had called her a few times.

She sneezed and dug a tissue out of her pants pocket. "I hate colds," she moaned, blowing her nose, which resembled Rudolph the reindeer's in color.

In Holly's frame of mind, it was bad enough to have a nasty head cold, but to suffer from one on her birthday was a fate worse than death. She was doomed to stay confined to the house and feel sorry for herself on what should have been an important day to her.

She happened to catch a glance of her face in the bathroom mirror as she got herself a fresh tissue. Her nose was red and raw-looking, her skin florid, and her eyes red-rimmed.

"I hate birthdays too." Holly sniffed mournfully, reaching for her bottle of cold medicine. She poured the proper amount of the green liquid and grimaced at the strong taste as she swallowed it.

In an effort to forget her misery, she curled up in bed and began reading a book she had been meaning to read for the past few months. With a cup of hot tea steaming on her nighttable and Ralph sleeping on the other side of the bed, Holly could have been posing for a picture of domestic harmony.

Holly was about ready to give up on her reading when the telephone rang.

"H'lo," she croaked into the receiver.

"Holly?" Jonathan's voice was questioning, as if he was wondering if he had been connected to a wrong number.

"It's me, Jonathan." She managed a feeble laugh.

There was a slight hesitation on the other end. "Are you working on a new voice?"

"I guess you could call it practicing someone with a cold the hard way." She gripped the receiver tightly. "How is your trip going?"

"I should be back in a week," he explained. "We're still finishing up the new system at this branch. Marian hopes to have it all set up by then."

"Marian," Holly repeated weakly. She had heard that name a great deal over the past ten days. Marian was a computer expert sent with Jonathan to work on the new system. She's probably tall, beautiful, and has a perfect figure, Holly mourned silently, looking down at the shapeless sweatshirt and jogging pants she wore.

"Holly, are you all right?" Jonathan's voice sharpened.

"No," she rasped, feeling very close to tears. She blamed them on her cold. "I'm sorry, Jonathan, but I'm really not feeling very well. I guess I'll see you next week then. Thank you for calling." She carefully replaced the receiver and pulled her pillow around to hug it tightly against her middle.

Jonathan sat in his hotel room and stared at the telephone. He had easily guessed that Holly was sick, but he hadn't missed the desolation in her voice that was much more than just a part of her illness. He switched his gaze to the pile of computer printouts laid out over the table.

Why was she so unhappy? he mused. Funny, he couldn't remember ever worrying about a woman's feelings before.

Even Liza had never raised any protective emotions in him since he knew she could take excellent care of herself.

Jonathan felt restless. He didn't want to admit that his disquietude was due to missing Holly. She was rapidly becoming a part of him, and he knew he would have to cut the tenuous ties between them before too long. His logical side told him it was best. His swiftly growing emotional side told him it would be impossible.

Jonathan checked his pocket calendar to figure out when he would be able to return to Los Angeles and noticed that the day was not only Halloween but Holly's birthday.

"No wonder the lady is feeling more than just ill," he murmured, staring down at the date. "She undoubtedly isn't happy to be confined at home with a bad cold on her birthday."

As she mixed a can of dog food with kibble, Holly loudly wished her head didn't feel as if it was stuffed with cotton.

"I never get sick," she grumbled, setting the large plastic bowl on the floor. "I mimic a better sneeze than the real thing." She proceeded to demonstrate the authentic action and was still sneezing when the doorbell rang. "Now what?" She moaned, walking to the front door.

Holly was stunned to find a delivery boy carrying a basket filled with autumn-hued flowers.

"Holly Sutton?" he asked cheerfully, holding the basket out.

She nodded her head as she took the flowers. Then she closed the door and carried the basket into the living room to set it on the coffee table, and wondered who had sent the flowers. She withdrew the tiny card and read the simple message, but it was the name that warmed her. Holly traced each of the eight letters and smiled. That was when she knew that Jonathan Lockwood was revealing that he had a heart after all.

The fall flowers sat on the coffee table for the rest of the week. Each day Holly carefully put water in the bowl and pulled out any dead blooms. She also religiously took her medicine at the prescribed times. She was determined to be well when Jonathan returned.

Holly was also glad when she could return to work because it would help pass the time faster. They were finishing up an hour-long television special celebrating summer and Holly was one of the main voices.

"Rhonda Robin." Holly gave an unladylike snort.

"She looks like a Rhonda, Holly," Hal explained, holding up a colored-pencil sketch of the little bird.

She sighed heavily. "Hal, I hate bosses who are so deeply involved with minor details such as what the birds are supposed to look like."

He laughed loudly. "Do you think you could give her an English accent?"

"Highbrow or cockney?"

"Highbrow?"

Holly thought about Jonathan and how his harsh-timbred voice sent shock waves through her body. "I think I can manage it," she said with a casual air.

"Holly, Mrs. Benson is here to see you," the receptionist's voice cackled over the loudspeaker.

"Thanks, Sherry," Holly called out.

Hal glanced up at the wall clock. "Luncheon engagement?"

Holly nodded. "If my mean old master will let me

leave," she squeaked, holding her hands out in supplication.

"Get outa here," he ordered, but his laughter cancelled out the mock ferocity on his face.

Holly jumped off her stool and knelt down, grabbing one of Hal's hands. "Oh, master, you're so good to me!" she trilled.

"And I used to say that you were the sanest of the group." He groaned. "I take it all back."

"It's working around here that does strange things to the brain," she said cheekily, jumping up. "See you this afternoon. And could we please come up with something besides Rhonda?"

Holly stopped long enough to grab her purse and jacket before heading for the lobby. Looking immaculate in a lettuce-green wool suit and a creamy vanilla ruffled blouse, Liza stood near the reception desk.

"Don't you look lovely today?" Liza said sincerely, noting Holly's hot-pink tailored shirt tucked into black wool pleated pants.

"I decided I needed to update my wardrobe," Holly muttered, steering Liza out of the building and down the street.

"By the way, how was your trip to San Francisco with your friend?" Liza asked. "I can't believe it's been that long since I've spoken to you."

"Fine," Holly mumbled, leading the way to a restaurant specializing in any kind of omelet imaginable.

"Did you and Chris take in all the sights?" Liza questioned, once they were seated in the cheerful dining room. "Holly, you're blushing!"

"No, I'm not!" she denied vehemently, taking a sudden interest in her water glass.

Liza watched Holly with an X-ray gaze. "Did you meet any interesting men while you were up there?"

"No." At least she could speak the truth regarding that!

"Did you meet a man on the plane?" Liza wasn't going to stop now.

Holly shrugged, preferring not to answer. She had forgotten how relentless her friend could be.

"Did Chris go with you?" Liza pressed, now suspicious of Holly's monosyllabic answers.

Holly shook her head and looked around silently begging the waitress to come.

Guessing that Holly didn't care to talk about her trip, Liza turned to her menu. "I think I'll have the spinach omelet," she decided. "What are you having?"

"I'm not sure, maybe the cheese and mushroom." Holly looked relieved that the subject had been changed.

"How are you and Jonathan getting along?" Liza asked brightly.

"Oh, fine." Her voice went up at the end. "He's away on a business trip right now."

But Liza hadn't missed the dull red flush along Holly's cheekbones and the way her fingers nervously fiddled with the silverware.

"Oh, did he have to fly up to San Francisco?" She took a stab in the dark. "If I remember correctly, the bank's headquarters are up there."

"I'm not exactly sure where he went," Holly prevaricated.

Liza thought back to her idea of throwing Holly and Jonathan together. In the beginning, she had felt that it was all for the best for the two of them. Now that it appeared her plan may have succeeded, she was experiencing second thoughts.

"Holly, are you and Jon having an affair?"

"Liza!" She didn't have to feign shock. Liza's question had certainly stunned her. "Are you accusing me of sleeping with your ex-husband?"

"No, but I'm hoping that you are," she replied with a serene smile.

Holly grabbed her water glass and drank deeply. "Liza, you have a very unusual attitude toward Jonathan," she finally said, gasping, still shocked by Liza's frank talk.

"I have a practical view," she corrected.

Holly was reluctant to reveal her and Jonathan's new relationship. Mainly because she didn't believe in "kiss and tell" and also because she wasn't sure what the end result would be.

"We've gone out a few times, but other than that there's really nothing to say," Holly supplied. "I told you once before that I'm not his type."

Liza looked over Holly's more sophisticated clothing and smiled knowingly. She had seen past her evasion and easily guessed that there was much more to their just being neighborly. Deep down, Liza still felt that Holly was right for Jonathan. She only hoped they would learn that fact before Jonathan moved into his new home.

"Sometimes we can be very surprised as to what our types can be, Holly," she said quietly. She thought of Harold, who might not be as handsome or compelling as Jonathan, but she couldn't imagine anyone else she would prefer to spend her future with. "Nature has a way of showing us who we belong with."

Holly was ready to protest but thought better of it. While the idea of getting to know Jonathan a great deal better was a tempting prospect, she knew that he didn't allow anyone very close to him. She might have been allowed access to his body, but he never relaxed the control on his mind. It was a sad thought that he didn't seem to trust anyone enough to reveal his true nature. There was also a bright spot. Holly couldn't imagine Jonathan sending flowers to her unless she did mean something to him.

CHAPTER TWELVE

Holly made a careful inventory of her kitchen supplies before sitting down to write up a grocery list. "Tell me, Sutton, do you honestly believe you can pull this off?" she murmured to herself.

She thought back a few days to when her brainstorm had germinated. Jonathan had been home almost a week, but Holly had seen little of him since he had been busy catching up on his work.

After coming up with her idea, she waylaid Jonathan early one morning before he left for work.

"I was wondering if you were doing anything for Thanksgiving?" she ventured. "And if you're not, perhaps you'd like to come over for dinner?"

Jonathan was frankly surprised by a dinner invitation issued by a woman who cheerfully professed to not having any culinary talent. "I'd like that," he agreed, silently wondering how Holly would conjure up a Thanksgiving dinner with all the trimmings unless she planned on serving TV dinners.

As she thought back to her impulsive invitation, she was beginning to wonder the same thing. It was the Tuesday before Thanksgiving and she was finally figuring out what she needed to cook a turkey. At the top of her list was a large roasting pan. She decided not to chance fate too much and would pick up a pumpkin pie at the bakery.

"I wonder if a turkey really needs dressing." She reread the recipe for a cornbread dressing.

"Holly, you cannot be serious about cooking a turkey!" Liza had exclaimed when Holly had called her to ask if a hen or young tom was a better purchase. "You create a disaster while boiling water!"

"I'm not that bad," she argued. She was just glad she hadn't mentioned whom she was cooking the meal for. She had only said she was entertaining other single friends on that day.

"You should do all right with a hen," Liza advised. "At least that's what I always buy. And don't forget to take the gizzards out of the cavity and wash it thoroughly. Holly, I have another call. I'll talk to you later."

"Take the gizzards out? Wash it thoroughly?" she wondered, trying to remember how her mother had handled cooking the large Thanksgiving dinner. The trouble had been that an energetic Holly with slippery fingers had been banished from the kitchen and she had only viewed the final results.

With the help of a cookbook, Holly did her grocery shopping and ended up filling her entire backseat with brown paper bags. She was glad to see that cranberry sauce came in cans and all it would need was refrigeration. After purchasing a pumpkin pie and rolls at a nearby bakery, she felt ready to tackle her most important dinner.

Holly was up early Thanksgiving morning to begin her preparations. She studied the cookbook to discover that she had to bake the turkey one hour for every five pounds and to baste it with melted butter to keep the skin moist

Holly took the turkey out of the refrigerator and placed it on the counter next to the sink where she had set the roasting pan. She peeled off the plastic wrapping and stared at the huge white-skinned mound.

"Ugh!" She dreaded the idea of probing the cavity to retrieve the gizzards. Holly closed her eyes and tentatively reached inside, but the feel of the cold, clammy poultry flesh stopped her. She couldn't understand why she couldn't cook the gizzards inside the turkey since she wasn't going to stuff it.

In an attempt to wash it, she poured warm water into the cavity and carefully tipped the large bird over the edge of the sink.

Holly encountered another problem. She couldn't find her pot holders and she refused to pick the turkey up with her bare hands. She rummaged through her utensil drawer hoping to find something in there to assist her.

"Better than nothing," she muttered, holding up two large serving forks. Holly stuck one on each side of the turkey the way someone would insert holders in an ear of corn. Using those, she carefully lifted the bird and got halfway over the sink when one of the forks bent and the turkey tumbled onto the floor accompanied by Holly's shriek.

"Holly! Holly!" The pounding on the back door coincided with Jonathan's shouts.

She opened the door and offered him a feeble smile. "Hi, you're early."

"Are you all right?" he demanded, gripping her shoulders.

"I'm fine, it's only my pride that's battered, not to mention our dinner," she replied ruefully.

Jonathan looked beyond to see the turkey lying on the

floor and the two forks, both badly mangled, lying nearby. "What happened?"

"I was putting the turkey in the roasting pan," Holly explained, as if every turkey had to land on the floor before cooking.

Jonathan bent down and picked up the turkey and put it in the sink to rinse it off. Noticing a bit of paper sticking out of one end, Jonathan probed and drew out the bag holding the gizzards. He then checked the other end to find the neck. "I think you forgot something."

"Uncooked turkeys feel horrible!" Holly declared with a theatrical shudder.

Jonathan placed the turkey in the roasting pan and picked it up, setting it in the oven. "I was afraid you might have hurt yourself," he told her.

She stared up at the ceiling. "I didn't think the disasters would begin so soon," she said, moaning. "You may not want to eat here."

A tiny smile flitted across Jonathan's lips. "If I go back to get my contribution for dinner, would you mind if I arrived early?"

"You're certainly welcome." Holly's voice softened as her eyes watched the enticing patch of dark hair peeking above the partly buttoned shirt. Holly's previous views of Jonathan had been either impeccably dressed or naked. This bare hint of disarray was very appealing to her senses. "In fact, you're more than welcome," she injected a seductive note into her voice.

Jonathan didn't miss the not-so-subtle wording. "I'll be back in a few minutes," he murmured.

He hated to admit how much Holly's cries had frightened him. Knowing her penchant for trouble in the kitchen, he had feared the worst as he had torn out of his back door and reached hers.

Jonathan returned home and took the time to finish dressing and smooth his hair before picking up a bottle of liqueur and returning to Holly's house.

"Irish Cream!" Her eyes lit up at her favorite drink. "How did you know this was my favorite vice?"

"Your favorite one?" he questioned, stroking her throat with his fingertips.

"Mmm, perhaps my second favorite." At that moment, Holly wanted nothing more than to curl up and feel those warm hands all over her.

"Would it help if you had a reminder?" he asked huskily, teasing her ear with his lips.

But teasing wasn't enough for two people who were literally starved for each other.

Jonathan's mouth fastened hungrily on Holly's. His tongue demanded an entrance she readily surrendered to as their bodies molded together.

He sought the soft mounds of her breasts by pulling the hem of her shirt free from her jeans and allowed her the same liberty with his shirt.

Holly felt lightheaded, as if she hadn't eaten for days. She flicked her tongue over Jonathan's lips and darted inside to sample his rich taste. She slid her hands over his naked back and down beneath the waistband of his slacks. A moan ripped through her throat in reaction to his fingers circling her taut nipple.

As before, their arousal was instantaneous. Holly pressed her curves closer to Jonathan's hips and rotated her pelvis against his masculine cradle.

"I've missed you, Jonathan," she murmured, gently digging her fingertips into the muscular skin.

"I've missed you too," he admitted in a grating voice. He swiftly unbuttoned her shirt and bent his head to cover the rounded tip of her breast with his lips.

Holly drew in a sharp breath at the intense pleasure shooting through her body as his lips tugged on the tiny rose-colored nub.

"How long before dinner?" Jonathan asked hoarsely, transferring his attention to the other nipple.

"Almost three hours," she breathed, holding on to his shoulders for fear she would fall into a nameless dark void before she was ready.

"It will do . . . for now." He pulled her up into his arms and carried her into her bedroom.

When Jonathan entered the room, he stopped for a moment, his eyes taking in the room he had been in before yet it wasn't the same. "Are you positive I didn't take a wrong turn somewhere?"

Holly playfully nipped his neck. "This side only has one bedroom and you're in it."

The pink ruffled curtains had been replaced with pumpkin-color drapes and the patchwork quilt was gone; now a pale-blue, pumpkin, and cream geometric-designed bedspread covered the bed. Even the Mickey Mouse telephone had somehow changed into a pale-blue Trimline model.

Jonathan set Holly on her feet and stripped off her shirt even as she worked at unbuttoning his shirt and pushing it off his shoulders. Loosening his slacks took a bit longer as he was pulling off her jeans at the same time. After he slid her jeans down to the carpet, he placed a heated kiss on the soft skin of her stomach and tickled her navel with his tongue. He used his teeth to pull her bikini underwear downward.

Holly gripped his shoulders and gulped much-needed

air. They had barely begun and she could already feel an imminent explosion. "No more," she begged, pulling at him to rise up.

They fell onto the bed together in order to explore each other more easily.

"You have a sexy body, Jonathan," she said softly, lightly scratching his chest and trailing her nail in a circle around one flat nipple that soon peaked from her touch. She leaned over to taunt it further with the moist caress of her lips and give him the same pleasure he had given her.

Jonathan lay on his side and slid a knee between Holly's legs, offering her a tantalizing taste of what was to come. Not to be outdone, she draped a leg over his thigh.

She sighed in ecstasy when his hands cupped her small breasts and grazed his thumbs over the extremely sensitive skin. "I don't see how either of us will be able to wait much longer," Holly whispered, tracing imaginary lines over his abdomen and lower. Her lips curved against his collarbone. "I'd say you're more than ready."

Jonathan's brief laugh was hoarse with frustration. He grasped her hips and kneaded the skin in circular motions. Would he ever get enough of her? he wondered.

He reacquainted himself with the satiny texture of Holly's skin and the warm, floral fragrance that he associated with her alone. Desperately hungry to taste her again, he placed his mouth over hers and explored the moist recesses. His tongue darted in and out in the same manner as his hand moved over her femininity and probed her depths.

Holly arched upward as if an electric current shot through her veins. She slid her hands through Jonathan's hair, keeping her mouth firmly against his as her tongue reciprocated his heated caress. She felt as if she were on fire, which wasn't all that unusual. Only Jonathan could bring about such a hot and instant arousal.

"I want you inside of me, Jonathan," she pleaded, using one hand to smooth over his jawline then following it with her lips. Her fingertips sought out the hollow in his shoulder and down over his chest. "I want you over me, filling me." Her hand wandered lower and captured his masculinity. "I need you!"

He pushed her back against the covers and entered her with one strong thrust born of familiarity with her body. Holly wrapped herself around him as if afraid he would leave her too soon. She needn't have worried; he couldn't have withdrawn if his life had depended on it.

Jonathan placed most of his weight on his elbows and looked down into Holly's rapt features. Had any woman ever looked at him with such sincere longing? This was more than lust between them, but he didn't dare dwell on what really held them together.

She lifted her head to keep her mouth against his, their tongues frantically mating as even their bodies came together. She raised her pelvis in countermovements with his thrusting hips and felt herself filled with him. She experienced his strength plunging to her very core and sending shock waves vibrating throughout.

Jonathan's throat was raw from forcing air through tortured lungs. How could one woman transmit him into such a mindless state? His pace increased until they were clinging to each other as they were flung into another world where only they existed. Holly's cries were muffled under his fierce kiss of possession. His body continued to move with hers until he stiffened and shared himself with her.

It took some time before they regained their senses.

Jonathan cradled Holly against him, smoothing the damp curls from her forehead. Each time he made love to her, the craving to lose himself in her receptive body grew stronger.

"I guess I should check on the turkey," Holly murmured, reluctant to leave the comforting warmth of his embrace.

Five minutes later, Jonathan commented, "I thought you were going to check on the turkey. I haven't seen you move a muscle."

"Yes, I have," she denied, tapping his chest with her forefinger. "See, I moved something."

Jonathan rested his chin on top of Holly's head and stroked her bare hip. This was something else that was new for him—the enjoyment of just snuggling together after lovemaking.

"Aren't you afraid of the turkey burning?" he asked, ten minutes later when Holly still hadn't stirred from her position.

"I get the hint," she grumbled, rousing from her nest of blankets and Jonathan's arms. She disappeared into the bathroom while he got up and dressed.

Jonathan halted in the middle of buttoning his shirt, his attention drawn to the partially open closet door. He walked over to the opening and reached out to finger the silky fabric of a Chinese blue caftan decorated with silver threads.

Holly walked out of the bathroom and picked up her clothes.

"Put this on instead." Jonathan pulled the caftan from the closet and held it out to her.

There was a faint flush to her cheeks. "I—ah—I might get it dirty while cooking," she mumbled, stepping into pearl-color bikini panties. Suddenly self-conscious of her small breasts, she twisted her upper body away from his view.

Still holding the caftan, Jonathan crossed the room and took Holly's shirt out of her hands. "I'd like to see you wear this," he insisted quietly.

She stood there vacillating between Jonathan's request and her own trepidation.

Jonathan was surprised at Holly's hesitation. Was there a particular reason she didn't want to wear it? He began to return it to the closet.

"No." Holly practically snatched the hanger out of his hand and carried the outfit into the bathroom, shutting the door firmly behind her.

Guessing she needed privacy for some unknown reason, Jonathan left the bedroom. The memory of her skin still glowing from their lovemaking and her naked breasts enticing him with their beauty was enough to tempt him into storming the bathroom.

Holly patted bath powder over herself before slipping on the caftan. She stared into the mirror and adjusted the low neckline several ways, none to her liking.

She had bought the caftan on impulse, not realizing until too late that the neckline was slashed almost to the waist. She didn't notice that the bright color added a new vibrancy to her skin and that her eyes were almost the same shade. All she saw was the material clinging to her slight figure. Holly had never been sensitive about her small bustline, but she remembered Liza's voluptuous curves and she was positive any woman in Jonathan's life had curves in all the right places. She also had never worn any article of clothing that showed off her charms so blatantly.

"I knew I should have tripled my vitamin intake during puberty," she mumbled, straightening the full sleeves gathered into tight cuffs. She brushed her hair again and left the bathroom before her courage deserted her.

Jonathan was seated in the living room reading the newspaper when Holly walked out of the bedroom. He glanced up, then stared intently at the sensual picture standing across the room.

Fearing that the gown was too sexy for her, Holly didn't realize how the fabric clung lovingly to her body and that the slashed neckline added a new sensuality to her form. A woman with lush curves would have merely shown off her assets in such a gown; for Holly, wearing the caftan *was* the asset.

Jonathan cleared his throat. For a moment, he found it difficult to speak. "You look lovely," he told her in a low voice.

"Thank you," she murmured with a nervous smile, surprised that he could look at her so hungrily after the hour they had just spent. "Would you care for some coffee or a mixed drink?"

"I think coffee would be more preferable at eleven o'clock in the morning."

"That depends on the drink," she corrected, moving toward the kitchen.

Holly first checked on the turkey and was pleased to see that it was still intact and baking nicely. She sliced off half a cube of margarine and placed it in a pan on the stove to melt. Then she uncovered her blender and took a carton of ice cream out of the freezer. She first filled the blender with ice cream then poured in some Irish Cream. Holly applied the top and flipped the switch. When the mixture blended to the consistency of a milkshake, she turned the blender off and poured the concoction into two glasses.

She carried the glasses into the living room and handed one to Jonathan, who eyed it warily.

"Go ahead," Holly urged. "It's really good."

He sipped cautiously. "I don't normally have a sweet tooth, but this is not bad. What's in it?"

"Cream 'n' Cookies ice cream and Irish Cream." Holly sipped her drink with obvious enjoyment.

Jonathan shook his head and smiled. "You're right, there are some drinks you can indulge in at eleven A.M."

"I wish you'd smile more often, Jonathan," she said suddenly.

"Bankers aren't allowed to look too happy," he explained.

"But you're not a banker at this moment," Holly argued, seating herself on the couch next to him. "You look like a different man when you smile and not half as intimidating."

"That's why it isn't a good idea for me to smile all the time," he countered a bit coolly. "Don't try to reform me, Holly. I manage well enough on my own."

She refused to lower her gaze under his frosty one. She now had an idea why Jonathan decided to withdraw from her. He used it purely as a self-defense measure. All she had to do was find out the reason why and then she could destroy his hard shell.

"What would you do to me if I called you Jon?" She affected a flirtatious smile.

He grimaced. "The mildest punishment I would come up with would be to boil you in oil. I deplore nicknames."

"Then why does Liza call you Jon?" Holly asked curiously, feeling a little uneasy talking about his ex-wife in such familiar tones.

"Because *Elizabeth* loves nicknames," he explained, releasing a long-suffering sigh.

Holly shifted her position until she was now curled up on the couch, her arm resting along the back. "To be honest, you don't look like a Jon," she confided blithely. "You're very much a Jonathan. The name suits you. I guess I'm lucky because no one could ever shorten my name!"

"What about your middle name?" Jonathan asked her.

She wrinkled her nose, an action he noted she did whenever something displeased her. "My middle name is so bad, I don't even use the initial."

"No name could ever be that bad," he chided.

"Want to bet?" Holly leaned forward as if confessing a terrible secret. "It's Beatrice."

"It's appropriate," Jonathan announcèd.

"Appropriate? You've got to be kidding!"

He shook his head. "It means someone who makes others happy," he explained.

Holly digested this new piece of information. She was tempted to ask if she made Jonathan happy also, but she had an idea he wouldn't answer her. "What's your middle name?"

"Something found only on my birth certificate," he stated firmly.

Holly was silent for a moment, wondering what name could be so bad he refused to use or speak of it. "Is it a family name?"

"Yes. I'm the third." Jonathan found himself wondering how they got started on the subject. "I just don't use the name."

"And are you the third banker in your family?" she probed.

He nodded. "Part of the family tradition."

"Family tradition," Holly murmured, more to herself. She wondered what it would be like to follow in someone's footsteps. Although Jonathan hadn't exactly taken up where his father left off. While he had remained in the same field, he still had left his home and everything familiar to attend school and work in another country and possibly begin a few traditions of his own. For a moment, she experienced a private fantasy of helping him with some of those customs.

Dinner turned out to be a great success for Holly. The turkey was cooked to a warm golden brown on the outside and juicy meat on the inside, the mashed potatoes were fluffy instead of watery, and the rolls turned out lightly browned instead of charred on the outside.

Her smile glowed from ear to ear as Jonathan carved the turkey and placed thin slices of white meat on each plate.

"I did it," she breathed, awed by her own accomplishment. "I actually cooked a full meal without burning anything."

"You're a capable woman, Holly," he told her. "You can do anything you set your mind to." Jonathan feasted his senses on her flushed features and big smile. He also concentrated on the enchanting strip of creamy skin visible from throat to midriff. He was incredulous that she couldn't believe she was a vitally sensual woman with so much to offer a man. Didn't she ever truly see herself in the mirror?

Holly was glad she had invested in a nice set of china a few years ago. She had decided earlier in the day that if her dinner hadn't come out right, at least the table decorations were perfect! But to her surprise, both turned out to be perfect. The meal was delicious, and she saw Jonathan enjoy every bite.

"You're not working tomorrow, are you?" Jonathan asked, after finishing a slice of pumpkin pie topped with whipped cream.

Holly shook her head. "We all threatened Hal with a mutiny if he wanted us to go in." She grinned.

"Would you like to take a drive up to Solvang tomorrow?" he invited. "I'd like to do some of my Christmas shopping in the shops there before I return home for the holidays."

"You're going to England?" She hadn't thought of him leaving although she would also be gone.

"I'm leaving on the tenth and returning on the twenty-seventh," Jonathan replied.

"Yes, I'd like to drive up with you. Perhaps I can find some gifts up there also," Holly went on to say. "I'm leaving on the twenty-third and returning just after New Year's."

"What about your dog?"

"I'll board Ralph at a kennel near here. He's been there before and they take excellent care of the animals," she explained. "The few times he's been there, he's come back spoiled rotten, but I don't mind as long as he's happy."

"What would you say to getting an early start tomorrow and we eat breakfast up there?" Jonathan suggested, carrying the turkey platter into the kitchen while Holly stacked the plates. Ralph had already been served his feast and put outdoors.

"For some of their fantastic Danish pancakes, I would

get up at dawn," Holly declared, adding. "At least, pretty close to it."

"I can promise you won't have to get up quite that early." He busily stripped all the meat from the carcass and piled it on the platter.

Holly rinsed off the dishes and put them in the dishwasher. As she worked, she tried to think of some clever quip to ask Jonathan to stay the night. Every line she ran through her head sounded either too blasé or too ridiculous.

In the end, she didn't need to worry. Later that evening, Jonathan merely pulled Holly up to her feet, steered her into her bedroom, and calmly undressed her. Their sensual explosion was simultaneous, and they were silently reverent because what they were sharing was so special it couldn't be put into words.

As Jonathan fell asleep, he sensed the bonds growing tighter around him. No matter what happened, he knew he would never be the same man again.

CHAPTER THIRTEEN

Holly realized it wasn't easy getting up early in the morning when Jonathan was lying next to her. Yet even with the temptation to stay in bed, they left the house early for the famous Danish town south of Santa Barbara.

"I suppose your sweet tooth will insist on stopping at each bakery," Jonathan remarked two hours later as he parked in a public lot near a large well-known bakery.

"I think I'll be able to make do with just the fudge kitchens." She laughed, waiting for him to open her door and help her out of the car.

"Perhaps you'll change your mind after eating a hearty breakfast." Jonathan marveled silently that Holly had been able to find a cowl-neck sweater the same cheerful color as her eyes. She had pushed the dolman sleeves up to her elbows and tucked the soft wool into dark-gray linen pants.

"We'll see," she mock-threatened, shifting her black leather hobo bag to her other shoulder and grabbing hold of his hand. She caught the fleeting look of surprise on his face. "Don't worry, Jonathan, this way I can protect you better," she promised, taking a tighter grip on his hand. This time she was determined not to allow him to draw back. Holly was going to prove to Jonathan that there certainly wasn't anything wrong with showing a bit of affection in public.

Naturally, I'll refrain from tearing his clothes off, she vowed whimsically to herself. No use in showing other women what a gorgeous body he has!

They walked across town to a small restaurant known for its aebleskivers, or Danish pancakes.

After being seated at a tiny window table, Holly studied the menu and decided on aebleskivers and Danish sausage. Jonathan chose the same.

Holly looked across the dining room at a woman making the round pancakes that were a bit larger than a golf ball. She watched how the woman poured a small amount of oil into holes in a brass pan then added some batter. In a few moments, the woman used something that resembled a knitting needle to turn the balls of dough. Soon there was a small batch on a plate.

"That can't be too difficult." She turned back to Jonathan. "After all, you only need a certain kind of pan."

"Cooking that turkey successfully has certainly given you a lot of confidence," Jonathan retorted, looking up with a polite smile when the waitress topped off his coffee cup.

Holly poured cream in her coffee. "Maybe that's all I needed," she mused, lifting the cup to her lips. "Especially after having my home economics teacher inform me that she had never flunked anyone before and she'd give me a D so she wouldn't ruin her record. She suggested that I stay away from stoves altogether."

"What did you do to prompt that?" he questioned.

Holly paused as the waitress set their food in front of them and added a ceramic pot filled with tart red raspberry jam.

"The stove I was using blew up," she confided, spooning jam onto her plate.

"Why am I not surprised?" Jonathan's comment earned a glare from Holly.

"It wasn't my fault!" she protested, cutting each pancake into fourths and covering them with jam. "They later learned the stove had faulty wiring. Everyone else had been cooking since the age of five while I wasn't allowed near the kitchen because of all the dishes I had broken. Therefore it wasn't surprising that unofficially I flunked Home Ec."

Jonathan read the bitterness in Holly's voice easily at the subtle reference to her family.

"Holly, will you smile again if I let you hold my hand during our tour of the city?" he asked almost formally.

She did smile at that. "Be careful or you might just revert to a much younger age. I know I feel like someone in grade school after speaking a simple language and mainly associating with small children," she said lightly. "After a while, I start using some of the strangest words!"

Jonathan's eyes turned bleak. "Then comes the day when you grow up and nothing is ever the same again," he murmured, turning his attention to cutting the sausage into tiny pieces.

"Yes," Holly agreed softly, realizing that was what she had been doing recently. The child-woman was maturing in a different way from the first time. The trouble was, were these growing pains ones she could endure?

The tiny Danish town was crowded with its usual tourists as Holly and Jonathan wandered through the shops. So far he had purchased a delicate crystal figurine for his mother and a painted plate for an aunt.

True to her word, Holly stopped at the first fudge

kitchen and purchased various flavors of the creamy candy.

"The source of one good old-fashioned tummyache," she announced, holding up the white paper bag filled with several boxes of the fudge. "Not to mention the addition of ten pounds." She glanced down at herself and muttered, "If only I could control where it would go."

"You're too sensitive about certain things, Holly," Jonathan reprimanded, guessing easily the turn of her thoughts.

She was ready to argue his statement, especially when she noticed his vague interest in a woman who more than filled out the tight sweater she wore.

At least his tongue wasn't hanging out like most of the men within a fifty-yard radius, she thought.

"How can people around here remain so calm with all the sightseers?" Holly wondered. "They're always smiling and never seem to lose their patience." She looked up at the large clock tower then at a shop featuring needlework. Her sister did a lot of needlepoint, and Holly thought of looking for a gift there. With Jonathan's assistance, she chose a meadow scene and then purchased the colored thread for the canvas.

Jonathan, in turn, found a needlepoint canvas resembling a medieval tapestry for his mother.

"It's hard to imagine someone could be patient long enough to finish one of these," Holly confided as they left the shop.

"What about all those hours you spend in your garden?" he pointed out.

"Pure therapy," she returned. "I can talk to the plants all I want and they never talk back!" She gave him a brilliant smile and grasped his hand. "I'm such a wicked woman," she murmured in a sudden attempt to change the subject.

Jonathan's amused gaze skimmed over Holly's figure, mentally visualizing what lay beneath the winter clothing. "You do have a few customs that are on the decadent side." To his amazement, he discovered that he enjoyed her public display of affection.

They halted in one shop for Jonathan to study the many beer steins displayed there. Then Holly purchased an elegant handbag for her mother and a wallet for her father in a nearby leather shop.

Jonathan groaned audibly when Holly dragged him into a large bakery. They sat down at a small table so they could relax and sample the rich pastries. Holly chose a tasty lemon tart and Jonathan decided on a cinnamon roll.

"If they wouldn't get stale before Monday, I'd buy some goodies to take to work," Holly thought out loud. "Chris could go crazy over these tarts."

"What about all that fudge you bought? Aren't you going to share any of that with her?"

"I'm very selfish when it comes to fudge," she replied, nudging the last bit of tart onto her fork.

"You'll need a bottle of bicarbonate afterward," Jonathan said dryly.

They both enjoyed the chance to sit down, and when they finally returned to the car late that afternoon, Holly couldn't remember ever feeling this tired.

"I wonder what it would be like to live in a windmill," she mused, looking at a brightly painted building with an adjoining windmill.

"You certainly wouldn't lack for power," Jonathan replied. "That or Ralph would constantly bark at it. Why did you ever give a dog such a ridiculous name?"

"Because he reminded me of Ralph Watson."

Jonathan knew instinctively this would be a story never to be forgotten. "I'll probably be sorry for asking, but who is Ralph Watson?" he sighed.

Holly half turned in the seat to face him. "He was in Mrs. Kane's kindergarten class with me and he pushed me in a mud puddle when I called him a frog."

"That still doesn't explain why you named a St. Bernard after someone who resembled a frog," Jonathan pointed out.

Holly nodded in agreement. "After Ralph pushed me in the mud, I threw some at him. The look on Ralph's face as a puppy with the dark-brown fur around his eyes reminded me of the human Ralph with mud on his face," she explained blithely, resting her chin on her folded hands that lay on the back of the seat.

"Tell me more," he invited with a brief smile.

Holly thought for a moment. "There was a young man from Grasse . . ." From there she proceeded to reel off limericks that any sailor would love to hear.

"Why do I feel that you didn't learn your poetry in school?" Jonathan commented, laughing.

"In my junior year in college, a bunch of us got together for a beer bust after finals," Holly told him. "Someone had brought a book of bawdy limericks and we took turns reading them to the group. It's amazing how the verses tend to stick in one's mind." She half closed her eyes, studying him through a veil of dark lashes. "I enjoyed today," she said softly.

"So did I." What surprised him was that he was sincere. He had enjoyed their time together. He had also noticed something else in the past few hours. Holly isn't the same woman I met a few months ago, he told himself. The trouble was he couldn't pinpoint the exact change. He glanced at Holly, who had been silent for the past ten minutes. No wonder she was quiet; she had fallen asleep! He leaned forward and switched on his favorite classical radio station, knowing the soft music wouldn't awaken her.

Holly didn't awaken until the car stopped in the driveway, and even then she was so groggy she had to be helped up to the house. Jonathan took her key ring from her and unlocked the door.

"You're—ah—" Holly blushed hotly. "You're welcome to stay the night."

He rubbed his thumb over her lower lip and briefly probed inside to the moist inner lip. "I have an idea we'd both be better off if we slept in our own beds tonight."

She stifled a yawn that threatened to stretch her mouth wide open. "You're always so damned logical, Jonathan," she complained sleepily.

"And you obviously become petulant when you're tired." He dropped a hard kiss on her lips, handed her her packages, and left. "Good night."

"I wonder if he programmed his brain at the same time he programmed that computer," Holly muttered, walking into the living room and dropping the packages into a chair. Yawning widely, she let a happy Ralph into the house and fed him. She moaned as she looked at the kitchen clock. It was only nine o'clock. She was glad they had stopped for dinner on their way back. She wouldn't have to worry about a growling stomach waking her up in the middle of the night. She yawned while showering and ended up with a mouthful of hot water, and she yawned while drying her hair. After throwing on a lightweight flannel nightgown, she slipped into bed and promptly fell asleep.

"Damn!" Jonathan threw his pencil down and resisted the urge to tear his hair out by the roots. After almost a month of quiet Saturdays, he felt secure enough to work at home again instead of making the drive into L.A. to his office. But today silence proved not to be the order of the day.

He looked out the window and counted ten children running and yelling through the backyard with a laughing Holly in charge of the chaos.

Jonathan returned to his desk and tried to concentrate on the paperwork in front of him.

"Earplugs wouldn't keep that noise out!" he gritted, breaking the third pencil in the past half hour. "Obviously she's deaf in order to put up with it."

Fifteen minutes later, Jonathan's patience had passed its limits as he stormed through the house and outside.

Even Holly's bright welcoming smile failed to dissipate his black mood. "Hi, is your work going all right?" she asked cheerfully.

As she looked up at his fierce scowl, her smile faded.

"Was." Jonathan ground out the word. "I found it difficult to concentrate with all that was going on out here." His eyes scanned the children who continued running, oblivious to the scene being played out.

"We're playing zoo," she told him.

Jonathan arched the eyebrow that could speak so eloquently. "Judging from the barking and growling going on, a majority of your animals chose to be sea lions and tigers."

"Perhaps you'd care to join us since we're minus an important animal," she invited graciously.

"Such as?" he asked suspiciously.

Holly's acid sweet smile should have warned him. "A jackass."

Jonathan's eyes were hard as stones. "The child in you seems to refuse to give up," he said harshly. He turned on his heel and walked back into his house. A few minutes later, the sounds of his car leaving told her enough.

Holly sighed wearily. "As usual, I put my mouth in action before my brain could take charge."

"Holly, come on!" one of the girls standing nearby demanded.

"I'm coming." But the excitement had gone out of the game after her confrontation with Jonathan.

Holly had been feeling unsettled a great deal lately. While she still enjoyed the company of the neighborhood children, she found it difficult to join in their games as readily as she used to.

You're finally growing up, Holly, she thought. All of a sudden you're discovering that there's more to life than playing kids' games and probing their minds.

Inside the recording studio, six people wearing headphones sat on stools reading from the scripts they held in their hands.

"Hey, guys, I've got a bad feeling about this place," Steve intoned in a voice meant to resemble a young boy's.

"Danny, you're just actin' like a 'fraidy cat," Holly chided in a syrupy Southern accent.

"Look who's talkin' about a cat," Steve jeered, acting like the self-righteous beagle puppy he was speaking for.

"Both of you be quiet." Chris spoke up in a crisp nononsense voice meant for a sleek greyhound. "If we're to get Tommy free from those kidnappers, we can't fight among ourselves."

"That's right." Warren put in his two cents. Speaking as a cocker spaniel puppy, he usually agreed with the winner of the argument. "Ssh! I hear a human."

"You imbeciles, what are you doing?" Rene, a recently hired voice, was speaking the park of the evil villainess.

"Cut!" Ron spoke up. "Rene, check your lines again. ' You imbeciles, why did you bring him here?' is what you're supposed to say. We changed the line this morning, remember?"

"Oh, I'm sorry." The pert blond woman smiled her apology.

Chris sent a speaking glance in Holly's direction. As far as they were concerned, Rene was more than appropriate for speaking the part of a vampish evil woman. In the scant two weeks she had been working for Carousel Productions, Rene had managed to wind half of the male staff around her little finger. She never had to worry about getting her own coffee, and Holly sincerely doubted a day went by without one of the men taking her to lunch.

"She can't be for real," Chris complained that day when she and Holly walked down to the Jack in the Box on the corner for a quick lunch. "Although I will admit she is excellent with voices. It's unbelievable someone could sound like a witch one moment and a breathy kitten the next."

"The breathy part I can understand," Holly jeered, moving inside the fast food restaurant. "How any air can get up to her throat is past me."

"You're just envious," Chris teased, taking her place in the quickly moving line.

"Pure kelly green," Holly muttered, just before the girl asked for her order. "I'll have a bacon cheeseburger, a large order of onion rings, a chocolate shake, and an apple turnover," she requested grimly.

"If nothing else, envy certainly hasn't affected your appetite," Chris commented.

There was no malice in Holly's thoughts regarding the sexy Rene. It was just that Holly had had a full view of the games a woman plays to gain a man's attention. It also appeared that Rene had a specific approach for each man and her ploy *never* failed.

Being an outspoken and straightforward person, Holly never indulged in games and saw no need for them. She smiled to herself. There certainly hadn't been any necessity for games where Jonathan was concerned!

"Are you going out with Jonathan tonight?" Chris asked after they had taken their trays of food to a table outside.

Holly nodded. She had finally told her friend about her neighbor but hadn't mentioned any of the intimate details.

"I wish you'd have him come around the studio, Holly," Chris urged. "He sounds absolutely delicious!"

Holly winked saucily. "Just like a hot fudge sundae!"

The other woman laughed at the sinful description. "Then perhaps you better wait until a time when Rene isn't around," she advised. "While you might not need to worry about him, you still would have to contend with that female mantrap."

Holly nodded and sighed. "I guess we can say truthfully that blondes *do* have more fun!"

Holly had a surprise for Jonathan that evening. She had planned on cooking him dinner with shrimp and mushroom ramekins for the main course. Her choice was made due to Chris's promise that it only took ten minutes to prepare and about twenty minutes to cook. After a careful study of the recipe, she assembled the ingredients and slowly began preparing the meal.

"Cut that out!" she ordered Ralph, who nudged her bottom with his nose. "Ralph, I can't cook with you doing that." Then she heard the unmistakable crackling and rustling of paper. She spun around and faced a guilty-looking St. Bernard carrying a bag of M&M's in his mouth. "I should have known. Bad dog!" she scolded, snatching the bag away.

Ralph looked up at her with a sorrowful expression in his eyes and bobbed his head up and down in silent plea for a few pieces of his favorite treat.

"No," Holly said firmly to the errant canine. "You go lay down so that I can finish this." She laid the bag on the counter and returned to slicing the mushrooms. A half hour later, she had the dish ready for cooking after Jonathan arrived. Chris might have said that the dish only took ten minutes to prepare, but she hadn't reckoned on Holly working slower than most cooks.

"Congratulations, Holly," she toasted herself with a glass of white wine as she wandered into her bedroom to shower and change her clothes.

When Jonathan arrived an hour later, Holly's freshly shampooed hair was dried into loose curls, her face and eyes highlighted with makeup, and a silky top and matching pants in a royal blue clung to her body.

"I don't smell anything cooking." He smiled down at her. She had already told him she was cooking him dinner although hadn't given any more of a hint.

"It doesn't take very long." She laughed nervously, praying that her turkey dinner hadn't just been a fluke and that this time her entire kitchen would blow up. "Would you care for a drink?"

"Some whiskey, if you have it." He sat down while she disappeared into the kitchen to fix his drink.

Jonathan glanced around the living room, feeling as if something were different. It took a few moments for him to realize the ruffled curtains at the living-room window had also been replaced with drapes.

While it wasn't a significant change, it was enough to force him to wonder what Holly would change next. He certainly hadn't missed the marked absence of jeans and dilapidated sweatshirts that used to make up ninety-five percent of Holly's wardrobe. He couldn't help but like her new way of dressing because it revealed the inner woman he glimpsed from time to time.

Holly returned to the living room with his drink and handed it to him with a bright smile.

"How is the Southern Persian cat?" Jonathan asked, accepting the short, squat glass with its amber liquid.

Holly wrinkled her nose. "I've gained five pounds from all the sugar I've been spouting the past few days. With luck we should be finishing the beginning of next week. How about you?"

Jonathan shrugged and swallowed his drink. "Very busy. I'm trying to clear my desk before I take my vacation." *What will it be like not seeing her for two and a half weeks?* he wondered. *Would it make it that much easier when I move into my house and have to make the break all around?*

Holly, in turn, sipped her wine. She knew she wasn't looking forward to spending the holidays with her family, but she hated the idea of Jonathan being gone even more.

"It's always more difficult working during this time of

year," she said softly. "Most people party all weekend and most of the week too. That's why this program will be the last one we'll work on until after the first of the year." She looked up when the timer went off. "There's our dinner," she said cheerfully, rising to her feet and hoping her fear wouldn't communicate itself to Jonathan.

Holly really had nothing to worry about. The dish smelled heavenly and looked perfect on the serving platter as she spooned the creamy cheese sauce filled with mushrooms over the shrimp. That, along with rice pilaf, which she was thankful came in a box, and mixed vegetables made up the meal.

Jonathan's first bite was cautious; then he dug into his meal with gusto. He usually was very fussy about what he ate but he didn't want to offend Holly by asking what he was eating. "This is delicious, Holly," he complimented sincerely, trying the rice pilaf next.

"It is, isn't it?" She was just as surprised with her accomplishment. "Cooking isn't such a nasty chore after all." She looked up and smiled brightly. Holly's eyes showed puzzlement as she gazed across the small table at Jonathan. "Are you feeling all right? Your face has red splotches on it." Alarm laced her voice as she cried, "Jonathan, you're puffing up!"

He looked down at his hands, which appeared swollen with faint red spots on the surface. "What is this?" he demanded hoarsely, gesturing to his dish with his fork.

"Shrimp and mushroom ramekins and rice pilaf," Holly replied, still confused by the abrupt change in him.

Jonathan uttered a sharp curse word. "Shrimp." He groaned. "I'm allergic to shellfish!" he almost roared.

Holly gulped. Luckily, she had always thought on her feet, and now she quickly jumped up. "Come on," she ordered, while running out of the room to find her purse. "I'm taking you to an emergency center."

Jonathan stumbled out of the kitchen and into the living room where Holly was rummaging through her purse.

"Here." He fumbled for his keys.

"I found mine," she told him, holding up her key ring.

"I won't ride in that wreck." He grunted.

"Jonathan, you have no time to argue." Holly led the way outside to her car.

He now found it difficult to breathe. "There is no way I will ride in your car," he said, gasping.

Rather than upset him further, Holly took his key ring, walked over to his sedan, and assisted him into the passenger seat. One thing she had to admit was that his car started up at a mere turn of the key instead of having to repeatedly pump the accelerator and mutter threats of sending the little Bug to the junkyard.

She silently wondered if the sedate automobile had ever traveled as swiftly as it did that evening while she maneuvered around the moderate traffic and whizzed through yellow lights.

"Holly, I'd like to arrive there in one piece," Jonathan demonstrated in a breathless voice.

"We will," she vowed grimly, narrowly missing a bus as she changed lanes and made an illegal U-turn to turn into an emergency medical center. She parked parallel along the slanted lines and ran around to the passenger door to help Jonathan out. She kept an arm around his waist as they walked up to the front door.

"I am not helpless," he informed her between thin lips.

"You're not exactly a lightweight either," she murmured as they passed through the automatic doors.

The nurse at the front desk took quick stock of the situation and showed a wheezing Jonathan into an examination room while calling out for the doctor.

Feeling as if she had just finished fighting a major battle, Holly collapsed in a chair in the reception area. She looked down at her hands lying in her lap and wasn't surprised to see them shaking badly. If she hadn't been feeling so frightened of the situation, she was positive she would have broken down in tears.

It was some time later before Jonathan was released. Holly jumped up from the vinyl chair, distraught to see him looking so tired.

"A good night's sleep is what he needs right now," the doctor advised, smiling at her.

She nodded, not returning his smile. She didn't feel very happy at the moment, only relieved that Jonathan was all right.

The drive back to the house was quiet. Jonathan wearily leaned back against the seat. Holly could have driven a hundred miles an hour the entire trip and he wouldn't have reacted.

Holly assisted him into the house and to his bedroom.

"I am perfectly able to put myself to bed," he said gruffly, hating to endure her maternal instincts. He sat down on the bed and unbuttoned his shirt then pulled it free from his slacks. "Go on home, Holly, and I'll talk to you later." That was when he looked up and saw the silvery trail down her cheeks.

"I am so sorry," she whispered. "I wouldn't have had this happen for anything." Her chin wobbled in anticipation of more tears.

Jonathan sighed and reached up to pull her down next to him. "Holly, this wasn't your fault," he assured her. "There was no way you could have known about my a lergy to shellfish. It certainly isn't an important topic of conversation." He brushed the salty moisture away with his lips.

"But you could have died!" she wailed, throwing her arms around his neck and hugging him tightly.

"But I didn't, thanks to your quick thinking," he reminded her. "I'm just grateful that you keep a cool head in an emergency."

"Just don't expect me to do it all the time." She sniffed, rubbing her forehead against his chin. "Oh, Jonathan, I don't know what I would have done if anything horrible had happened to you."

"But nothing did," he insisted.

Holly wasn't easily convinced and she sobbed even louder. All she could remember was the look on Jonathan's face as his breathing became more labored.

"Holly." He spoke softly, in an attempt to calm her. "I would appreciate a glass of water."

"Of course." She jumped up, ready to do his bidding. She left the bedroom and headed for the kitchen. It took a little time for her to find the proper cabinet, but she soon filled a glass with ice and water, carrying it into the bedroom and placing it on the nightstand. "Are you going to be all right?" she asked, still afraid for the worst.

"I'll be fine," he reassured her. "All I would like is some sleep."

Holly nodded, obviously reluctant to leave although Jonathan strongly hinted that he preferred to be alone. "Will you call me if you need me?" she requested.

"I promise," Jonathan said wearily. "Good night, Holly."

She stood in the doorway looking at him with soulful

eyes. "I hope you don't mind my saying that this wasn't the way I expected the evening to end," she said softly.

He smiled briefly. "To be perfectly frank, I had hoped it would end differently also."

Holly took her leave still feeling guilty over the turn of events. As she undressed for bed, she thought about the somber furniture filling the bedroom next door. She remembered seeing a few pictures on the walls, but little else to give the room any personality.

She huddled under the covers wondering why he didn't put his stamp on the rooms even during his short stay there. Was Jonathan afraid of people seeing the inner man that would be revealed by his furnishings? She wished she could bring out the man she had come to know, because he was so very special.

Despite her tumultuous thoughts, Holly soon fell into a fitful sleep fraught with dreams of Jonathan blowing up into a balloon and exploding into tiny pieces. Her sleep-filled mind swore she would never eat another piece of shellfish again. The potent memory of the evening wouldn't allow her to.

CHAPTER FOURTEEN

Jonathan studied the contents of his suitcase. Every shirt and pair of slacks was folded neatly to prevent too much wrinkling during the long flight to London.

For the past week, Holly had kept a sharp eye on him as if fearing he would have a relapse. He shuddered at the memory of the incredible strength it had taken to force air in and out of his lungs that night. What he remembered even more was the naked fear in Holly's eyes during those few hours. While she had competently bundled him into the car and driven like a maniac to the emergency center, she hadn't realized she had left her purse at home after taking Jonathan's car keys from him. Or that all the lights in the kitchen and living room had been left on. It hadn't taken much for him to realize that her main concern had been to get him immediate medical care.

He also recalled her tears and misery over an event that had been beyond her control. Jonathan hadn't known that a woman could feel such empathy for a man's pain until he watched Holly that night.

He quickly flipped the top of his suitcase over and locked it. A glance at the bedroom clock told him the airport express van would be there any moment.

Jonathan picked up a small wrapped package and

slipped it into his jacket pocket before reaching for his suitcase.

Holly stood outside when Jonathan walked out and set his suitcase down nearby.

"Have a good trip." She parroted the proper words, but her smile didn't quite reach her eyes.

"You too." He handed her a key. Holly had given him her extra house key earlier to use in case of emergency since he would be returning to Los Angeles before she did.

Holly ducked around her open front door and pulled out a large square box. "This way you'll have something to open when you get back," she said softly, handing it to him.

Jonathan smiled. "Then I'll return the favor." He handed her the small box before putting his present inside the house.

She turned it over in her hands as if that alone would reveal the contents to her. She didn't acknowledge the dark-green van with white lettering that pulled up.

"Have a good Christmas," she whispered, slowly raising her face.

Jonathan experienced a strong blow to his midsection under the force of the shimmering blue-green eyes looking up at him. Without a word, he picked up his suitcase and walked swiftly toward the waiting van. Now he knew why he hated public good-byes.

"If the airline serves you a meal with a sauce on it, make sure it isn't shellfish!" Holly called after him with a wobbly voice.

Jonathan's faint nod of the head was his only reply.

Holly remained outside until the van was out of sight. Then she ran through the house to let Ralph in and turned on the stereo with the volume on high. She craved the noise to keep from thinking of the empty half of the duplex.

Holly stared down at the brightly wrapped box she held.

"There is no way I am going to wait two weeks to open this," she muttered, tearing off the gold ribbon and the gold and silver foil paper. She lifted the box top and gasped when she looked inside. The silver chain was delicate with a brilliant sapphire in the middle with just a hint of green in its depths. She didn't have to look in the mirror to know that the stone matched her eyes. Holly immediately put the chain on, feeling the cool metal caress her throat.

For some time, she had been investigating her feelings toward Jonathan more thoroughly. Holly knew that there was so much more to the man than he allowed the world to see. She could only wonder if she'd ever glimpse even a hint of his private self. Jonathan had erected a barrier around himself that Holly doubted an atom bomb could blast away. At the same time, she was one very stubborn lady and was determined to knock every inch of that barrier down and learn the real man. She wanted to learn what made him withdraw from the emotions all human beings suffered from and, in learning, she knew she would get close to the real man and not the one revealed to the world.

Holly had figured the time would pass slowly with Jonathan gone, but she was grateful that it flew instead—even if it meant she would be leaving for her hometown that much sooner.

She wasn't surprised to find little had changed there. As she walked down the main street on her second day back, she felt as if she had never left.

Holly visited with old friends, duly congratulating them

on new children or new jobs, and listened to some of the same old complaints from her mother.

"I don't see why you felt you had to waste good money to fancy up your teeth at your age," Iris Sutton complained during Holly's first evening home. She had whipped up a meal that contained more food than Holly usually consumed in a week and Holly heard exactly how much time each dish took to prepare. Naturally, her offer to help was brusquely refused.

"Because they now look and feel better," Holly argued mildly. All the time during her flight, she had promised herself that she wouldn't argue with her parents; it looked as if her vow would be broken in record time.

"If you're making such good money to afford something as frivolous as braces, you should think about helping out your family," Cal Sutton brought up in his raspy voice. "Fred is out of work and hasn't had a job in more than six months. He and Darlene could use some extra cash."

Holly contained a loud sigh. She knew she wouldn't help her brother if he had been out of work for six years! She doubted there wasn't an occupation Fred hadn't tried at least once. Since he had trouble holding down a job due to heavy drinking, it was up to his wife to provide for them and their three children. As always, everyone in the family preferred to ignore Fred's drinking problem and mourn his lack of employment.

"My group insurance covered them," she lied, hoping they wouldn't know that braces usually weren't covered for adults.

"Sarah Tolliver is expecting again," Iris told her, glancing sharply at her daughter's flat abdomen.

Holly raised an eyebrow, unaware that she had picked

up one of Jonathan's favorite gestures. "Herman's still trying for a boy, is he?"

Iris frowned. "She's made him a good wife, Holly. Herman bought up Claude Jackson's north fields and is doing very well." Her words implied that Holly had missed out on a gold mine.

Holly maliciously wondered what her mother would think if she told her she was having an affair with a successful banker. She decided Iris would probably ignore the affair part and concentrate on the banker part.

From there, her visit went from bad to worse.

As usual, Holly wasn't allowed in the kitchen on Christmas Day while her sister and sisters-in-law helped Iris with the dinner preparations. Even Holly's proud declaration regarding her successful Thanksgiving dinner brought little remarks.

"How could you have forgotten to fix sweet potatoes?" Iris had asked scornfully after demanding Holly's menu for that day. "Thanksgiving dinner isn't proper without sweets."

Holly ended up wandering about the house fighting the urge to go out into the backyard and indulge in some primal scream therapy. Her peace of mind was further ruined when one of her teenage nephews cornered her, asking if she had brought any drugs with her. He was astounded to hear that she didn't use any and then had the nerve to ask if the prices were any better out there and if she could procure some for him. Holly's reply to that was to the point, and he left her alone after that.

Dinner was spent with her siblings avidly discussing family gossip with an occasional question thrown Holly's way, though no one waited for an answer. Holly felt as if time had stood still and she was back to being the baby of a family that hadn't wanted any more small children cluttering up the house.

I wish I was home, Holly mourned silently, barely tasting her food and then having to bear her mother's scolding about wasting "perfectly good food."

Jonathan was bone tired when he let himself into the house. It was early evening and promised to be a cold night judging from the frosty temperature inside the house. He hurriedly turned up the thermostat, listening to the hum of the heater coming on. After his years in Southern California, adjusting to the colder and damper English climate had been a shock to his system.

He had enjoyed seeing his parents again and meeting with old friends, but he also had strange hallucinations of Holly there. At one point, while talking to his father, he instinctively knew the older gentleman would enjoy the vivacious woman. He also knew that his mother would read the fears in Holly's soul and in her usual no-nonsense way set out to put her at ease.

Stop it, he ordered himself. You can't wish for it so stop thinking about her. But that was difficult to do when his mother was still hinting that she'd like to see him married again.

Jonathan grimaced, slipping off his coat and hanging it up.

He glanced at the small pile of mail on the coffee table and the large box next to it.

"This should prove interesting." He smiled, picking up the box and carefully unwrapping it. He laughed out loud when he finally saw the contents. Two pair of jeans lay side by side; one pair was of the designer variety with a note pinned to one leg stating they could be drycleaned. The other pair was soft and faded as if washed many times. Those carried the instructions that they were *not* to be drycleaned. Jonathan checked the labels. Holly had even gotten them in the correct size.

He smiled, wondering what she was doing and if her visit was going better than she had feared. Then he yawned widely. He was ready for bed; ten to twelve hours of uninterrupted sleep would be heavenly.

Holly lay in bed feeling more alone than she ever had in her life. Each day she had listened to her mother talk about Herman's triumphs and subtly tell Holly she had made a mistake in letting him go. She also hinted that Holly wasn't getting any younger and had better do something about her single state before it was too late.

Fred had taken her aside and asked for a loan, then he turned belligerent when she turned him down. Kathy, her sister, demanded the gory details of all the men who traipsed through Holly's bed and refused to believe her when she said orgies in hot tubs weren't her style. Even her father found ways to belittle her accomplishments. He reminded her that her years of higher education hadn't done her any good and all she seemed to be good for was to work on kids' shows and what kind of job was that?

Holly wondered how anyone could have such a cold and unfeeling family. She hastily corrected herself. She had no family.

After realizing that, her decision was easy. She got out of bed and crept downstairs to the kitchen so no one would overhear her using the telephone. Her first call was easier than she thought. Her second call was a bit more difficult since she required the operator's assistance. She glanced at the clock and noticed that it was after three o'clock in the morning, but she had no one else to call.

Holly couldn't remember ever feeling as exhausted as she did during those early-morning hours when the jet arrived at Los Angeles International Airport.

It hadn't helped when her flight had been delayed for three hours before taking off and then encountered another delay during her layover in Denver due to a snowstorm. It was after two in the morning when she finally staggered off the plane and down the tunnel.

She looked wearily around the waiting area where only a small number of people, none of them familiar, stood or sat. If the position had been reversed, would she have waited all these hours? Then she looked to her left and knew her question had been answered.

Jonathan stood near one of the columns looking disgustingly fresh despite the late hour. Once he spotted her, he walked toward her, taking her tote bag out of her hand and setting it down. Then he did something very unexpected and very beautiful. He enfolded her in his arms. His comfort and strength flowed into her veins, infusing her with his vitality.

That was when Holly knew she was fully and irrevocably in love with Jonathan. There were no bells ringing or fireworks shooting off. Not even one roman candle. Instead, she felt warm and cherished.

"Jonathan." Her voice trembled with the new emotions running through her body. "Please take me home."

He kept an arm around her shoulders during their long walk to the main part of the terminal and the baggage carousel. Luckily, Holly's suitcase was one of the first unloaded and they were soon walking to Jonathan's car, which was parked nearby.

Holly curled up on the front seat with her head resting on Jonathan's shoulder. As if her body was aware she was safe now, she promptly fell asleep. She was still asleep when Jonathan carried her into his house and carefully undressed her before putting her to bed. When he climbed into the bed next to her, Holly stirred enough to curl up to his welcome warmth.

Jonathan lay back staring up at the ceiling. All he could see was the mental picture of Holly standing in the middle of the terminal resembling a lost waif. It hadn't taken a genius to figure out that something had happened to force her to cut her visit short. Her middle-of-the-night collect call asking if he would pick her up at the airport the next evening told him she was distressed about something.

Holly made a small sound and shifted her position. Jonathan tightened his hold and rested his chin against her hair. He soon fell asleep.

When Holly finally awoke, she felt groggy, a warning that she had slept too long. She slowly turned her head, seeing the late-afternoon shadows crossing the room. For some unknown reason tears pricked her eyelids.

"I see you finally decided to join the rest of the world."

Holly turned her head and found Jonathan standing in the doorway. Her spirits lightened at the sight of him wearing jeans.

"You look very sexy," she said, half sitting up and drawing the sheet over her bare breasts.

He looked down with a rueful smile at the faded denim riding low on his hips before his gaze returned to her. "I will admit they're very comfortable."

"Probably because I must have run them through the washer about fifteen times," Holly said lightly.

"Would you care for something to eat?" Jonathan asked her.

Holly focused on his mouth, remembering it thin with anger and fuller, moist with desire. It was the latter she wanted to see.

She shook her head, allowing the white sheet to drop to her waist. "Perhaps later," she murmured, keeping her eyes trained on his face.

"A shower first?" He deliberately misunderstood. Although his body was already tightening with anticipation, he wanted to prolong the pleasurable agony as long as possible.

Holly shook her head very slowly. "What I want is you making love to me." She sat up further so that the sheet fell from her nude body.

Jonathan's eyes caressed the creamy skin of her throat before moving down to her breasts, which swelled under his visual contact. The nipples peaked to tight rose-color buds as if they had been physically touched. His contemplation of her tiny waist and slender flared hips only fueled his own desire. He moved away from the doorway and walked slowly toward the bed. With each step, his eyes never left the pulse beating madly at the base of her throat. When he reached the side of the bed, he halted. His hands fastened on her forearms and she was pulled to her knees as his mouth descended on hers.

Holly was convinced there was never a sweeter, more gentle kiss than the one Jonathan bestowed on her that moment; nor one that could arouse her as quickly. He nibbled along her lower lip and even brushed over the thin moist inner skin. It was apparent that he was in no hurry as he tasted every millimeter of her lips. Once he had memorized her lower lip, he moved up to tease the corner before concentrating on the slightly bowed upper lip and just beyond it. His tongue swept lazily over the surface of her teeth but made no effort to probe the interior just yet.

A tiny sound of delight traveled up Holly's throat, out her lips, and into Jonathan's mouth. He absorbed each murmur, needing to hear her enjoyment from his touch.

Holly's tongue darted out to transfer the moisture from her mouth into his. She already knew that one taste wasn't enough. She craved him the way an alcoholic needed spirits and insisted on giving in to her hunger. She wrapped her tongue around his and folded her arms around his shoulders in an effort to pull him down onto the bed. Jonathan widened his stance so that he wouldn't lose his balance. The feel of her naked body against his clothed one was more erotic than anything he had ever felt before. Actually, anything to do with Holly was capable of arousing him to mindless heights.

His hands moved up her shoulders to her head, cradling her face in a gentle grip. His mouth traveled leisurely over her mouth and to the outer perimeters of her face. He inhaled the soft fragrance of her skin, positive no other woman could have such a beautiful scent. Jonathan laughed deep in his throat when Holly shivered under his nibbling exploration of her ear. He fastened his teeth on the lobe and bit gently then soothed the faint hurt with the laving heat of his tongue. He nuzzled the area behind her ear and investigated the ultrasoft skin of her nape.

"Oh, Jonathan," Holly breathed, kissing the side of his neck as she unbuttoned his shirt and endeavored to push it free from his shoulders. "This isn't enough for me and I doubt it is for you."

He slightly pulled back and gazed down at her face with its lips moist from his kiss. "No, it will never be enough," he vowed, lowering his mouth to hers again.

Holly's mouth opened wider under his probing tongue even as she searched out his own. She wound her arms around his neck and slid her body along his. She could feel his bulge fighting the soft denim and reached down to unfasten the button and lower the zipper. She laughed throatily at her discovery.

"No underwear, Mr. Lockwood," she murmured, sinking her teeth into his shoulder in mock punishment. "My, my, we are getting risqué, aren't we?" It took some time, but she finally pushed his jeans down to the floor.

This time, Jonathan offered no resistance when Holly pulled him down onto the bed. He rolled over until she lay sprawled wantonly over his naked body, leaving him free to caress her.

Jonathan traced her body with reverent fingertips as if this was their first time together. He wanted to rediscover her all over again and did so with his hands then his lips. Not one inch of Holly's quivering body was left untouched.

She, in turn, caressed him with equal care. "I feel as if I should keep you under lock and key," she whispered, circling his nipple with her tongue until it peaked as boldly as her own. "No man as sexy as you should be allowed to run loose." She slightly raised her head to look down at him with a feline smile. "Those three-piece suits aren't as good a disguise as you think they are."

Jonathan probed the silky area between her thighs and was not surprised to find her ready for him. He smiled as Holly threw back her head and almost purred under his expert touch. He created the beginning of a tiny explosion as he caressed the tiny bud that gave her more joy than she could imagine. Her hips moved with each motion of his fingers, which also generated heat against his own pelvis. Jonathan's hips arched up against hers as she rubbed against him and the more insistent touch of his fingers sent explosions throughout Holly's body.

She could feel her entire body moving faster, then tightening in reaction to his touch. Before she was allowed to come down, he lifted his hips and entered her with a thrust that sent Holly spinning outward once more.

Jonathan kept his hands spanned over Holly's buttocks in order to keep her close to him as he thrust upward into her welcoming warmth that held his velvety length so lovingly. Both kept their eyes open, gazing into each other's souls as they became one being.

Holly cried out as the eruptions began again. In the space of a breath, Jonathan rolled over until she lay on her back. For a second, he halted, looking down at her. Both could feel the tension in their bodies coiling and were powerless to halt what would come. Holly held her breath, fearing that Jonathan would leave her in this pleasure-pain of agony.

"You are more beautiful than any woman, Holly," he murmured. "And at this moment, you are as much a part of me as any vital organ."

Holly sobbed as Jonathan increased the rhythm until she was sure she would explode into tiny pieces. She wrapped her arms and legs around him so that she wouldn't lose him in the moment of a greater love than known to any human being. For a moment, her surroundings dimmed as if she were in another world.

Jonathan stiffened before giving up of himself. For a moment, he could only lay to one side working to control his erratic breathing. Holly also gasped for air as her body still trembled. Even as she felt her nerve endings calming, she remembered that for the first time Jonathan had spoken in the midst of their lovemaking.

He does feel something for me, her brain insisted, infusing her veins with new warmth.

Jonathan remained quiet, stunned by the intensity of what had just happened. He was only too aware that what they had just shared was an experience few lovers realized. It convinced him of something else equally astounding. Holly had not only given all of herself, but he had reciprocated by sharing all he had. He instinctively knew that if he made love to thousands of other women, he would never experience such a mind-shattering encounter again. Only Holly could give him the glimpse of heaven he had just received. The thought was frightening.

Holly could feel the tension in Jonathan's body and knew it wasn't from desire. She sorrowed at the idea that he feared what had happened to them and knew she would have to keep most of her emotions to herself.

She burrowed her face against the hollow of his shoulder. "Jonathan, is the offer for breakfast still open?" she asked softly.

His body shook with suppressed laughter. "Don't you think dinner would be more appropriate?"

"Just as long as it's food," Holly replied. "I vaguely remember lunch yesterday and quite a few cups of coffee during the rest of the day."

"I'm surprised that you were willing to put a meal second." Jonathan commented in his dry voice.

She lifted her head and grinned saucily. "I've just managed to work up an even larger appetite. How about pizza? A large one with everything on it sounds nice."

Jonathan shook his head. "You have quite a proclivity for junk food, don't you?"

"Pizza is an excellent source of protein," Holly informed him as she sat up and ran her fingers through her damp hair. "I hope you don't mind if I make use of your shower?"

"I'll get you clean towels." He got out of bed and reached for his jeans.

"Hmm, perhaps I should have gotten you those in a size smaller," she mused, enjoying the sight of the denim fabric hugging his lean buttocks.

"You are definitely a hedonist at heart," Jonathan accused her, but he didn't seem to dislike the idea.

Holly shrugged. "I think it was programmed in my genes," she said flippantly.

He turned his head deciding to ask the question that had been tickling the back of his mind. "You didn't mention how Christmas with your family went."

Her face paled momentarily. When she finally spoke, her voice was devoid of all emotion and her eyes stared blankly into space. "You must be mistaken, Jonathan. I have no family."

CHAPTER FIFTEEN

Jonathan sensed it wasn't the proper time to question Holly further about her aborted trip. Instead he provided clean towels for her shower and obtained the telephone number of a pizza restaurant.

An hour later, Holly, dressed in a mauve terry robe, enjoyed the large pizza Jonathan had ordered and picked up. She persuaded him to wear only his jeans for their intimate meal.

"I told you this was an excellent source of protein," she said smugly, lifting her wineglass in a toast. She sipped the rich red wine and reached for another slice of pizza dripping with extra cheese, mushrooms, and sausage.

"Tell me about your trip, Holly," he urged quietly, keeping a sharp eye on her face.

All the animation left her features. She set the pizza slice down very carefully and swallowed part of the burgundy in her glass before replying.

"It was as if I had never left there." Her voice lacked its usual vibrancy. "My mother is still moaning the fact that I let good old Herman get away. Did you know that he bought Claude Jackson's north fields? Oh, yes, he's become quite a successful businessman." Holly twirled the stem of her glass between her fingers and sipped more of her wine. "My father feels I should not have bothered having something so ridiculous as braces when the money could have helped out my brother, Fred, who's been unemployed more than he's been employed for the past fifteen years. Fred asked me if I would loan him five thousand dollars and wasn't too polite when I turned him down. My nephew, Tommy, asked if I had anything to smoke, sniff, or shoot and couldn't believe that I wasn't into drugs. And my sister is convinced that I have a different lover for every day of the week!" Her voice rose with every word. "Naturally, I wasn't allowed in the kitchen because who knows what havoc I might have caused there!" she ground out, reaching for the wine bottle and topping off her glass.

"Didn't your mother take the time and sit down to talk to you at any time?" Jonathan quizzed, leaning back against the couch, one arm dangling over a raised knee.

Holly laughed, a bitter, harsh sound that chilled the air around them. "My *mother* was more concerned with getting all the files in order for the office and bemoaning the fact that I've grown away from a family who had conveniently forgotten that they had never wanted me in the first place."

"Holly, you know that's not true," Jonathan said sternly, in an attempt to break through her protective shell.

She stared down into the ruby depths of her wine. "Isn't it?" she whispered. "When I was five, I overheard my parents arguing because neither cared to take the time away from their work to attend the school play I was starring in. In the end, they both didn't show up." Holly's delicate features hardened with distaste. "That was when she let him know that she had resented a pregnancy she didn't want and she didn't care to raise another child during a time in her life when she should be doing what she wanted without worrying about the measles, mumps, and chicken pox." She drank the wine as if it could warm the cold knot in her heart. "After that, I didn't bother telling them about any of my school activities. I didn't want them there."

Jonathan reached out to take Holly's hand, shocked to find the skin ice cold. "What was your parents' reaction to your returning ahead of time?" He rubbed her chilled fingers between his own warm palms.

Her lips twisted in a smile devoid of mirth. "My mother felt that I was thoughtless to leave so suddenly and on a weekday at that. My father wasn't too pleased to take a day away from his hardware store to drive me to the airport. If there had been an airport express bus service available, I certainly would have taken it."

Jonathan grasped Holly's other hand and pulled her over onto his lap. He pressed her cheek against his bare chest and held her quietly in an attempt to allow the pain to flow from her body.

It isn't right! The words bounced around in his head. But how can I hope to heal her hurts when I can't even heal my own?

Still he held her and she buried her face against the curve of his neck. "I never did thank you for my necklace," she murmured. "It's very beautiful."

"I gather you can tell that I like my gift," he whispered into her hair. "I congratulate you on the excellent fit."

"A tape measure and a pair of your slacks does wonders." Now her laugh was the one he enjoyed hearing. Her fingertip ran teasingly down his bare chest to the denim waistband. "Actually, I'd say they're a perfect fit." Her breath was warm and moist against his skin. She wildly wondered if she would ever have enough of him and seriously doubted it.

"I suggest you eat that slice of pizza you chose before you finish seducing me," Jonathan recommended with a husky catch in his voice.

"Any reason why?" Holly's words were muffled. She laughed when he stood up, keeping her cradled in his arms.

"That excellent source of protein would have helped you keep up your strength," he said gruffly, heading for the bedroom.

Holly tilted her head back and looked directly into his eyes, easily reading the lambent flames in the dark irises. "Then we'll just warm it up in the oven"—she directed a small breath in Jonathan's ear—"later."

Later turned out to be the early-morning hours when Jonathan discovered that warmed-up pizza could be a feast when shared with the right person.

Since Holly wasn't due to return to work until January 2, she decided to revel in an unexpected vacation. Jonathan had accompanied her the next day when she had picked up a happy Ralph at the kennel.

She also spent one morning wallpapering her bathroom and the afternoon fitting a dusty-rose carpet to complement the new wallpaper.

At the end of the day, she sat back on her heels viewing her project with pride. "An excellent job, if I say so myself." She thought nothing of complimenting herself.

Holly had always been a happy person, but the past few days had added a fourteen-karat-gold lining to hers and Jonathan's time together. If she cared to examine it further, she would have admitted that the smile on her face for the past few days was due to more than a sunny nature.

Suddenly laughing out loud, she flopped back on the

bedroom carpet, her arms thrown out over her head. She closed her eyes and rolled her hips from side to side enjoying the feel of the plush carpet beneath her.

"I was correct when I called you a hedonist."

Holly opened her eyes and treated herself to an upside-down view of Jonathan.

"Hi," she greeted him in a breathy voice.

He smiled and shook his head. "Don't tell me you've been drinking at this hour?" he inquired.

She shook her head, still in her prone position. "What do you think?"

"I hope you didn't go to the door while wearing that shirt, although I'm certainly not one to complain."

Holly glanced down and let out a horrified shriek. A tear in the front gave an observer a perfect view of the curve of her breast and just a hint of the dusky nipple.

"I was talking about the bathroom." She held up her arms in a silent request to be helped to her feet.

Ignoring her plea, he bent down on one knee, pulling at his slacks. "The job looks very professional," he murmured close to her mouth.

"Since the front door is locked, how did you manage to get in?" she whispered, flicking the tip of her tongue over her lips and noticing his reaction to the sensual peek of her breast.

"I still have your key and coming in through your back door was no problem since your faithful watchdog merely sat there and watched me walk in." He spoke softly, still keeping his mouth a breath away. "That could prove to be dangerous, Holly. What if I were an attacker?"

"It depends on what kind of attacking you were planning on doing." She lifted her arms and circled his neck. Something undefinable kept nudging Holly's brain as she looked up at him. Suddenly the light bulb clicked on with the intensity of a one-hundred-watt bulb. *"Jonathan!"* She squealed, jumping up and bumping heads in the process.

"Holly!" he mimicked, scowling as he rubbed the sore spot on his forehead and straightened up. "If this is a new way of greeting people, I don't think I'm modern enough to like it."

"Oh, Jonathan, you did it!" Holly laughed, hopping around him before hugging him tightly.

"I don't see how I could accomplish anything if I'm to be almost rendered unconscious and still have my clothes on," he pointed out in his dry voice.

"Cute, Lockwood, real cute," she scolded, placing her hands on her hips.

He fixed her with a not-so-patient stare. "When do I find out the reason behind your sudden excitement?"

Holly jabbed her forefinger against his shirt front. "That."

"What?" Jonathan asked, although there was just the faintest hint of a gleam in his eye that warned her of his knowledge regarding her exhilarated chatter.

"Your shirt," she persisted.

"I always wear a shirt, especially if I'm wearing a suit."

Holly waved a mock-threatening fist at him. "Not a shirt with color in it," she referred to the faint blue stripes running through the white cotton. Her smile was brilliant in its intensity. "Oh, Jonathan, you're wearing a colored shirt!" She threw her arms around him again. "You've always worn nothing but white shirts before."

"I needed new shirts," he mumbled, feeling a bit uneasy under her elation.

She planted a smacking kiss on his lips. "A colored shirt isn't so bad after all, is it?" she teased affectionately.

"The effect is positively corrupting," Jonathan retorted, uneasy under her happy agitation.

Holly sampled the salty skin along his jaw. "Mmm, I like you corrupted," she murmured, sliding her hands just under the waistband of his slacks. "I like you in your jeans much better," she whispered provocatively. "They have a snugger fit."

"Holly." He groaned, trying to loosen her hands from their erotic wanderings.

"Jonathan C. Lockwood, do you realize that you haven't made love to me in almost twelve hours?" She burrowed even closer. She caught her lower lip between her teeth and looked up under lowered lashes. "I'd hazard a guess that you were also cognizant of the fact."

"Possibly because you've already set certain events in motion." He couldn't help chuckling at her wanton actions.

"Oh, is that what you call it?" Holly concentrated on unbuttoning his dark blue vest. "What does the *C* stand for?" She was determined to learn his middle name.

"None of your business."

"That doesn't start with a *C*," she pointed out, stopping at the last button. "Now, carnal begins with a *C*, crave also begins with a *C*, not to mention concupiscence." She referred to someone with strong sexual desires.

Jonathan's facial muscles tightened with the control he exerted over his body. "That"—he swallowed—"that is not the proper way to speak to your banker."

"Well then—" Holly's voice lowered to a sexy register that raced through Jonathan's veins like hot wax. "Perhaps we should discuss deposits then." She carefully loosened his blue and silver striped tie and tugged it loose. "And withdrawals." She tugged the top shirt button free, then the next. "What about the interest rates rising?" Her finger drew an imaginary line down to his belt buckle and toyed with the cool metal.

In retaliation, Jonathan slid his finger through the strategically placed hole in Holly's shirt and caressed the nipple into a pouting nub.

"I can't stay. I stopped by to pick up some papers for a dinner meeting," Jonathan explained in a hoarse voice, reluctantly withdrawing his hand from further temptation.

Holly's face revealed her disappointment. "You came in here to tell me that?" she grumbled.

He nodded. "I know we had talked about driving in to Westwood to see that new play and I wanted to apologize for having to cancel our plans. I had forgotten about this meeting until I looked over my calendar this morning. Since I had to return home for the papers, I decided to tell you in person instead of phoning."

Holly hid her smile. She found it amusing to find out that Jonathan's impeccable memory could slip at times!

"Of course I understand," she soothed and assured him readily. "We can see the play another evening. I admit that after all the physical labor I've put into this bathroom, I wasn't sure that I would be the best company tonight anyway."

She's too complacent. Why isn't she the least bit distressed about our evening out having to be cancelled so abruptly? Jonathan asked himself, but said out loud merely, "I'll see you later then."

"Yes," she agreed in a voice that would melt butter. Her smile remained on her lips long after a confused Jonathan left the house. "Yes, I'll see you later," she murmured, turning back to doublecheck the fit of the carpet before taking her shower.

Holly kept her promise. When Jonathan arrived home late that night, he found her sleeping peacefully in his bed. And just like Prince Charming discovering Sleeping Beauty, Jonathan found a most satisfactory method to wake up his nocturnal lovely. The only difference between his method and Prince Charming's was that Jonathan didn't just stop with a kiss.

On New Year's Eve, Jonathan arrived to pick Holly up for dinner and found her limping as if her foot hurt badly.

"I told you, I stepped on a cigarette," Holly argued, vainly trying to pull her foot from Jonathan's firm grip.

"Since you don't smoke, how were you able to step on a cigarette within the past hour?" he clipped, manacling her wiggling ankle with his hand and tipping the bottom of her foot up for his inspection.

"Ouch!" she yelped, jerking away.

"Holly, I'd like to hear the truth on how you burned the bottom of your foot." He pinned her with a merciless gaze.

Holly drew in a deep breath. "Do you promise not to laugh or scold me?"

"The two do not go together."

"I want your promise." She grimaced, looking down at the small strip of raw flesh. "Or I won't tell you a thing."

Jonathan silently counted to ten. He was fully determined to shake the truth out of Holly, but he knew that would only bring out her stubborn streak.

"I promise." The two words came out in a staccato procession.

Holly squirmed. "My hose are ruined," she mourned, looking down at the lacy patterned black silk stockings lying on the carpet.

"Holly," he reminded her of the reason for this conversation.

She released a deep sigh. "I had a tiny hole in my stocking," she explained. "They were new and expensive plus I was running late so I tried a trick I had heard about. I sprayed hair spray on the hole to stop it from running."

"I thought nail polish was the trick," Jonathan countered.

"I don't have any nail polish," Holly argued. "I could see that the hair spray wasn't working, so I used a drop of instant bonding glue," she mumbled, running the words together in rapid succession.

"You *what?*" Jonathan hoped that his ears had deceived him.

"I figured the glue should work but it began smoking and that's when I started yelling," she finished lamely.

Jonathan shook his head in disbelief that someone would do something that could be potentially dangerous. "And here I thought you couldn't surprise me any longer." He stood up. "You'll have to have a doctor look at your foot and treat the burn."

"We have a dinner reservation!" she protested, beginning to stand up until her injured foot sent up a quick stab of pain. She hurriedly shifted her weight to her other leg. "Jonathan, I am not spending New Year's Eve in an emergency clinic!"

"We have enough time before dinner." He rose to his feet and walked over to the closet near the front door. "I doubt you'll be able to wear high heels. We see a doctor first or I cancel the reservations."

"You're a tyrant," Holly accused loudly.

"If that's what it takes to get you to a clinic, I'll act like any of the more popular ones," he replied calmly.

"A dab of first aid cream and a bandage would do just as well," she argued.

"Not by my standards." He draped her coat over one arm. "You have to ensure there won't be an infection. I doubt that you're a person who enjoys staying in bed for long periods of time, and that is exactly what could happen."

"It depends on who shares it with me." Holly sent him a seductive smile, but he wasn't giving in to her ploy this time. As she limped into the bedroom, she told herself that arguing with Jonathan was the same as talking to a stone wall; neither took any notice of a person's words.

At first, Holly panicked when the doctor asked her how she burned her foot. She dreaded hearing the kindly man's laughter when he heard the story of her endeavoring to stop a run in an expensive pair of hose. But she had no choice if she wanted to be helped. As she was thinking of how to explain what she'd done, Jonathan inserted smoothly what had happened, saving her any further embarassment.

And they say chivalry is dead, she thought, smiling gratefully at his quick intervention.

After the burn had been treated, they arrived at the restaurant just in time.

As they ate their rack of lamb and delicately seasoned potatoes, Holly silently wondered what the new year would bring for them. She knew that Jonathan's house would be ready for him to move in sometime in January. She also knew that he had visited the site several times in the past two months, but he had never asked her to accompany him.

Holly's tactful conversations with Liza had only revealed that Jonathan was an intensely private person and over the past few years he had made his work his life. It was as if he wanted to make sure there would be no room in his life for one special person. At least, that was the way Holly read it. What she hadn't told Liza was that there had been some interesting changes in Jonathan's personality over the past week.

Holly still remembered the warm comfort of Jonathan's arms surrounding her at the airport when she had returned so hurt and exhausted. It was also the first time he had touched her affectionately in public. And lately, he murmured words of hunger and praise during their lovemaking. Holly would bet everything she owned that for Jonathan, speaking during the act of love was new. She could sense it from his hesitation between words, as if he was afraid he might say something that might bind him to his lover. Or was he afraid of encountering something he wouldn't be able to handle?

She dutifully sipped her champagne and smiled at Jonathan while wondering if she could crack the last remnants of his reserve. Holly had already decided that she didn't want Jonathan just for an affair that could fizzle out any time. She wanted him for the duration of their lives, and she only hoped that she could make Jonathan see the wisdom in her thinking. She noticed that the tension he once carried around the way one carried a coat was gone. Now she only had to seek his trust and his love.

Jonathan was doing some inner reflecting of his own during that time. The woman he had once described as a kook turned out to be more woman than any man could dream of. During the past few times they had made love, he sensed a new warmth in her response. He knew no woman had ever given him as much as Holly had during their hours together. No woman had crept into his soul either, but Holly had done that and so much more.

He lowered his eyes quickly so that she wouldn't see the stark terror he felt inside at the idea that Holly could hurt him more with her innocence than any other woman he had known over the years. Even Liza hadn't left him feeling so raw and exposed.

I can't let Holly go! his soul cried out. His saner half intervened with the reminder that he must so that another man could give someone with so much unboundless love in her heart what she truly deserved.

Holly didn't need to see Jonathan's face to know that all wasn't right. She could sense his distress and instinctively knew she couldn't intrude upon his thoughts.

"I wrote out my New Year's resolutions today," she announced, hoping to banish the tight lines from his mouth.

Jonathan looked up with a blank expression as if he had been pulled back from another world. "How many pages did it turn out to be?" he asked with wry amusement.

"More than I'd care to think about. That's why I burned it," Holly declared airily. "I'd just break all of them anyway. Every year I vow to think before I speak and every year I put my foot in my mouth without a bit of trouble."

"I'd like to suggest that you also stay away from instant bonding glue from now on," Jonathan murmured, glancing down at the bill discreetly nestled in a small leather portfolio that the waiter had placed near his coffee cup.

"That was one lesson I certainly learned the hard way." Holly sighed. "Only good ol' Elmer's Glue-All will cross my threshold."

"I didn't realize cartoon voices have their dramatic sides," Jonathan commented.

"When the glue started hurting, I learned all about tragedy and drama." She smiled, fingering her sapphire necklace, which matched the dress she wore. She willed him to smile and banish the darkness in his eyes.

"As long as it's a lesson you don't forget," Jonathan replied, placing his credit card within the folder.

Holly had never been so happy as when she could take her low-heeled sandals off. While they had been comfortable during the first part of the evening, the throbbing in her foot refused to allow any pressure against the sole. The moment they entered Jonathan's living room, she slipped her shoes off with a loud sigh of relief.

"Brandy is supposed to be an excellent painkiller," Jonathan recommended, disappearing into the bedroom to hang his suitcoat and tie up. He had to admit that Holly's casual attitude toward clothing had its advantages.

"Brandy sounds heavenly." Holly dropped onto the couch and curled up in the corner.

Jonathan left the bedroom and walked over to the small bar to pour brandy into two balloon glasses. He handed one to Holly and stood in front of her.

"Happy New Year." He held his glass against hers.

"Happy New Year," she murmured, listening to the melodic tinkling of the crystal.

Jonathan sipped the strong alcohol and glanced at the clock on a nearby table, noting the time to be a quarter to twelve.

"We don't have long for me to fulfill my first New Year's resolution," he commented, setting his glass on the coffee table.

Holly smiled, feeling the male hunger reach across the small space to her. "And what is that?" She deliberately injected a throaty vibration to her voice.

"That when the clock strikes twelve, the first sounds I'll hear are your cries of passion." His eyes centered on her moist parted lips with a drop of the amber liquid glistening on the lower lip.

Holly sipped her brandy and set the glass down. She stood up and with a deft flick of the fingers released the hidden hook that sent her dress slithering to the carpet, leaving her clad in the barest of bras, a wisp of underwear, and a lacy garter belt.

"I certainly can't allow your fulfillment not to come true, can I?" she asked softly.

It hadn't taken long for them to make Jonathan's resolution come true.

Many hours later, Jonathan lay awake while holding a sleeping Holly in his arms. He didn't want to admit that when the time came for them to part, it would be much harder than he expected. While he hadn't indulged in a great many affairs after his divorce, he hadn't lacked for women in his bed. He also never worried about breaking off before emotions got in the way, but then he hadn't known Holly.

"If only there was a way," he whispered to the air o perhaps to some ethereal being who kept watch over him "If only."

They missed the first viewing of the famed Rose Parad the next morning and settled for the replay with a break fast of buttermilk pancakes, sausage, and kisses thrown i for spice.

All during the day, Holly could see the same disquiet i Jonathan's manner that she had glimpsed during dinne the previous night. She wasn't completely sure what ha caused his change of mood, but she had the good sense no to intrude on his thoughts when he truly needed to work his worries out on his own.

I wish I could tell him I love him, she thought, curled up in an easy chair watching Jonathan concentrate on the Rose Bowl game. But I am so afraid that he would run so far I'd never see him again. *Oh, God, I can't lose him now!* she wailed inside.

Holly slowly rose from the chair, walked into the kitchen to pour two glasses of wine, and carried them into the living room. She handed one to Jonathan, accepting his absent smile of thanks, and returned to her chair to watch his every facial expression. She wanted to press them into her memory book in case her worst fears did come true.

CHAPTER SIXTEEN

Holly was more than ready to return to work the day after New Year's. The previous day had taken a lot out of her emotionally, and she needed the crazy people at Carousel Productions to make her laugh again.

"How was the old hometown?" Chris greeted her. The two women had arrived in the parking lot within a few moments of each other.

Holly shook her head. "I flew home ahead of schedule," she replied.

Chris threw her a sympathetic grin. "That bad, huh?" While they hadn't exactly compared family backgrounds, Chris also came from a small town, but she had parents who were supportive and loving. "Wolfe said you can't return home and I guess he's right."

Holly nodded, still smarting from her mother's anger when she had announced she was flying back to L.A. ahead of time. As far as Iris Sutton had been concerned, Holly had no love for her family. Holly felt that she couldn't love when that emotion wasn't returned. "How has it been around here?"

"Quiet. No one really wanted to work over the holidays. Hal is talking about closing the offices during the week between Christmas and New Year's this year." The two women walked toward the building. "You and Sherry were smart to take the time off. During that week, our idea of having fun was taking turns at the reception desk. It's probably just as well she's coming back today. We've really messed up her filing system and I bet she won't be able to find anything for days." Chris laughed as she pushed the glass front door open.

"You're certainly right on that count," the perky receptionist spoke up.

Holly and Chris turned to greet the young woman, but their words halted on their lips.

"Sherry, what did you do to yourself?" Holly blurted out, then reddened as she realized how her less than tactful question sounded. I was right about that resolution not lasting long, she thought.

The receptionist pointedly smoothed the pale-blue sweater that covered a great deal more than it would have two weeks before.

"I'm hoping Denny won't run after Rene so much any more," Sherry grumbled, mentioning her boyfriend as she took a deep breath. "This took most of my savings." She looked at them with a bright smile on her face as she stood up and walked over to the lateral filing cabinet. The knowledge of her more voluptuous curves had added a new bounce to her walk.

"I'm surprised that Sherry would have breast implants just because Denny had been chasing Rene around. Especially since just about every man in the building who wasn't blind has been sniffing at her heels," Chris told Holly as they walked to the back of the building.

"I guess she was tired of taking a back seat to Rene. Sherry really loves Denny, and she must have felt it was as good a way as any to hold on to him," Holly replied absently, recalling that Sherry's bustline had been as small as her own. She also remembered that Jonathan didn't seem to touch her breasts very often. The rare times he did she loved the pleasure he gave her. She wondered if her less-than-ample proportions turned him off.

"If that's what she thinks will hold him, she better think again." Chris spoke more forcefully. "The time will come when Denny realizes the ability to hold an intelligent conversation counts more than a C-cup bra."

"He's only twenty-two and she's nineteen. It's going to be a while before either one realizes that what truly counts in a serious relationship is more than perfect measurements," Holly murmured. "At least the lechers around here will have two women to chase after." She could speak confidently, knowing that Chris wasn't interested in anyone but Jay.

"I've seen some members of the male sex look your way," Chris pointed out as she headed for the coffeepot and poured herself a cup.

"Sure, all the creeps like Steve," Holly groaned.

During the next few days, Holly watched Sherry gain a great deal of attention from the men who worked in the studio. It wasn't difficult to see that the young woman was in seventh heaven.

"You must really feel that the surgery was a success," Holly said as she stopped by the reception desk one morning.

Sherry's smile revealed smug satisfaction. "Holly, it's changed my whole life," she announced with a pseudomaturity. "Dr. Tanner, the plastic surgeon, is a wonderful man." She pulled out her purse and dug into the roomy interior, drawing out a pamphlet. "Here, just in case you're interested."

Holly hesitated before accepting it. "Well, ah . . ." she muttered before walking away quickly.

She didn't have a chance to read the brochure until she arrived home that evening. After looking over the information, Holly studied herself in the mirror and drew in a large breath.

"It would sure beat those exercises," she told herself, pulling her bright red sweater down around her hips.

"What have you done?" Jonathan's roar of outrage brought Holly running to the front door and outside. When she skidded to a halt, she found three boys looking up at an angry Jonathan.

"We didn't mean nothin'!" one of the boys said plaintively when he saw Holly. "You let us do it to your car."

"Possibly because it wouldn't make a bit of difference to that piece of junk," Jonathan gritted, facing the terrified boys with his fiercest glare.

"Oh, boy." She sighed, walking around to find an abstract design painted on the driver's side of Jonathan's car. "Brian, this was done with watercolor paints, wasn't it?"

The boy nodded. "It's just that his car is bigger than yours and we can paint bigger pictures."

"I suggest you wash your artwork off right away." Holly glanced at a still-fuming Jonathan. "And tell Mr. Lockwood how sorry you are for painting his car without asking his permission first."

"As if I'd give it," Jonathan breathed at the same time the three boys offered their apologies and promised to wash his car right away.

"At least it washes off without any damage to the paint job," Holly pointed out, walking back into her house with Jonathan following.

"Next thing you'll know, they'll be painting the house," he rumbled.

"Don't be so pompous, Jonathan," she chided. "Brian and the others apologized. As he explained, I do allow them to paint pictures on my car. And no more disparaging remarks about my car either!"

By now Jonathan's attention was now centered elsewhere. He leaned down to pick up the pamphlet lying on the coffee table. He quickly skimmed the contents before spinning around to face her.

"I sincerely hope you're not considering *this.*" His voice was tight with barely restrained anger.

"Why not?" Holly countered flippantly, surprised by his ire. "It's sure made a difference in Sherry's life."

"Sherry?" He waited for a further explanation.

Holly told him about Rene and the effect she had on the men at the studio, including Sherry's boyfriend. Sherry's idea of competing was to have breast implants.

Jonathan crumpled the brochure in his fist and tossed it on the table. "And what is *your* reason for having something like that done?" he demanded in an all-too-quiet voice.

Holly found that she couldn't look at him. "I'm—ah—I'm not very desirable in that area so I don't see why it wouldn't hurt to fill me out a little."

Jonathan looked away and raked his hands through his hair. His muttered words were filled with the frustration he felt. "Have I ever given you that impression?" he challenged, turning back to face her.

Holly stepped back a pace under the fierce fire of his rage. "You . . ." She looked away, discovering that candid speech in the light of day was different from during heat of passion. She looked down at her hands clenched i front of her. "You rarely touch my breasts, and I figured that they probably turned you off. I know I don't have a lot there while Liza is in perfect proportion and I'm sure any other woman you've known is similar in build."

Jonathan swore explicitly. "Is that what you've honestly thought all this time?" he asked quietly, once he had calmed down.

Holly nodded.

Jonathan crossed the room and placed his hands on her shoulders, sliding them down to her breasts and cupping them gently through the soft wool.

"Every time I touched your breasts, you'd flinch or draw away from me," he explained in a gentle voice. "I didn't know if they were extra sensitive or if you didn't like to be touched there. Therefore, I didn't caress or kiss them half as much as I wanted to. Holly, don't you realize how beautiful you are all over?"

"I am?" she breathed, unable to believe him even though deep down she knew he would never lie to her.

Jonathan exhaled a sharp breath. "Are you telling me that after the many times I've made love to you, you've always assumed that I saw the size of your breasts as undesirable?" he questioned, incredulous that she would think he could be so cold-blooded.

Holly shifted uneasily under his harsh regard. When he pointed it out so logically, she could see there was no reason for her to presume Jonathan would make love to her if her breasts had turned him off.

"When you put it that way, I can see how I was wrong," she admitted, then burst out, "Jonathan, you know how good I am at not looking at the obvious."

"I suggest that you start thinking with the logical side of your brain," he grated, reaching out to pull her to him. His mouth captured hers at the same time his hands moved under the edge of her sweater to cover her breasts. When she unconsciously drew away, he muttered, "Now do you see what I mean? Every time I touch your breasts, you pull away from me. For once, just remain still and enjoy."

Holly was stunned to see the truth in Jonathan's statement. Had she always feared that he would be displeased with her small breasts and therefore rejected his attentions? She followed his request and looped her arms around his neck to allow him easier access.

He easily unclasped the lacy froth of her bra to bare the firm flesh.

"You fill my hands, Holly," he said thickly, demonstrating the fact. "No man in his right mind requires any more than that." He pushed the soft wool up and bent his head to catch hold of one of her nipples with his teeth, drawing it into his mouth.

Holly gasped at the contractions in her abdomen under the force of Jonathan's suckling motions. She dug her fingertips into his scalp, pressing him even closer to her.

"I want you, Holly," he muttered against the warm skin as he slipped one hand beneath the waistband of her jeans.

"Yes!" Holly rasped, listening to the bells ringing in her ears until she finally realized that the ringing wasn't in her head but rather the doorbell! She could hear Brian calling out her name. "Jonathan, I better go." She pulled away and hastily straightened her clothing before moving toward the door.

"We got the car all clean," the boy announced, not noticing the smoky color of Holly's eyes and her jerky movements.

"That's fine, Brian," she said huskily. "Thank you."

"Sure." He grinned before running off to join his friends.

Holly closed the door and leaned back against the wood surface as she watched Jonathan. "You confuse me at times, Jonathan," she said softly. "I've said things to you I've never said to any man. You make me feel things I've never felt before."

"Then I believe we're even." The desire in his eyes seared her across the room as he walked toward her.

He brushed his fingertips over her lips, watching her face as she circled his wrist with one hand to keep it steady as she moistened each fingertip with her lips, laving the slightly salty skin with her tongue. Keeping her eyes fastened on his face, she turned his hand to place a kiss in the palm before placing it on her breast.

"Do you have a dinner meeting this evening?" she murmured.

His hand rotated gently against the softly rounded flesh as it swelled against his touch. "No."

"Then we could discuss my problem further," Holly suggested in her provocative voice.

"I'd be open to such a discussion." His lips whispered over the curve of her ear and he dipped his tongue inside.

"Perhaps we should continue our talk in more comfortable surroundings." She led him into her bedroom, where they undressed each other with great care before pulling back the covers and lying down on the cool sheets.

"I shouldn't feel like this." Holly sighed when she lay sprawled over Jonathan's supine figure.

"Feel like what?" He ran his hands over her trim buttocks and down over the back of her thighs to the moist curve between.

Holly laughed as she slid a leg between his thighs. "I'm turning into an insatiable woman," she warned him with a saucy wink of the eye.

"I would never have guessed," he retorted, moving sinuously under her slight weight. He trailed a warm palm over her breast, cupping the fragile weight in his palm and rotating the nipple between thumb and forefinger. He smiled at the sound of her deep groan. He reached up and enclosed the dusky nub in his mouth, grazing the sensitive tip with his teeth.

Holly's eyes were closed, her cheeks flushed, and her lips parted with desire. She felt the familiar heavy ache in the center of her body and only wanted to sate the hunger that went with it. A soft incoherent sound left her mouth just as she bent her head to his. Their mouths mated hungrily and their tongues dueled in frantic need. Jonathan arched his hips and withdrew in countermovements to Holly's circling pelvis against his fiery strength.

"I want you so much," she pleaded hoarsely, lowering her head to sink her teeth gently into the taut skin of his shoulder. "Perhaps it's an old line, but I could die with wanting you." Her lips moved moistly over his throat to taste the salt of his skin.

"If so then we'll die together."

Holly gasped as Jonathan thrust himself so deep within her that she was positive he had reached the very center of her body.

"Look at me, Holly," he commanded, reaching up to grab hold of her head. "Open your eyes and watch me possess you." For a brief moment, his hips ceased their loving action until she slowly opened her eyes and looked at his features, taut with sensuality. At that moment, aware by her soft cry that he wasn't hurting her but giving her supreme pleasure, he probed even further into her silken recesses.

"I want to please you, Jonathan," she told him in her smoky voice.

His smile brought another kind of warmth to her. "You *are* pleasing me," he replied, lifting his head to place a hard kiss on her lips and darting his tongue inside.

Holly was soon lost in the tempest Jonathan had wrought. She sought his mouth again and with the security of his arms around her, she climbed the cliff and dove into a fire-filled sea. Her body coiled with a tension she couldn't recall ever feeling and for a moment it frightened her. The darkness that surrounded her wasn't frightening but it was unfamiliar. It was only with Jonathan's hoarsely whispered encouragement that she gave in to the turbulence around her. She wasn't aware of her cries of joy piercing the air because his rumbling voice joined hers as they reached ecstasy together.

Moments later, they lay among the rumpled covers, stunned by the impact of their shared joy.

But Jonathan soon felt a much stronger emotion. He felt a chill run through his veins as he realized the new significance of what he and Holly had just experienced. His mind-shattering conclusion frightened him more than anything he had ever encountered in his lifetime. She had entered into his heart as easily as if she had been there all his life. Jonathan knew he couldn't remain with her any longer. Earlier he had left Holly because he needed to get away and regroup his thoughts before being with her again. This time he had to leave her for good. Now there would be no coming back.

He pulled away from her warm body and sat up abruptly, reaching for his clothing scattered on the carpet.

"Jonathan?" Holly's voice was husky and sated. She propped herself up on one elbow and watched as he picked his clothes up and began to dress. "Is something wrong?" She was alarmed by his continuing silence and refusal to look at her. "Jonathan, please tell me why you're acting like this," she insisted.

Holly sat up straighter and draped the sheet over her shoulders, watching as Jonathan walked out of the bedroom without a backward glance. She felt numb as she heard the back door open and close with a strange finality.

"Jonathan?" she murmured, confused and hurt by his sudden rejection. She knew that he hadn't acted so cold even during those horrible days in San Francisco, and she couldn't imagine what brought his sudden moodiness on.

Holly lay back and piled the covers over her cold body. She had no idea how long she remained in bed. Only Ralph's mournful whining from the backyard roused her to get up and feed him.

All through the evening, Holly searched her brain to discover what could have happened to turn Jonathan away from her. What they had experienced together was so moving that she couldn't imagine anyone else ever sharing such complete fulfillment.

Then why did he leave? her brain kept asking. Unfortunately, she couldn't come up with the answer.

That evening Jonathan drank the better part of a bottle of scotch, cursing himself for his weakness the entire time. No one had ever given him the rapture Holly had nor had he scaled the heights simultaneously with a woman, as he had with her only a few hours before. He had done what he had sworn he would never do—he had fallen in love knowing he would never be able to follow it through. His only recourse had been to cut the ties with as little pain as possible. Now he knew that no matter how brutal a leavetaking was, it still hurt like hell.

He pressed the heels of his hands hard against his eyes. "I can't keep her." His voice was raspy from the alcohol and his lack of sleep. "I have to let her go before she finds out and hates me."

For the first time in his life, Jonathan C. Lockwood was more than intoxicated; he was dead drunk, and he couldn't have cared less.

Holly found the time passing slowly. For the next two nights, her sleep was minimal until she looked as exhausted as she felt. In order to sleep at night, she began running early in the morning and taking Ralph for a run in the early evening. She saw nothing of Jonathan and noticed his car never pulled into his driveway until late at night. She dreaded to think where he might be spending his evenings and with whom. Holly wished that Jonathan would have told her what had happened between them to make him leave so suddenly and without any explanation.

Holly's true shock came the following Saturday when she heard loud noises and looked out the living-room window to see a moving van parked in Jonathan's driveway. "No," she whispered tearfully, gripping the drape so tightly she almost tore the fabric. "He wouldn't do this without saying something to me. He *couldn't!*"

She continued looking out, watching him standing near the moving van speaking to one of the men. She was certain that Jonathan's face appeared leaner and his features more austere than she remembered them. But dressed in black slacks and a cobalt wool sweater, he was the same commanding figure she had watched move in months before.

Holly was frantically trying to think of a way to talk to him when the matter was taken out of her hands. Ralph had somehow gotten loose from the backyard and ran up to Jonathan, jumping up on him and barking.

"Ralph, down!" Jonathan ordered, pushing at the effusive dog.

Holly was out of the house immediately but kept her distance by remaining on the porch. "Ralph, come here," she called out.

Jonathan looked up. "He still hasn't learned any manners," he grated, sounding angry in an attempt to hide his true feelings.

Holly could have cried at the deep lines of tension she saw in the corners of Jonathan's mouth. He had reverted to the cold and indifferent man she had first met.

"Ralph sometimes forgets that his love can't always be returned," she replied quietly, finally coaxing the St. Bernard to her side. "What happened?" She asked the question that had been plaguing her for days.

Jonathan moved closer so that no one could overhear their conversation. "The house is ready and I'm moving in today."

Holly shook her head. "You know very well what I mean. Why did you leave the way you did that day? That isn't like you."

The arctic stones that doubled for his eyes chilled her to the bone. "Don't try to analyze me, Holly," he said coldly. "You never finished your psychology course, remember? I don't think that allows you to probe people's minds."

She refused to flinch under his frosty sarcasm. "Perhaps that's why I can see your desire to push people away for fear they'll discover the real you and leave of their own accord," she shot back.

"You're the one with the fears, Holly." Jonathan's quiet voice resembled a deadly blade. "You not only resent your parents' indifference toward you, but you also feel bitter about your missed childhood. So for these past years you've made up for it by becoming the neighborhood children's best friend. You're afraid to grow up, Holly, because it means taking on responsibilities you don't want. You don't want to face the real world so you remain in your little niche by saying cute words into a microphone and playing games with anyone under the age of ten." This time she did flinch under his cruel words.

"And that's why you left without a word?" She forced the words past a dry throat. "Because I'm too immature for you all of a sudden?"

He shrugged as if the subject had no meaning for him. "I never made any promises to you. It's time for the both of us to move on."

"On to bigger and better things." Holly choked. "That sounds like an excellent idea, Jonathan. I've missed my former wild and crazy life. It will be good to get back to it. Good luck in your cold and sterile cell. You'll need it." She turned on her heel and walked into the house, slamming the door behind her.

Jonathan whitened at her verbal slap in the face, and he stood there for a moment before returning to the truck. He was grateful that he would be gone within a few hours. He knew he wouldn't be able to hold his frozen composure much longer.

As he later moved through the empty rooms, he muttered several curses regarding "cruel to be kind." He hadn't realized just how painful their parting would be. At that moment, he felt as if his guts had been ripped out without the benefit of anesthesia. Holly had looked as if the same operation had been performed on her because of his verbal stabbing.

"Damn," he muttered to himself, wishing he could take his pain out in a more physical manner. Punching his fist through the wall would help immensely. He would carry the image of her face to his grave; with luck, it would be sooner than he thought.

Before he left, Jonathan looked at the closed front door, positive that he could hear Holly crying through the thick walls. He knew it wasn't his ears that heard her sobs but his heart.

Holly lay on her bed crying as if she would never stop. If loving someone hurt that much, she decided she'd rather never love again. She sobbed into her already-soaked pillow. The trouble was, she knew that he was wrong for her and she had been stupid enough to take the chance of falling for him anyway. With that thought she only cried harder until a painful bubble from her vocal cords halted her tears. "Oh, hell, *hic!*" she practically screamed, pounding her pillow with her fists.

When she later heard the sounds of the moving van and Jonathan's car driving away, she wondered if the pain could grow any worse. After that, Holly spent the longest night of her life, alternating between crying and her hiccups.

Jonathan had accused her of refusing to grow up. He was correct in his assumption that Holly wanted to remain a child. What he hadn't known was that her tenuous hold on the past had been released with a vengeance. Holly had indeed grown up.

CHAPTER SEVENTEEN

At the end of two weeks, Holly had tried every known cure for the hiccups. As a last resort, she had gone to her doctor, who suggested it might be more a mental problem than a physical one.

"I was thrilled to pay someone to tell me that they're in my head," she grumbled to Chris one day during lunch.

"It really hit you hard, didn't it?" Chris gazed sympathetically at her.

Holly nodded, hoping to keep the tears from falling as they had so often during the past weeks.

Chris shook her head slowly in disbelief that a man would be so deliberately cruel. "That he could break up with you in such a nasty way is horrible to even think about. Why would he be so cold to you for no reason?"

"Maybe he thought it was a kinder way of getting me out of his life," Holly murmured, toying with her salad. "Many people believe in being cruel to be kind," she mused, unaware that she had parroted Jonathan's thoughts on the matter.

"Stop playing with your food and eat it," Chris ordered briskly. "You look as if you've lost fifteen pounds."

"Only eight." Holly speared a lettuce leaf with her fork and slowly lifted it to her mouth.

"On you it looks double." Chris slathered butter on her

roll. "You should talk to him, Holly. There has to be much more to this than those crazy reasons he gave you."

Holly shuddered at the suggestion. "No, thanks, the wounds haven't healed from the last time."

Chris sipped her coffee and studied Holly covertly. She's taking this much harder than before, Chris thought, noting the hollowed-out eyes and wan features. How could he be so monstrous to someone as sweet and loving as Holly? He should be shot! she decided silently.

"I know a good cure." Chris spoke up with a teasing grin. "Go out with Steve."

For the first time in days, Holly flashed a faint resemblance of her old smile. "That kind of cure would more than likely kill me," she said wryly.

"You'd probably be exerting all your energy evading his very nimble hands," Chris went on.

Holly's smile faded. "It hurts, Chris," she whispered, looking down at her plate. "Sometimes I wake up in the middle of the night crying and I don't even know what woke me up."

"Oh, honey," Chris soothed, wishing she could do something for the pain Holly was going through. But she knew only time would ease the hurt. The trouble was, she was afraid this pain wouldn't heal as easily because the love Holly had felt for Jonathan ran too deep. That kind never disappeared.

"Do you know what?" Holly asked, unaware Chris had even spoken. "I cleaned out my closet the other day and I found one of Jonathan's shirts." Her fork viciously stabbed a cucumber slice. "One of his lousy, pristine white shirts!"

"Tack it up on the wall to use as a dartboard," Chris advised crisply.

"No, I've done something else with it that's much more appropriate." Holly gazed blankly into space.

Jonathan wasn't taking the separation much better. His staff had decided that working for Frankenstein would have been preferable, and his headaches were growing more intolerable each day. He knew the reason behind them but that didn't make them go away.

Jonathan gazed down at the stack of papers on his desk but had no desire to go through them. He took his glasses off and rubbed the bridge of his nose with his thumb and forefinger, scowling irritably when the intercom buzzed.

"I didn't wish to be disturbed, Arlene," he rapped out.

"I realize that, Mr. Lockwood," his secretary said hesitantly. "But there's a messenger out here with a package for you."

"Then just sign for it," he ordered.

"He said it has to be delivered personally," she explained.

Jonathan sighed. "All right, send him in."

The young man handed Jonathan a rectangular box and took his leave. Since there was no return address and the address had been typed, Jonathan tore the brown paper wrapping off to investigate the contents. Inside the box, he found a shirt, which he recognized as his, and draped over the buttoned collar was a silver chain with a sapphire winking insolently at him.

Jonathan carefully replaced the top of the box and set it aside. It was impossible for him to concentrate on his work for the rest of the day.

When he drove home that evening, he parked his car in the garage and entered the house. He walked through the airy rooms not seeing the large glass sliding door leading to a flagstone patio and spa. The rooms were still a little bare since his furniture had been chosen for a small apartment. He hadn't bothered looking for more just yet.

Jonathan's movements were mechanical as he changed from his suit into a pair of jeans and a lightweight sweater.

"Well, old man, what's on the agenda next?" he asked his reflection in the bathroom mirror. "Stab a few butterflies, pull the wings off flies? You've already hurt a lovely woman. Surely you can find a few more atrocities to perform during your time on earth." His tone was cynical as he left the bathroom. He had sounded like that for quite some time. The cold-blooded Jonathan Lockwood was back.

In the beginning, Jonathan had wondered if another woman would ease the pain. He had soon found out differently because he had only been disgusted with himself for even considering such a remedy.

Jonathan dropped onto the bed and buried his face in his hands. He knew he wasn't wrong in what he did. But he still felt like a bastard for the cruel words he had spoken to Holly.

"You look like hell," Liza announced when Holly opened the front door.

"Thanks," she said dryly. "It's because I don't have any makeup on." Holly stepped back as Liza breezed in without an invitation. "Come in, why don't you?"

Liza shook her head, ignoring her sarcasm. "I called the studio this morning. They said you haven't been in for the past three days."

"I've been sick." Holly sounded defensive instead of ill.

Liza's eyes critically scanned Holly's shadowed eyes, sunken cheekbones, and unnaturally pale features.

"I stopped by Jon's office yesterday to drop off his deposit and he looks as bad as you do," Liza stated bluntly. Her voice softened. "Did the two of you break up?"

Holly turned away. "It was time for us to move on to bigger and better things," she said. "A mutual parting of the ways."

Liza's comment on that was to the point. "There's more to it than what you're telling me."

"Do me a favor, Liza, don't do me any more favors," Holly said bitterly. "I can't handle it."

"Damn," she swore softly. "You're really hurting, aren't you?"

"I'm too numb to hurt any more."

Liza couldn't help but see the raw agony in Holly's face and eyes. "Would you care to talk about it?" she asked gently, her question stemming from deep concern.

Holly uttered a harsh laugh. "That would really be a joke, wouldn't it?" she gasped. "My talking over my defunct affair with my ex-lover's ex-wife." She paused to gulp. "No, thank you, Liza. I'm sure you can understand why."

Liza sighed and nodded. "Yes, I can. More than you know." She picked up a microscopic speck of lint from the skirt of her orchid wool suit. She looked up and fixed Holly with an expression that spoke of hidden secrets. "Do you love Jon, Holly?"

There was no hesitation. "I love him so much that I'm dying without him," she replied, combing her fingers through hair that obviously hadn't seen a brush in days. "I only wish I knew what I did wrong."

Liza groped in her handbag for her cigarettes and lighter. She lit one and drew on it deeply before speaking.

It was apparent she was debating about the choice of her words.

"Don't question me any further about what I'm about to ask." She blew out a gray stream of smoke. "If Jon had only a year to live, would you still love him?"

Holly's eyes widened. Questions were ready to trip off her tongue, but she restricted herself to a simple "Yes."

Liza nodded as if that was the answer she expected to hear. "No matter what you would still love him?"

Holly leaned foward and spoke with the intensity of a woman who loved deeply from the very depths of her soul. "Liza, Jonathan could have two wooden legs and a glass eye, and I'd still love him."

Liza finished her cigarette before speaking again. "If you truly love Jon, you'll go to him and demand his love in return."

Holly shook her head. "He doesn't love me." Her words were laced with bitterness.

Liza wagged a finger at her. "Holly, you're a stubborn woman who knows how to go after what she wants and won't allow one bull-headed man to deter her. You love Jon, so go after him and give him all the love you have."

Holly felt a cold shaft of fear pierce her body. "Liza, are you trying to tell me that something is wrong with Jonathan?"

Liza reached over to stub her cigarette out in a nearby ashtray. "Go to him, Holly," she advised. "He needs you just as much as you need him."

"I can't handle your matchmaking schemes any more, Liza!" she wailed.

Liza smiled. "I'm not matchmaking, Holly. All I'm saying is that if your love is sincere, you'll go to him." She pulled a card from her handbag and dropped it onto the coffee table. "Take care, sweetie." She walked out of the house.

Holly remained sitting for some time before she rose slowly and walked over to the coffee table to pick up the card Liza had left. As she had anticipated, an address was written on one side. Holly instinctively knew that it was Jonathan's.

She paced the carpet, tapping the card against her lips as she considered Liza's words. Holly loved Jonathan, but she didn't want to be the target of his rapier-sharp tongue again. She had spoken the truth when she said the wounds hadn't healed yet. In fact, she wasn't sure if they would ever heal. Holly halted to look out the window to the backyard, watching Ralph snoozing peacefully in his favorite corner. Why couldn't she have such an easy life instead of loving someone who was too cold-hearted to return it? Her entire body jerked.

"Hic!" Holly looked up at the ceiling as if the Fates had added their advice to Liza's. "Oh, damn!" She hurried into the kitchen to try drinking a glass of water again in hopes of curing her hiccups. As she drank several glasses, she decided she was crazy enough to take Liza's advice.

Holly sighed as she looked up the steep hill to the house standing among several trees to lend privacy. Her little Volkswagen had refused to climb any further and she had left it parked off to the side of the road.

She began walking up the sloping road, muttering irritably every step of the way. Holly grumbled, thinking how she should have worn her tennis shoes. Instead, she had wanted to make a good impression and wore boots, which were turning her feet into gigantic blisters. She looked down at the maligned black leather boots and her black wool pants now turned a dusty gray from the dirt she was kicking up as she walked.

With each step, Holly grew more positive that Jonathan would refuse to speak to her and her stomach churned at an alarming rate. She knew she should have eaten something before making the drive, but she had been afraid she couldn't keep food down. She looked around at the trees that lent a false serenity to the area.

"Lions and tigers . . ." she began to chant just as Dorothy and her three friends had done on the way to Oz. Holly winced when she set one foot down a little too abruptly. She hated to think what she would finally look like when she arrived at the house. She had dressed so carefully for her meeting with Jonathan and she would probably more resemble a street urchin than the sophisticated woman she had worked so hard to seem. She pulled the cowl neck of her pale rose sweater away from her throat. While the air was cool, her climb was warming her up quickly.

By the time she reached the top of the hill, Holly found herself huffing and puffing. She looked around with interest at the pine trees standing guard over the spacious ranch-style house with its flagstone walkway to the front door.

Holly attempted to brush some of the dust from her pants and fanned the heated skin of her face as she slowly walked to the door. Now that the time had come, she wasn't entirely sure she was ready for any kind of showdown. She took several deep breaths to calm her erratic pulse and reached for the doorbell.

She waited for a moment listening to the melodic peal soar through the house. Holly wasn't sure whether the sound relieved or disappointed when she determined that he wasn't home. She had just turned to leave when the door swung open. Holly spun around to face a visibly shocked Jonathan.

"Hello, Jonathan." She managed to sound much calmer than she felt. For one brief second, she could have sworn that she saw joy in his eyes before they became opaque.

"Don't tell me that you just happened to be in the neighborhood," he said sardonically. "I'm afraid that explanation won't wash."

Holly's spirits plummeted. This was going to be much harder than she thought. Damn Liza for suggesting this! And damn her for going along with it. "You'll never have to worry about door-to-door salesmen with that hill," she quipped.

Jonathan continued to stare at her with a harsh expression on his face. He exerted an inhuman amount of control over his emotions so that she wouldn't know how happy he was to see her. He couldn't help but notice how pale and thin she looked. He remained standing in the doorway, afraid that if he allowed her inside, he wouldn't be able to let her go this time. He glanced over her head toward the empty driveway. "Where's your car?"

"It didn't like your hill." She glanced down and noticed she really hadn't gotten too much of the dirt off her clothing. "If I had known, I would have worn jeans." She looked pointedly at his faded denims then up at his face. "May I come in?"

"Why?"

Terrific! Holly's brain screamed. Okay, Sutton, come up with an excellent reason for his allowing you inside. "Because I feel that you owe me the courtesy of talking things over." She hoped he wouldn't demand a more detailed explanation, because she doubted she could think of something logical.

Jonathan stared at her for another moment before silently stepping back.

Holly walked inside and surveyed the living room with interest. The cathedral ceiling and sliding glass door gave the room a light and airy feeling. The couch sat against the wall facing the stone fireplace and a brass free-standing lamp was positioned next to the black leather easy chair. She easily pictured a painting over the fireplace and a pair of brass candlesticks on the mantel.

"Where did you get my address?" Jonathan asked abruptly, jarring the quiet mood of the room.

Holly shrugged. "Does it matter?"

"I guess not, since you're here. I suggest that you say your piece and go," he said crisply. "I have little time for unexpected visitors."

For a moment, Holly wondered if a woman was waiting for him in his bedroom. While she was tempted to investigate for herself, she tamped down her feelings of sick jealousy and turned around.

"You look tired," she commented.

Jonathan's lips twisted. "I've been . . . busy."

I'm certainly not about to go into that, she thought heatedly. She took a second to organize her thoughts. "I'm sure you would rather I don't sit, so I'll take as little of your time as possible." Holly laced her fingers in front of her. "For the first time in my life, I'm going to be so serious it could hurt," she stated quietly, facing him squarely. "I'm in love with you."

Only Jonathan's frozen stance gave her any indication that he believed her statement. "If you expect me to applaud or swear undying love, you can forget it," he rapped out. "Unlike you, I don't allow my emotions to get the better of me. It's much healthier."

Holly cocked her head to one side. Some hidden instinct told her that Jonathan was lying and her only hope was to batter down his cynical façade.

"Is it?" She circled the room leisurely. "Let me tell you the exact moment I knew that I was in love with you." She kept on talking, refusing to allow him to interrupt her train of thought. "When I returned from Iowa I was not only exhausted physically, but emotionally as well. My parents still saw me as some kind of misfit who didn't belong in their well-ordered niche. I was hurt and angry that they refused to see me as the pretty normal, not-so-bad person that I hope I am." She stopped to stroke the cool leather surface of the chair. "I stepped off the plane that night tired and pretty well fed up with the human race. I had even decided that you had gotten tired of waiting for me and had left. When I saw you standing there, I wanted to cry with happiness." Her voice lowered to a throbbing intensity with the memory of that important night. She slowly raised her head, looking at him with glowing eyes. "That was when you did something very beautiful. You walked over and took me in your arms. Jonathan, that was the first time you had ever touched me in an affectionate way in public and that was when I knew that I loved you with everything I had."

He remained standing under the archway with his hands jammed in his jeans pockets. Only his tense stance betrayed that he wasn't completely unmoved by her words.

"There's nothing left for us, Holly," he said flatly.

She shook her head in a strong denial. "You said some things to me the day you left that really hurt. The reason they hurt was because they were true," she murmured. "I was trying to keep my childhood because grownups have all the problems children don't. I was also afraid that there would be some chance of my turning out like my mother, who had no idea that life could be fun and for whom laughing wasn't allowed. I'm still afraid it could happen, but as long as I remain playing a child, it won't."

"It won't," Jonathan assured her. "From what you had said of your mother, she wouldn't have traveled to a state where she didn't know anyone and begin a new life. If you were like the rest of your family, you would have remained in Iowa and married that farmer."

"You can't hate me, Jonathan," she challenged, holding her hands out in supplication. "If you did, you wouldn't have made such beautiful love to me all those times. I think there's more to your reason for breaking off."

"Have you been talking to Liza?" He gazed at her warily.

"She gave me your address," Holly evaded.

Jonathan swore under his breath. "She always did enjoy interfering where she wasn't wanted. What did she say?" His question was casual, but the expression in his eyes revealed suspicion.

"Nothing," she replied honestly. After all, Liza hadn't said anything. What was Jonathan hiding from her? She hesitated for a moment before speaking in a rush. "I know I'm putting my pride on the line here, but what is so wrong with us being together? I know that you don't want to get married, but what if we just lived together?"

"Go home, Holly, and forget all about me." His voice was pure steel. "Find yourself a very upstanding man who will give you all the things you should have because I can't give them to you."

She was past the point of backing down. "Is that wha

you really want me to do, Jonathan?" she demanded, fighting hot tears. "Shall I marry that upstanding man and make love with him the same way I made love with you? Shall I carry his child instead of—"

"Yes!" Jonathan roared, spinning away to pound his fist into the nearby wooden column. He turned to face a stunned Holly. "Yes, find that damn upstanding man, marry him, love him, and have his children because I sure as hell can't give them to you!" He stood there, breathing hard from the emotional pain running through him. He seemed unaware that his knuckles were red and scraped.

Holly felt as if she were frozen in time. She licked her dry lips. "You can't give me love and marriage?" She hated to prolong the conversation because she couldn't miss the agony Jonathan was enduring at that moment, but she had to know what he meant. She had to force him to face whatever it was that he didn't want to admit.

The cords of his throat stood out from the tension radiating through his body. "You really enjoy making me bleed, don't you?" he gritted. "To be blunt, I'm sterile, Holly. I was unfortunate enough to be stricken with the mumps when I was twenty. One of the typical aftereffects for a man is sterility. I couldn't get you pregnant if we made love from now to doomsday. Is that plain enough English for you? Now I'd appreciate it if you would get out and never return." He stared at her blindly, his face nothing but harsh planes.

Fragments of conversation filtered through Holly's mind. She remembered his wince when she had once coldly informed him that he wouldn't have to worry about any complications since she was on the pill. Then not all that long ago she told him to live in his sterile cell.

She thought quickly. The worst thing she could do was

show pity. "Is that why you ordered me out of your life?" she asked softly, taking a tentative step toward him. She was afraid that if she moved too quickly, he might react negatively.

He raked his fingers through his hair and looked away as if he couldn't bear the sight of her. "Yes," he ground out.

"Liza knows, doesn't she?" Holly persisted. "She never even gave me a hint, Jonathan," she assured him.

"She wasn't interested in having a family, so that had nothing to do with our divorce," he said grimly. "You're a much different story."

"Why?"

Jonathan closed his eyes and pressed his thumb and forefinger against the bridge of his nose. "Because you love children and it's only right that you have a family. You would lose that right if you remain with me." He laughed harshly. "Now will you get out?" he demanded in a pained voice.

Holly shook her head and crossed the room until she stood in front of him. She reached out and grabbed his hands, placing them on her hips. "Did you ever stop to think that our positions could have been reversed? I might have been the one not able to have children," she informed him gently. "In case you haven't noticed, I have a very small pelvis. Jonathan, I don't love you for an X- or Y-chromosome. I love you for the man that you are. I love the man who can make such sweet, gentle love to me one moment and inspire me to savage passion the next! I love you because you make me stop and think about who really am. And I just bet that if you cared to consider it you'd admit that you love me too." She dropped her head to one side and offered him a tiny smile.

The muscles in Jonathan's throat moved convulsively. "Damn you." His laugh revealed raw frustration. "Yes, I love you, but I can't allow you to stay with me because I wouldn't be able to let you go later on."

"If we want children later on, there's always adoption," Holly pointed out, then rushed on in exasperation, "Oh, Jonathan, you're not going to make me propose to you, are you?"

For the first time, his mouth relaxed in a faint smile. "I don't think so, although I'm so afraid you're making a mistake. I've loved you a long time, Holly, but I was afraid to admit it, even to myself."

She moved forward and slipped her arms around his waist. "Then kiss me, you fool," she ordered, looking up at him.

Jonathan's mouth covered hers with a fierce hunger that told her more than anything he could say. His tongue explored familiar territory and drew her tongue into his mouth. The wild sounds that came from their lips only confirmed their fierce need.

"Jonathan, I suggest you give me a tour of your bedroom, preferably of your bed, before I attack you here and now," Holly whispered, nibbling the rough skin of his chin and rubbing her pelvis suggestively against him.

He put his arms around her and lifted her off her feet until their faces were even. "I'm not entirely sure I can wait that long," he admitted roughly, carrying her down the hallway to the spacious room at the end. He slowly slid her down over his body then drew back far enough to draw her sweater over her head and unfasten her slacks. Holly was equally busy unbuttoning Jonathan's shirt and working on his jeans' zipper. He gently pushed her onto the bed and leaned down to pull her boots off.

Holly dropped back onto the deep-rust quilt and laughed like she hadn't laughed in a long time. "Come here, my crazy lover," she murmured, holding her arms out. She uttered soft sounds of joy when Jonathan joined her and stripped her of her bra and panties.

"I can't wait any longer, Holly," he whispered, worshipping her breasts with his mouth and tongue. "It's been too long."

"Then don't." She tempted him with a caressing hand moving over his velvety length. "Love me."

Jonathan thrust deeply into her and they melted into each other's bodies. There was no time for slow and easy loving as they ascended the heights simultaneously in moments. Holly's cry of joy was smothered under Jonathan's mouth as they moved together until they floated back down to earth.

Holly lay in his arms breathing deeply to calm the erratic pulse still raging through her body. "You're not going to make me leave now, are you?" she asked, confident of his reply.

"I just hope Ralph enjoys the larger yard and stays out of the spa," he mused, staring up at the ceiling. "Do you think you could take the day off tomorrow?"

"They haven't seen me in four days, I don't think one more day will matter. Why?" Holly smothered a yawn. Her many nights of fitful sleep were catching up with her as her body relaxed in the most natural way. "I can wait until Saturday to move my clothes over."

"The license bureau isn't open on Saturdays," Jonathan explained.

Holly's eyes widened. She turned over and propped her elbows on his bare chest. "The license bureau as in marriage licenses? You want to marry me?" she breathed.

His eyes were a soft dark gold as he gazed up at her. "If you're willing to put up with a bad-tempered Englishman who loves you," he said quietly. "But if you have any doubts. . . ."

She squealed and threw her arms around him. "My only doubt is whether you'll live past the first month on my cooking." Holly began laughing and talking all at once. "I'll take a cooking course, Jonathan. And I'll work hard at being the kind of wife a bank executive should have," she promised fervently.

He wrapped a hand around her nape and pulled her down for a lusty kiss. "Just be yourself and I'll have the wife I want." He nibbled the corners of her mouth. "I'll tell you now, Holly, I still have a few reservations about us succeeding. I'm afraid that the day will come when you'll decide that having a child of your own is more important than me."

Holly shifted until she lay fully on top of him. She placed a hand on either side of his face and put her nose to his nose. "Listen to me very carefully, Jonathan C. Lockwood. *No one* will ever matter to me as much as you do. And by the way, since we're going to be married, what is your middle name?"

"Back off a bit or I'll end up cross-eyed," he ordered gruffly. "And there's no reason for you to know my middle name."

"You'll have to give it for the marriage license," Holly reminded him.

Jonathan sighed. "If you really must know, it's Cyril."

She tightened her lips to keep her laugh from escaping. "Cyril?"

He speared her with a frosty glance, which she ignored. "It's a family name and a secret as far as I'm concerned."

She nodded solemnly, although her lips twitched with silent mirth. "Don't worry, Jonathan, I'll still love you anyway," she cooed.

"One more thing," Jonathan added, frowning at her teasing remark. "I have an excellent idea for your wedding gift."

"Oh." Holly bent her head to nuzzle his neck. "I would like my necklace back," she murmured.

His arms tightened around her. "I hated to see that in the box although I think I can understand why you returned it. It's in the small box on my dresser. As for your gift, I believe we should look at another car for you."

"But, Jonathan!" she protested. "My little car has character!"

"Your little car is a time bomb on four wheels," he countered. "I worried every morning when you started it up. The fact that it didn't make it up the hill convinced me. You'd be better off with a heavier car, say a Buick or a Ford."

Holly wrinkled her nose. "What about a used Porsche?" she asked hopefully.

"Plymouth has some nice sedans," he pointed out.

"One of the men at work is selling his MG." She playfully bit his earlobe.

"What about a Chevrolet?"

"A Fiat?" Holly's hand wandered over his chest and down below his waist.

Jonathan gripped her wrist and pulled her hand from temptation. "I gather this is the beginning of our compromises?" he asked wearily.

Holly blew in his ear. "Let me seduce you and we'll talk about cars later."

He released her hand. "Will you listen to my suggestions?"

"As long as you listen to mine." She pressed nipping kisses along his jaw.

Jonathan's wedding gift to Holly turned out to be a used Toyota station wagon with enough power in the engine to make her happy and there was enough car surrounding her to make him happy. And the back of the car had more than enough room to make Ralph happy.

Now you can reserve February's Candlelights before they're published!

- ♥ You'll have copies set aside for *you* the instant they come off press.
- ♥ You'll save yourself precious shopping time by arranging for *home delivery*.
- ♥ You'll feel proud and efficient about organizing a system that *guarantees* delivery.
- ♥ You'll avoid the disappointment of not finding *every* title you want and need.

ECSTASY SUPREMES $2.50 each

- ☐ 61 **FROM THIS DAY FORWARD,** Jackie Black 12740-8-27
- ☐ 62 **BOSS LADY,** Blair Cameron 10763-6-31
- ☐ 63 **CAUGHT IN THE MIDDLE,** Lily Dayton 11129-3-20
- ☐ 64 **BEHIND THE SCENES,** Josephine Charlton Hauber 10419-X-88

ECSTASY ROMANCES $1.95 each

- ☐ 306 **ANOTHER SUNNY DAY,** Kathy Clark............10202-2-30
- ☐ 307 **OFF LIMITS,** Sheila Paulos 16568-7-27
- ☐ 308 **THRILL OF THE CHASE,** Donna Kimel Vitek......18662-5-10
- ☐ 309 **DELICATE DIMENSIONS,** Dorothy Ann Bernard 11775-5-35
- ☐ 310 **HONEYMOON,** Anna Hudson..............13772-1-18
- ☐ 311 **LOST LETTERS,** Carol Norris..................14984-3-10
- ☐ 312 **APPLE OF MY EYE,** Carla Neggers 10283-9-24
- ☐ 313 **PRIDE AND JOY,** Cathie Linz 16935-6-23

At your local bookstore or use this handy coupon for ordering:

Dell DELL READERS SERVICE – Dept. B507A
P.O. BOX 1000, PINE BROOK, N.J. 07058

Please send me the above title(s). I am enclosing $_____ (please add 75c per copy to cover postage and handling). Send check or money order—no cash or CODs. Please allow 3-4 weeks for shipment.
<u>CANADIAN ORDERS: please submit in U.S. dollars.</u>

Ms./Mrs./Mr._____

Address_____

City/State_____ Zip_____

FALCON CREST

Wish you could spend more than just an hour at Falcon Crest? Now you can, with this fabulously readable new paperback

A mighty novel, it lets you experience all the life, power, and excitement of the phenomenally successful TV series that inspired it. And rather than end in 60 minutes, it gives you hours—even days—with the family that's consumed by their fierce power struggles: Chase Gioberti, Angela Channing, her dangerous daughter Julia, and her chameleon-like grandson Chase. All set against California's rich wine country, the Tuscany Valley.

12437-9-41
$3.95

At your local bookstore or use this handy coupon for ordering:

Dell DELL READERS SERVICE—Dept. B507B
P.O. BOX 1000, PINE BROOK, N.J. 07058

Please send me the above title(s). I am enclosing $_____ (please add 75¢ per copy to cover postage and handling). Send check or money order—no cash or COD's. Please allow 3-4 weeks for shipment.
CANADIAN ORDERS: please submit in U.S. dollars.

Ms./Mrs./Mr._____

Address_____

City/State_____ Zip_____

All-new Candlelight Newsletter

An exceptional, *free* offer awaits readers of Dell's incomparable Candlelight Ecstasy and Supreme Romances.

Subscribe to our all-new CANDLELIGHT NEWSLETTER and you will receive—at absolutely no cost to you—exciting, exclusive information about today's finest romance novels and novelists. You'll be part of a select group to receive sneak previews of upcoming Candlelight Romances, well in advance of publication.

You'll also go behind the scenes to "meet" our Ecstasy and Supreme authors, learning firsthand where they get their ideas and how they made it to the top. News of author appearances and events will be detailed, as well. And contributions from the Candlelight editor will give you the inside scoop on how she makes her decisions about what to publish—and how *you* can try your hand at writing an Ecstasy or Supreme.

You'll find all this and more in Dell's CANDLELIGHT NEWSLETTER. And best of all, *it costs you nothing*. That's right! It's Dell's way of thanking our loyal Candlelight readers and of adding another dimension to your reading enjoyment.

Just fill out the coupon below, return it to us, and look forward to receiving the first of many CANDLELIGHT NEWSLETTERS—overflowing with the kind of excitement that only enhances our romances!

Dell DELL READERS SERVICE—Dept. B507C
P.O. BOX 1000, PINE BROOK, N.J. 07058

Name_____

Address_____

City_____

State_____ Zip_____